A Deadly Affair

The Deadly Series
Book 1

R.M. Connor

ISBN: 978-1-7367139-3-8

Cover design by: Cover Villain
Editing: Black Quill Editing
Formatting: Champagne Book Design
Library of Congress Control Number: 2018675309
Printed in the United States of America

To my Gramsie
I wish you were here to see this.

A Deadly Affair

Welcome to Wildewood

Chapter 1

"Let me see it." Tessa motioned for me to show her my pumpkin.

She sat across the table from me in the large meeting hall. The air was stale and smelled of pumpkin innards. Half the town was crammed in the room so we could get as many jack-o-lanterns as possible ready for the Halloween Festival only a few days away.

I shook my head refusing, but she gave me a *do it now* look: one eyebrow raised and her lips pursed. Her arms were crossed and she tapped her index finger on her forearm. I groaned. This was embarrassing. I wasn't good at carving pumpkins. Seriously, I was *really* bad at it. But Tessa had insisted I come with her.

I turned the finished jack-o-lantern around to face her. I wrinkled my nose as Tessa averted her eyes from the hideous creature I had created.

"It's not that bad." She bit her lip and turned the pumpkin back toward me.

Tessa Anderson was my best friend. She was probably the only real friend I'd ever had in my entire twenty-eight years. She was a woman of many talents, but lying was not one of them.

I looked down at my pumpkin and wiped away strands of orange guts that still clung to the face. The two triangles that made up its eyes were lopsided. One was too close to the mouth, and the other, I mean, come on. How had I managed to carve it so crooked? This was what happened when I didn't use a stencil. I had accidentally cut off a few teeth when my knife slipped and tried to secure them back in with toothpicks but it just made it look worse.

I heard a giggle. My eyes flicked to Tessa. She had one elbow resting on the table and her hand pressed against her mouth. The corners of her eyes were pulled tight enough to create wrinkles like chiseled spider webs stretching outward from her emerald eyes.

If I had been able to use magic to carve it, it would've been close to perfect. But being a witch was a secret I hadn't shared with anyone, not even Tessa. Though, it hadn't been a secret I'd been keeping for long. After I moved to Wildewood, I woke up one morning suddenly equipped with magical abilities and what a strange morning it had been.

I woke up late the day of my café's grand opening. The Witches Brew had been a dream of mine—a charming little café and bakery—since I decided to move to Wildewood. But that morning had not gone the way I had intended. I had run down the stairs to rinse off in the shower. I had snapped my fingers when I remembered I had laid out an outfit on my dresser while simultaneously thinking about starting a pot of coffee before getting ready.

In horror, I watched my perfectly planned outfit fly down the stairs like a baseball toward me. The lid to the black canister that held the coffee grounds spun violently and landed on the ground at the same time the ball of clothes hit me in the chest so hard I fell backward. I sat on the floor with the pile of clothes in my lap and stared at my hand. My fingers were hot and tingling. I remember feeling completely freaked out, and yet excited. What girl didn't dream about having powers?

I took a chance and thought about filling the back of the coffee maker with water and snapped my fingers again. The water turned on full-force and the sprayer attached to the faucet pulled out and floated toward the coffee maker but the hose wasn't long enough to reach. I threw the ball of clothes off me and scrambled to the sink. Water had gotten everywhere. All over the counter, the floor. By the time I slammed the handle down to turn the water off, the kitchen was soaked.

Needless to say, I had been late to my grand opening and had been very careful about snapping my fingers the rest of that day. It took me a few months to control my abilities. Though I was still a novice, I could now make a pot of coffee without flooding my kitchen. I still didn't understand where the magical abilities came from. I supposed it was possible it had been lying dormant my whole life but I couldn't ask anyone about it.

I placed the lid on the pumpkin. "There will be so many, I doubt anyone will notice." The lid slid sideways and threatened to fall inside. I leaned back against my folding chair and crossed my arms. I had been defeated by a squash.

"I think next year you should volunteer for something else." Tessa grinned and, this time, didn't try to hide her laughter.

I stuck my tongue out at her. "That's probably a good idea."

Tessa stopped laughing. When I looked up, her already big green eyes were wider and she was staring behind me.

"Oh dear," a disgruntled voice said and I stiffened.

Hesitantly, I turned around. Wildewood's long-time mayor, Esther Miller, stood with her arms crossed. The wrinkles on her face deepened as she frowned. Her gray curls laid neatly in a clip, pulled back from her face. Her dark blue eyes, that always seemed to know too much, focused on to me.

Shit.

"It's okay, dear. We will find a spot for it." She patted my shoulder. "In the back."

My cheeks burned and I groaned as I wrapped my thin flannel jacket closer to my body and sunk further into my chair. Esther hosted the pumpkin carving meeting every year. This would be my first time participating, and by the disapproval on Esther's face, probably my last.

Tessa leaned across the table and whispered as Esther walked away, "It's okay, Riley. At least the cupcakes you're making for the festival will make up for it."

Oh, yeah. The cupcakes.

Every establishment was asked to participate in some way with the festival. I had decided the café would bring a few hundred cupcakes. I may have been a bit over-ambitious.

I scrunched my nose and said, "I get it. I'll stick to what I'm good at."

Grinning, Tessa bobbed her head up and down.

Esther made her way to the front of the large room and cleared her throat loud enough for us to hear in the back. The room went quiet, as it always did when she demanded the attention of a crowd. Her presence was much larger than her petite frame and hard to ignore. I suppose that's how she managed to be mayor for the last few decades—no one could compete with her.

Tessa crouched underneath the table to get to the side I was sitting on. We watched as Esther clapped her hands together, her demeanor transforming as a large grin appeared on her face, erasing the frown lines my pumpkin had given her.

"I am so pleased with the turn out of this year's pumpkin carving night. The festival would be nothing if it weren't for every one of you." She spread her arms out and took a moment to look around the crowded room.

My assistant at The Witches Brew, Leah Crane, walked into the meeting hall dressed in a pair of form-fitting jeans and a plain white t-shirt. Her shoulder-length blonde hair was pulled up into a rare ponytail. She usually wore it down and straight, curling at the ends toward her neck. Jennifer Mitchell, an employee at Wildewood's bakery, Just Treats, came in behind her. She was a few inches shorter than Leah, with long brown hair. I usually only saw it pulled back in a hairnet but tonight it was hanging loosely around her shoulders.

I watched as they propped the doors open, glimpsing a large wheelbarrow sitting outside. Alice Starr, the owner of Just Treats, stood in front of the wagon holding the handle as she spoke with a man I had never seen before. He smiled and a dimple formed in his right cheek above the line of his neatly trimmed beard. I wonder if he had a dimple on both cheeks. His caramel-colored hair was long, falling to his neck but cut in layers that had slight waves. Leah and Jennifer hauled finished jack-o-lanterns to the wagon, blocking my view.

I squirmed in my seat, trying to catch another look at Dimples. Who was he?

Giving up, I asked, "Has anyone ever been banned from pumpkin carving night?"

"Nope." Tessa's grin stretched across her face. "But there is always a first time for everything."

Esther cleared her throat, her eyes focusing on us. I tried to slink further into my chair, trying to hide from her gaze. "My daughter Samantha will be passing out tea lights. Please take one and place it inside your pumpkin. If you cannot put yours out in the square, Alice will take them for you. Thank you again, Wildewood!" She gave one last smile and walked around the room, making small talk.

Samantha came walking toward the two of us with a small box of battery-powered tea light candles. Her dark brown hair framed her face, falling right above her shoulders. Impeccably dressed, just like her mother, she wore a black pencil skirt with a gray turtleneck tucked in, adorned with a thin black belt showing off her small waist. Her black stiletto heels tapped the ground as she came to a stop in front of our table. She held out two candles to Tessa.

"Are you coming over this week to work on costumes?" Tessa asked Samantha who handed me one of the small candles. The two of them had grown up in Wildewood together and had been friends since kindergarten, but recently Samantha had been distant, distracted with her upcoming wedding. She was planning it mostly by herself instead of hiring someone to do it for her. The only help she had was Esther's assistant at Town Hall.

"I'm not sure." Samantha shuffled the box to her other arm. "Who all is going?"

"Riley." Tessa nodded toward me. "Maybe Leah and Jennifer."

Samantha shrugged. I could tell by the look on her face she was uninterested. "I think I'll just buy my costume this year."

"That's no fun." Tessa poked her bottom lip out in a pout.

"I'm not in the mood for fun right now," Samantha replied, her face solemn. She looked past us for a moment before walking away to continue handing out candles.

Tessa turned back to face me, resting on her elbows on the table and mumbled to herself, "I wonder what's gotten into her."

Peeking behind me, I saw Samantha's fiancé, Trey Brewer. He was leaning against the back wall of the room, a trash bag in one hand and the other resting on the wall above another woman's head as they talked. The woman twirled her blonde hair in her finger, laughing at whatever he was saying. Trey was a handsome man but looks only went so far.

"Probably that." I tilted my head in Trey's direction. It was common knowledge that he was a flirt but it was still unsettling that he was so unashamed about it, especially in the same room as Samantha.

Tessa glanced behind me and I saw her nose scrunch before she looked away. "I can't stand him."

Changing the subject, I said, "Do you think I should ask Esther where she wants me to stick this guy?" I patted my pumpkin. Tessa could be a hot head when it came to her friends and I didn't think Samantha would want another scene in front of so many people. Trey was doing a good enough job of that.

"I'm sure she'll sniff it out tomorrow morning when you aren't looking." Tessa stood, her chair scraping along the cement floor. Her eyes flicked up to spot Trey once more. "Come on." She pulled her jacket on. "I'm hungry."

We walked out of the warmth of the meeting hall and into the chilly autumn night to find a spot for our pumpkins. The Halloween Festival was only three days away. There were promises of a hay maze in one of the four corners of the square, but it was currently nothing more than bales of hay stacked in a large pile. The stage where a band would be playing was being set up. Esther didn't seem to be bothered by the lack of progress. As far as I knew, this was normal.

Walking through the middle of the square, past the large oak tree in the center, we found a spot along the path where the maze would be. I placed my pumpkin down and it tipped and teetered, daring to fall over onto its side.

"I hope no one will notice." I fumbled with the lid, trying to keep it from falling inside. How did this even happen? It should fit like a puzzle piece but somehow the lid was smaller than the hole.

"I think it would take actual magic for no one to notice." Tessa chuckled, setting hers next to mine to help prop it up.

I tensed at the words she chose. Sometimes I wondered if Tessa knew more than she let on. But there was no way she knew I was a witch because I had never used magic around her.

"I'm not even sure magic could fix this thing." I stared at the lopsided mess.

"Want to go get something to eat?" Tessa asked. It was her turn to change the subject.

"I think I'm going to just go home." The Witches Brew opened at seven in the morning, but I had to be in earlier to prep for the morning rush.

I waved at her; Tessa wiggled her fingers in return. She headed in the opposite direction toward her favorite late-night eatery, Mike's, Wildewood's only bar. I waved at Leah and Jennifer as I walked past but then slowed. I looked back at my pumpkin. Though I had tried to stop it, the lid had fallen sideways in the hole pushing the teeth off their toothpicks. Maybe I could use a little magic to fix it.

I brought my hands in front of me, curled my index finger, and whispered a simple Latin word to conjure the magic I possessed. I had learned to use simple terms to better control what I wanted to do. Heat blossomed at the tip of my finger— it happened every time. The pumpkin lid wriggled upward then set back in place, where it belonged. Using the same motion, I breathed out another spell. The teeth secured themselves in the pumpkin's mouth without support from the toothpicks. With a smirk forming, I turned back and continued on my way, picking up my pace to get to Cattail Road. A quiet, narrow street with overgrown oaks lining both sides and my cozy little cottage nestled between a row of old houses in the forest of Wildewood.

Chapter 2

The horizon was still dark as I left my house the following morning. The sun wouldn't be up for another two hours, giving me plenty of time to bake the goods my regulars had grown to expect. The wooden broom stayed airborne as I swung a leg over the handle to dismount. My boot made a slight tapping sound as the toe touched the ground. Whispering, I took away the broom's ability to fly and it fell, clattering loudly to the ground.

Grabbing the handle, I leaned it beside the back door of the café. My legs wobbled as I began to walk. No matter how many times I flew, my legs always felt unsteady afterward. I ran my hand along the brick wall lining the alley between my café and the neighboring bookstore for support as I walked to the storefront. The brick was damp from the storm that had moved through last night. A strong wind had howled between the clapping of thunder. It would be just my luck that the storm carried away all of my Halloween decorations.

I touched the thin, wrought iron fence separating The Witches Brew patio from the sidewalk. It was wrapped in a lighted garland, with red, orange, and yellow leaves. Plastic spiders and bats were weaved through it. Heavy, black chairs and two small, circular tables matching the fence sat outside. The patio was slightly covered with a large black and white striped awning that offered a small amount of shade in the afternoon. Under the awning on the large window were black letters that spelled out *The Witches Brew* with a silhouette of a bubbling cauldron.

Everything appeared intact until I noticed one small pumpkin lying face down beside the front door. I wiggled my index finger in an upward motion at the magically carved jack-o-lantern and muttered a word under my breath. It sprung up, sitting back against the brick wall where it belonged and gave me a toothy grin. Stepping back to see the entire patio, I felt content with how it had been set up. I snapped my fingers. *"Accendere."* The yellow lights of the garland lit up, creating a soft glow around the café.

The street was barely illuminated by the weak light from the short, black lamps lining the sidewalk. Banners hung from every other one to remind everyone of the annual festival. Each storefront was decorated, ranging from spooky to kooky, representing the individual business owners' personalities. I had chosen to decorate simple compared to some.

The café looked out onto Town Square, the only grassy area in the dense forest of Wildewood. I noticed more progress had been made after I went home last night. String lights were wrapped around the trunk of the large tree then strung from its branches to posts on the perimeter of the square. It gave the impression of a Big Top at a circus. The lights shone brightly in the dark morning. More jack-o-lanterns lined the pathways, creating a magical, orange glow.

The cold air was sharp in my lungs, reminding me winter was right around the corner. I wrapped the knee-length black peacoat tighter against my body, thankful I had decided to wear it instead of my go-to flannel shirt, *again*. Pulling my hat further over my ears, I was ready to go inside and get warm. As I dug through my coat pockets for the keys, I had an urge to look down the street. The air had grown still and the hairs on the back of my neck stood. I took a few steps toward the corner of Oak Avenue and noticed flashing lights behind the buildings.

A second later a siren wailed. A fire truck turned the corner, rushing past me. A gust of wind followed and the thin toboggan was swept off of my head and went bounding down the street after it. I dropped my messenger bag in front of the café door and chased it. Getting close enough, I stomped my boot on the bottom corner of the hat and bent to pick it up. My heart was racing, not used to running and my breathing was strained. Wiping the hat off as I straightened up, I saw Tessa, running toward me, panic flashed across her face. Her long black hair bounced around her small frame wildly. She stopped in front of me and sucked in a deep breath.

"What's going on?" I asked, sliding the hat back in place. Tessa was the owner of the Wildewood antique store, Odds 'n' Ends, located on the same street as The Witches Brew. When she wasn't at Mike's, she was at her store. And if I didn't know better, I'd swear she lived there.

"Just Treats!" she exhaled loudly and pressed her hand to her chest as she sucked in another deep breath. "It's on fire!"

Looking past Tessa to the horizon, I saw the flashing red lights of the fire truck in the distance, the siren muted. Just Treats sat by itself in an empty lot used for overflow parking for downtown Wildewood. Black smoke swirled upward into the sky a short distance away. The scent of burning wood hit me. Panic sank in.

Tessa and I raced down the street in the direction she'd come from to stand outside the front entrance of the hardware store. We watched as the firemen pulled the hose to the building. Bright orange flames lapped out of a hole in the roof. Another gust of wind shook us at the same time as the firehose was turned on, misting us with the water as they began to extinguish the growing flames.

Wildewood began to wake up from the commotion, and a crowd of curious onlookers gathered in the street. Scanning the group of people, I spotted Alice Starr and Jennifer Mitchell standing together in the grass near the sidewalk. Alice's long silvery hair was pulled back into a tight braid that fell to the small of her back and her white apron was tied tightly around her waist. Jennifer had her hands pressed to her mouth, shaking her head. I pointed them out to Tessa. In unison, we weaved through the crowd and crossed the street to stand near them.

"Alice," I called out to her.

But her attention was transfixed on the burning building. She jumped as my fingers brushed her arm and she turned to me. Her honey-colored eyes were large, wide with fear, tears hovering in the corners glistened in the lights from the fire truck. She was chewing on her bottom lip and her arms were wrapped around herself, making her appear smaller than she already was. She looked ten years older as worry created deep creases on her face. Her shoulders sagged though she was holding on to her composure better than I think I would be able to.

"Riley," Alice's voice cracked as she said my name. The tears she had been holding back began to run down her cheek. Jennifer put her arm around Alice's shoulders to comfort her.

"Why would someone do this?" Alice asked.

Raising an eyebrow, I said, "What do you mean?"

Just Treats was an iconic part of Wildewood and had been for over seventy-five years, owned only by the Starr family starting with Alice's mother. She had lived here her whole life and provided the best cakes in all of Northern Georgia. Who would want to put a stop to that? I wasn't able to come up with a single person who would want to ruin her, let alone who didn't enjoy their famous soda cake.

Sniffling, Alice regained some of her composure and wiped at her eyes with the bottom corner of her apron. She whispered, "I swear I saw someone run through the parking lot when I got here. By the time I got to the bakery, smoke was pouring out the back door."

Tessa and I exchanged a confused look. She scrunched her brows and said, "Someone set fire to the bakery?"

Alice blinked and more tears formed. "I just don't know why."

I didn't know either.

A familiar voice called from behind me. Leah waved her hand in the air and jogged toward us through the crowd. She was huffing, out of breath, and pulled her black toboggan off of her head. Her blonde hair was matted with sweat against her forehead. It looked like her, Tessa, and I needed to form a running club to get in better shape. Coming to a stop next to me, Leah took in a deep breath, running her fingers through her hair to straighten it out. She looked toward the bakery, her mouth opened in awe. She whispered, "What happened?"

The firemen were turning the hose off and rolling it back into the truck. The smell of wet, burnt wood filled the air. The Fire Chief walked into the building and yelled incoherent commands to his crew. As the firemen went to work loading the truck, the chief found Alice and removed his hat from his head then the gloves from his hands.

"Fire's out, Mrs. Starr," his voice was apologetic.

Her hand was swallowed up by his massive bear claw dirtied with soot and ash.

Alice mumbled a thank you and then she was called over by a police officer.

"It looks like we have a firebug in Wildewood." A pit formed in my stomach.

Alice walked toward the officer. The lights of the firetruck were turned off as they backed out of the parking lot and onto the street but the blue lights from the police car remained.

Chapter 3

The crowd dispersed and Alice was given a ride to the police station. Leah and I said goodbye to Tessa as we walked past her store. Picking my bag up from in front of the door where I had dropped it, we walked into the dark café. I ran my hand along the wall to find the light switch. Large fairy lights flashed on, strung from one end of the café to the other. Larger pendant lights hung above the bar, reflecting on the black surface and on the glass-domed cake stands that held day-old pastries for half price. The larger display case attached to the bar was empty.

I loved walking into the café. The smell of coffee and warm muffins always lingered in the air. The black countertops contrasted with the white subway tiles on the walls and under the bar. A large, chrome-colored, industrial-sized coffee machine sat behind the bar on another counter against the wall. There were four large coffee bean dispensers, filled to the brim with small, brown beans of various strengths. Behind the fixtures was a ceiling-to-counter sized chalkboard where we wrote the menu.

Along the white walls were slender black shelves that held vining plants. I had draped the vines at different heights with hooks—the kind with adhesive so as not to damage the tiles.

There was a long, slender black table placed in front of the window for customers to people-watch as they drank their coffee. On the right side of the cafe was a set of black, plush chairs and a forest-green coffee table. The rest of the café had black, round tables with two to four chairs spaced out equally for comfort.

I looked at the clock above the kitchen door and my shoulders slumped, knowing we wouldn't have enough time to fill the display case as much as I preferred. We were a half-hour behind schedule and my second employee was late.

Maisie Law had come to Wildewood only a few months ago. She'd been desperate for work and I had been desperate for another set of helping hands. Blinded by my own needs, I hired her and instantly regretted it. Her attitude with customers was unpleasant and she was late for her shifts more often than not. Problematic from the start, I should have let her go but something stopped me. I wasn't sure what it was, except that I'd never fired anyone before. I had one employee who was less than mediocre and another beyond exceptional. Something had to give or I would end up losing both employees.

I kept hoping that if I gave her *one more shot,* she would finally become reliable. I thought giving her some responsibility would help her grow up—though we were the same age. I wanted to help her. She was alone and I understood that feeling more than she knew. I had been born in Wildewood but abandoned at birth and placed in foster care. I had moved from one family to the next, all over the state of Georgia until I reached eighteen. I had only been back home, in Wildewood, for a year after searching for my birth parents. I found my father, but just like everyone else, he was gone now too.

"I'll go get started." Leah quietly made her way to the

kitchen through the salon-style swinging doors. Her face was long and solemn. Normally, she was chatty in the morning. After watching the fire at the bakery, I couldn't hold it against her. I didn't feel like talking either.

I could count on one hand how many times I had seen flashing lights race down the street. Crime was not common here. We lived in what I thought was a very safe community. The kind in which people don't lock their doors at night before going to bed. I had a feeling that was going to change.

In the kitchen, Leah was standing in the middle of the room, kneading the purple-tinted dough for the scones on the metal island. She barely glanced up at me as I moved past her to the left and clicked on the two ovens to preheat. I pulled all of the ingredients I would need to make the café's staples and set them on the counter.

I tapped my nail on the island. "Just work on the scones and I'll get the rest done."

Leah made a small noise in response.

Okay. She still doesn't want to talk.

I poured flour into one of the four chrome mixers on the counter near the door and thought about how I was no stranger to keeping my feelings tucked away. It was hard to open up when you weren't sure you'd be with the same person the next day. Slowly adding the wet ingredients into the mixture, I let the machine whisk it together and stared into the off-white batter, lost in my thoughts. I never could open up. Not to any of my foster parents and I never allowed myself to have a friend, it was easier when I moved—I never had to say goodbye. It was hard for me to let someone in completely—even with Tessa, I always maintained a slight distance.

I shook my head, trying to dismiss the sad thoughts.

Turning my attention to the stove, I flicked on a small burner and melted butter to dissolve the powdered espresso. I took in a deep breath, filling my lungs with the potent, earthy smell. I understood why my customers loved this particular treat—Espresso Chocolate Chip Muffins, a must-have in the morning.

As the batch of muffins and scones were pulled out of the oven to cool, I heard the little bell above the front door chime. I poked my head over the swinging doors, having to stand on my toes, and saw Maisie. Falling back flat on my feet so she couldn't see my face, I pushed down the immediate irritation upon seeing her. I closed my eyes and took a deep breath. There was something going on with her and I was trying to be patient but I was wearing thin.

I pushed the doors open and walked into the café. She flicked her hazel eyes up at me, putting her small bag under the counter. Standing, she brushed her long hair back into a ponytail with her fingers. Her long, layered hair was a light brown with red undertones. Maisie fixed a thick bandage wrapped around two of her fingers.

"I know I'm late. I—" she started.

I stopped her, holding my hand up.

"I don't want another excuse." I closed my eyes for a second, forcing my frustration down. I ran my hand over my mouth. "We open in ten minutes. Please get the coffee started." I turned my back to her and walked through the doors.

I could hear her shuffling behind the counter, banging things around and filling the coffee machine with water. I took a deep breath. I wasn't going to let her get under my skin. All I had to do was fire her, then no more problems.

"She can be such a bitch sometimes," Leah grumbled as we loaded two trays with three-dozen muffins and scones.

We carried the trays into the café. By the thinness of Leah's lips, I could tell she was fed up with Maisie's excuses as well. I set the tray I was carrying beside Leah's on the counter. She began to arrange the baked goods in the large display case. Turning around to the thin refrigerator, I grabbed the leftover pumpkin spice muffins from the day before and proceeded to arrange them neatly on the domed cake plates on the counter.

As we finished our morning preparations, I motioned for Maisie and handed her my apron. "I need you to start making the coffee cake muffins for the delivery later."

Her face hardened and her mouth opened. Before she could say a word, my eyes narrowed and her mouth quickly closed, her lips becoming a thin line. She snatched the white apron out of my hand and both she and Leah made their way into the kitchen to change.

Before they could come back, I touched the two carafes of the coffee machine, the hot liquid heating the palms of my hands. I closed my eyes, clearing my mind of all distractions—which was harder this morning than usual—and whispered a spell.

"*Evigilo*," I repeated it three times. The magic pulsed through my fingertips and into the dark liquid. It was dangerous to do in public, but this was a secret routine of mine every morning when no one was looking.

We served all types of coffee drinks at The Witches Brew, but my regulars got a caffeine-free boost to help them wake up and start their day, the Hocus Focus. Anyone who drank the brew—most of the town did every morning—would get an extra boost of energy helping them see out the rest of their day.

Leah came through the swinging doors, wearing a different apron just as I was removing my hands from the carafes.

She handed one to me. I tied it tightly around my waist. It was a short black apron with The Witches Brew embroidered in white lettering with a cauldron on the pocket. Making my way through the cozy sitting area, I weaved through the small black tables to the door and flipped the closed sign to open.

Chapter 4

"Riley!"

The bell above the door chimed and the high-pitched squawk of my name rattled my ears. I looked up from my position behind the coffee bar and saw Esther Miller pushing her way through the café.

Shit, I winced bracing myself.

There were some people who no matter how old you were, made you feel like a child in trouble. Esther Miller was that person for me.

She had her hand wrapped around Samantha's wrist, towing her behind. Trey was right on their heels. Reaching the counter, Esther took the white handkerchief she had in her hand and wiped the black bar stool with a back and forth flick of her wrist before sitting down.

Samantha took a seat next to her, her back bowed and her arms wrapped around her midriff. She was wearing a velour athletic outfit, burgundy-colored sweatpants and matching sweatshirt. Her long black hair was pulled up into a rather messy ponytail. Unusual attire for her. Trey stood a distance behind the two of them, his hands shoved into his trouser pockets, eyes roaming around the room.

Blowing her nose in the lacey fabric, Esther exclaimed, "This is terrible!"

I glanced down the bar to Leah where she had been watching the scene unfold. She shook her head and busied herself with customers sitting on the other side of the room, leaving me to fend for myself. Thanks, Leah. But how could I blame her? I wouldn't have come over either.

"What's going on, Madame Mayor?" I remembered Samantha told me Trey had stomach ulcers and only grabbed two white coffee cups and placed them on the counter in front of them. He used to come into the café every morning until a few months ago. Samantha blamed it on stress.

"The fire, Riley!" Esther wiped her nose. "Where have you been? The fire at the bakery."

Pouring coffee into the cups, I nodded. "It's really terrible. I hope there isn't too much damage."

"Oh, who cares." Esther took the cup.

Startled by her words, I raised an eyebrow and watched her pour sugar into the hot liquid. I looked at Samantha for an explanation. Had I missed something?

Samantha sniffed and rubbed her nose with her sleeve. Her eyes were red. "My wedding cake—"

"Ruined! It's all ruined!" Esther interrupted, dropping the small stirring spoon into her coffee splashing tawny liquid on the counter. She patted her daughter's knee, though it seemed she was the one who needed the comforting.

Samantha put her hands around the coffee cup and pulled it closer to her. Trey placed his hand on her shoulder, her body went rigid. She stared into the coffee for a few seconds before pushing it away.

"I don't know what we're going to do. The wedding is four

days away," Esther started back up. "Alice had finished the entire thing. It was big enough to feed the whole town!" She dabbed at the corners of her eyes with her handkerchief. "Everything is ruined now."

Trey slipped away, going to the other side of the bar. Leah was giving an older couple change out of the till. I watched out of the corner of my eye as he walked up to her. He rested his elbows on the counter, his arms going across, almost touching her. Leah's body tensed and she took a step back. I could barely make out him asking for a to-go cup over the noise Esther was making. Trying to hide my confusion, I turned my attention back to Samantha. Maybe his ulcer had healed?

"I'm sorry about your cake but that doesn't mean your wedding is ruined. You can still get married." I was pretty sure the cake wasn't the most important part of a wedding. But, *hey*, what do I know? I've never been married and probably never will be.

Esther put her hand over her heart dramatically. "Riley, the daughter of the mayor cannot have a wedding without a cake."

Okay. I cleared my throat and stuttered, "I—I'm just saying—"

"No. There will be a wedding cake or the wedding is off." Esther clenched her jaw. "But with Alice out of business for who knows how long ..." She rolled her eyes up to the ceiling. "I don't know how we can find someone on such short notice."

Shrugging, I crossed my arms and shifted on my feet. What was that saying? Not my circus, not my monkeys. I want no part in this. No one could finish a cake big enough to feed a small town in only a few days.

Leah squeezed behind me and grabbed one of the carafes. The movement brought the mayor's attention to me. We made eye contact. It was as if a lightbulb blinked on above her head and I realized what had just happened.

Oh, no. No. Nope.

She pointed with her handkerchief. "Riley. You can bake." I shook my head as she spoke. "You basically have a bakery in the back."

Not my circus! Not my circus!

"You can make the cake." She clapped her hands in front of her, the somber look on her face slowly disappearing.

Taking a step back, I waved my hands in front of me. "Oh, no. I am not qualified to make a wedding cake."

"Of course you aren't. You're not Alice." Esther rose from her seat. "However, you are the next best thing in Wildewood. I'll call Alice and have her fill you in on the details."

"Madame Mayor," I took a step closer, "I cannot make a wedding cake." There wasn't enough time.

Patting the counter, Esther smiled. "It's settled. You're hired, Riley Jones." Shoving the handkerchief into her purse, Esther placed her hand on Samantha's elbow. "Let's go tell your dad everything has been worked out. The wedding is still on!" she said the last part loudly.

I watched my other customers look over at the commotion.

As Samantha stood, I noticed her demeanor had not changed. The mayor was excited, relieved even, but Samantha seemed just as distressed as when she came into the café. Her eyes flicked to Trey as he chatted with Leah. He noticed they were leaving and made his way toward them, a to-go cup in his hand. I had a feeling Samantha's issues had nothing to do with whether or not she had a cake at her wedding.

Esther rushed them from the café and I stared after them, trying to wrap my head around what I had been forced into. Stunned, I had no idea how I was going to finish the dozens of cupcakes for the Halloween Festival and now make a town-sized cake in less than four days.

Leah inched her way over. "What was that all about?" She placed the carafe back on the warmer.

I swallowed and put my metaphoric top hat on, it looks like it was my circus after all. "I'm making a wedding cake."

Leah's mouth opened forming a perfect *O*. It expressed how I felt perfectly.

A stress-induced headache formed behind my eyes as I rubbed my temple. This was going to be a long few days. Who needs sleep anyway? Maybe I could figure out a spell …

Placing my hands down to my side, I looked up to see Officer Pete Kelley waddle to the counter.

His smile faded as he looked at me. "You look like you just got run over."

I felt like I was run over.

Pete was a large man with short stature. He took his dark navy patrol hat off and placed it on the counter, exposing a large bald spot on the top of his head, his gray hair flattened by the hat. He had been my father's best friend and partner on Wildewood's small police force. When I came back to Wildewood, my father had recently retired. I didn't get to spend a lot of time with him before he passed away, but Pete tried to keep an eye on me. He was like the uncle I never had.

Blinking, I opened my mouth then closed it, not sure where to begin. Drawing in a deep breath, I finally replied, "Esther Miller."

Chuckling, Pete nodded as he sat down on one of the barstools. "Yep, that explains it."

I pushed away the shock still reverberating through me and tried to give Pete a real smile. "The usual?"

Returning the smile, he nodded.

Sliding him a to-go cup of Hocus Focus and an espresso muffin, I studied him. His face lit up when he took a bite. He was my favorite morning regular, though today he was much later than usual. The fire at Just Treats had the entire town in a tizzy. I'm sure every police officer was on high alert. Twitching my nose, I wondered if he had any information he was willing to share. It had been a few hours since the fire had been extinguished and surely, they knew something by now. Right?

"Have you seen Alice?" I prodded.

"Poor girl," Pete said with a mouthful of muffin. He poured sugar into his coffee and stirred enough cream in that it changed to a light caramel color. "Alice was just a wreck at the station."

"I would've been too." I nodded.

After washing down his muffin with a sip of coffee, he said, "It's terrible to think we might have an arsonist in Wildewood."

Oh? "So, someone did set the bakery on fire?" I leaned across the counter on an elbow. Alice thought she'd seen someone. Did this mean the police believe her?

"Oh, yep. The glass on the back door was—" Pete stopped mid-sentence.

I zipped my lips with a hand motion. "My lips are sealed."

As Pete looked down to dust crumbs from the belly of his uniform, I reached into the display case and took out another muffin. While my fingers were still touching the wrapper, I muttered under my breath, "*Garrio.*" A simple spell to persuade someone to reveal a small secret or piece of gossip. Placing the new muffin in front of him, I hoped he would continue to chat.

"You sure do know how to spoil an old man." Pete's smile reached his eyes as he picked it up. He pinched the top of the muffin and placed the small morsel in his mouth.

Counting five Mississippi's, I hoped enough time had passed.

"The glass?" I said, reminding him where he left off to test out the spell.

"It was broken. The tech team is looking to get the surveillance footage in the parking lot, but I'm pretty sure those cameras haven't worked in a decade. They're mostly for show."

"Have you guys been able to figure out where the fire started?" I crossed my fingers behind my back, hoping I could get a little more intel out of him.

Nodding, Pete swallowed a larger bite. "It looked like the fire started on the stove and spread."

Straightening my posture, I crossed my arms over my chest. "You think Alice left the stove on?"

I turned to grab a carafe to refill his cup. "Oh, not Alice. She swears up and down everything was off when they closed yesterday." Pete leaned closer and lowered his voice. "But that's not even the weird part."

"There's a weird part?" I asked, raising an eyebrow as I poured the liquid into his cup.

"When we did a walkthrough, Alice noticed one cake was smashed, absolutely destroyed. Though," he added, "everything in that fridge was damaged from the smoke. The door was left wide open."

"Just one cake?" That was an interesting tidbit and I knew exactly whose cake it was.

Pete nodded as he finished the muffin.

Chewing on the inside of my lip, I tapped my fingers on my arm. "Let me guess, Samantha Miller's?"

Pete gave me a puzzled look. "Yes, how'd you know?"

Raising my shoulders, I responded, "Just call it a hunch."

Scooting off of his seat, Pete laid a ten-dollar bill on the counter. As he turned, I stopped him. "Hey. One more thing—" I was curious about how Esther already knew about the cake. "Was Esther at the walkthrough?"

"Nope. I haven't seen her today." He patted the counter and placed his hat on his head. "See you later, kid."

Pete took his coffee and left me staring through the large window of the café, deep in thought. How could Esther know Samantha's wedding cake was ruined if she hadn't visited the crime scene?

Running a hand through my hair, I pushed it back behind my ears. There was only one reason I could think of, but would the mayor really destroy a business in her own town? That seemed ludicrous. It didn't make any sense. This town was all the mayor had.

Though, perhaps it wasn't the mayor, but her daughter ...

Chapter 5

The morning shift was over before I knew it. Time seemed to have flown by after Pete left. The Witches Brew was only open until noon then again in the evening for a few hours. During the break, we took catering jobs and it just so happened that the mayor requested the coffee cart for a luncheon at Town Hall. To tell the truth, I was feeling uneasy about seeing the mayor after my conversation with Pete.

The front door chimed and Maisie walked through and toward the counter. Her ponytail was disheveled and beads of sweat glistened on her forehead. She had pulled the coffee cart from around the back of the building. It wasn't an easy job to move it through the alley, the wheels had a tendency to get stuck in most of the divots in the concrete.

"The cart is ready," Maisie said as she sat down on a barstool. She wiped the sweat from her forehead then leaned on her elbow on the counter.

I grabbed my flannel jacket and tied it around my waist. "Good. Let's go."

"What?" Maisie stood, her mouth clenched in protest. "Why me?"

Walking to the front door, I held it open with my back. "Because you were late, *again*. Let's go." The door shut before I could hear any more of Maisie's argument. By the look on her face, I was glad it shut when it did.

I helped Maisie pick the cart up to get it over the curb and then again once we crossed the street to the square. As I listened to her grumble under her breath, I couldn't help but let out a sigh. Maisie was always arguing with customers or me. I started having her do other work to keep her away from the customers as much as I could. This wasn't a situation that could last long term. I couldn't hide her from the front of the café forever.

"Riley," Maisie's voice jerked me out of my thoughts.

"What?" My tone was harsher than I meant it to be.

Jaw clenched, she pointed to the curb. "I can't lift the cart by myself."

"Right." I apologized. I picked up the front of the cart as Maisie lifted the back. We crossed the busy street and together lifted the cart again onto the sidewalk in front of Town Hall.

"Riley!"

I cringed at the sound of my name being squealed for the second time today. Esther Miller was waving a hand in the air as she walked toward us. Pulling black gloves off of her hands, she slapped them on her palm. I think I heard her mumbling about needing to replace them. She had a bandage on her index finger and she smoothed it back down.

I don't remember her finger being bandaged at the meeting hall last night.

I wondered if she got that from the broken glass at Just Treats? What a sight that would be—seventy-year-old Madam Mayor using her petite fist to break the glass on the back door of the bakery while wearing matching black blazer and slacks, escaping in her Jimmy Choo pumps. I bet she didn't even own a pair of sweats. I bit the inside of my mouth to stop myself from laughing as the visual played out in my head.

"Maddie," Esther yelled out, "go set the cart over there." She pointed to the cement picnic tables in the courtyard between Town Hall and the police station. Glancing at Maisie, I saw her nostrils flare ever so slightly as she took in a deep breath.

"It's Maisie," she corrected.

Clicking her tongue, Esther waved her hand in the air dismissively. "Right."

I saw Maisie's jaw clench again. I didn't know much about her, except for what was on her application, and that she had a temper. We were the same age and yet she reminded me of when I was a teenager. I had been angry at the world during my teenage years. I reached this age where I was just *angry*. I saw the same intensity in her eyes, especially when something irritated her. I could tell she was holding on to something big, something she needed to let go of. Though, I didn't have much room to talk—I hadn't let my own anger go until a year ago.

Esther hooked her elbow in mine and pulled me toward the courtyard. I was stumbling over my boots to keep pace with her. She moved quickly at her age, not to mention the heels she wore. Maybe she could have pulled it off?

Patting my forearm, Esther said, "I am so glad you can work magic."

Licking my lips, I cleared my throat. "Excuse me?"

"The wedding cake, dear," she explained.

"Oh." As if she had given me a say in the matter. She wasn't too far off though; I was going to have to use magic to get Samantha's cake complete in time. I wondered why she would be so pushy about a replacement cake if she had been the reason it was destroyed.

Maybe the mayor had nothing to do with it. That still didn't explain how she knew about the extent of the damage so quickly.

Turning her attention back on the coffee cart, Esther waved and pointed. "Maddie, put it on the other side."

"It's Maisie." Maisie was grinding her teeth, her chin jutting out and her body stiff with fists by her side.

"Maddie, Maisie. Just push it to the other side." Esther waved her gloves in the air.

Maisie stopped. My posture straightened and I gritted my teeth. She turned toward us, leaving the cart between two picnic tables and took a step away from it. Her chest rose and fell as she drew in a deep breath. "No."

Esther stopped pulling me toward the tables and let my arm go. "Excuse me?"

Untying the black apron from around her waist, Maisie looked at Esther. Her eyes narrowed. "My name is Maisie, not Maddie."

"Maisie," I hissed through my teeth, trying not to scream, but I was beginning to feel embarrassed. "Knock it off," I begged.

"No!" She walked toward us, honed in on me. "She's treating me like crap and you're always sucking up to everyone."

Esther pressed her hand against her chest, the gloves slapping together. "Excuse me!" her voice was louder.

Ignoring the mayor's obvious displeasure, Maisie shoved the apron into my chest and looked me in the eyes. "Stop acting like you have to be perfect all the time."

My mouth gaped as she moved past us.

Esther clicked her tongue. Her voice was filled with disapproval, "Something really must be done about her attitude, especially if she's going to stay here long term."

Shoulders dropping in defeat, I sighed. "I couldn't agree more."

Chapter 6

I finished moving the cart where Esther wanted it. There were platters of three-inch sandwiches probably from the deli across the street. I highly doubted they were from Mikes, though he made an amazing club sandwich—he and the mayor weren't on the best terms. Madame Mayor didn't like the type of crowd Mike's brought in at night. I didn't care, as long as he kept the buffalo wing basket on the menu. My mouth watered at the thought.

I took a step back and looked over the coffee cart. I should've been mad at Maisie, fired her on the spot. Instead, I was feeling torn between worry and frustration. It wouldn't matter if I fired her, she would still be stuck on the destructive path she was walking on. I wish I knew what her problem was. I knew exactly what mine had been.

Just shy of a year ago, I had finally worked up enough courage to begin the search for the parents that had abandoned me. I only had my own last name and the location of where I was found to help in my search. I had been found at a fire station two-miles outside of Wildewood. My name had been written on a piece of paper tucked inside the blanket I had been wrapped in.

These people had named me and then left me. I wanted answers. I knew it wasn't going to change anything from my childhood, but I had always felt like a piece of me was missing. I wanted that hole filled.

Even if it hurt.

When I found out where my father lived, I went straight to Wildewood. The closer I got, the angrier I felt. I had been high on adrenaline. What if I got there and he turned me away? I had banged on his door so hard I thought I was going to break it down. I had questions. I wasn't going to be ignored. And then Andrew Jones opened his front door and welcomed me in as if he knew I'd return one day.

Unfortunately, our time together had been cut short. He had been terminally ill with lung cancer and only had a few months to live. The anger I'd carried around for so long turned to sadness and I spent every weekend with him until he passed. I had finally found my father and then he was gone *again*.

Chatter behind me pulled me away from my thoughts. Esther's guests were arriving. Her husband, Robert Miller—a graying man with thick-rimmed glasses—and Arthur Saccardi, Wildewood's prominent lawyer, were the only two I recognized off-hand. Arthur's tall frame towered over me. He was dressed sharply in a gray suit that looked as if it had been made just for him. He had a white beard that made his blue eyes pop. He searched over me and my breath caught in my throat. It felt as if he was seeing me for what I was. Peering into me. Knowing my biggest secret. The hairs on my arms stood as if the air around me had gotten colder.

I rubbed my bare arms, unsure what his look had been for and backed away, slinking toward the front entrance of Town Hall. Arthur Saccardi was not a man I wanted to spend too much time with. He made me feel like I had forgotten to get dressed and walked out of the house in nothing more than my underwear.

I had only met him once before and, thankfully, it had been very brief. When my father passed away, Arthur's secretary sought me out to inform me Andrew had left everything to me, including his house and a large inheritance. His generosity was the reason I had been able to open The Witches Brew.

I tightened the flannel shirt that hung around my waist as I walked up the steps to Town Hall. Rose bushes lined the ground in front of the porch. I noticed some pruning shears and wondered if that's how Esther got the cut on her finger. Maybe she had gotten pricked by a thorn. I pulled the large door open and poked my head into the lobby. The receptionist's desk was vacant. Great, how was I supposed to pick up my check for the coffee cart? I looked across the hallway and noticed the desk to the mayor's assistant, Aaron Hall, was empty too. Had everyone gone to lunch? New policy—I was taking payment upfront.

I heard a voice yell somewhere down the hall.

"Then call it off!"

The voice sounded familiar and I found myself inching closer.

Another voice responded louder, "You know I can't. My mother would be devastated."

The front door slammed behind me and I yelped, flinching from the noise.

Shit. I did not want to get caught in the middle of whatever was going on down the hallway. I just wanted my check!

"—then let it go!"

I could only make out every few words, so I took a few more steps inside the building.

"You just constantly—"

I reached the edge of the receptionist's desk. Standing on my toes, I leaned closer with my head turned to the side in hopes I could hear the voices better. Wait—what in the hell was I doing? I began to lose my balance when a door was flung open. Jumping, I skittered to the other side of the desk and ducked underneath, trying my best to stay hidden while peering around the side. Since when did I become an eavesdropper?

Now. I was one now.

I rubbed my temple. How in the world would I explain this away if I was caught? I should've just backed out of the building and came back later.

"I wish you would drop dead!"

I moved my hand to cover my mouth, my eyes widening. Someone was *really* angry. I peeked around the side of the desk and saw Samantha run past my hiding spot with her head in her hands.

"Sam, we aren't done here!" Trey called as he ran after her, stopping right before the receptionist's desk.

I held my breath, hoping I would go unnoticed.

"Go to hell!" she yelled and then I heard the front doors being flung open, banging against the wall.

My attention drifted to the floor where the laces of my left shoe stuck out from underneath the desk. Panicking, I whispered a spell as quietly as I could and both laces rose. Muttering another word and moving my index finger, the laces crossed as my finger drew an *X* in the air. One bunny ear. Two. Loop-de-loop. Voila! Tied.

Another door closed and I flinched, the tied loops of my laces going limp against my boot. Peeking around the side to see where it came from, I spotted a pair of brown loafers in front of me. Raising my head up, I saw Aaron Hall. He stood with his arms crossed, his dark brown eyes narrowed slightly. His short blond hair was neatly combed to the left. He must use a ton of hairspray. There was no way it could still look that nice after being outside in the wind. Not one hair was out of place.

"Hey." My cheeks began to burn. He moved backward and I crawled out from under the desk. I pushed myself up off the ground, dusting my knees off. "I was just trying to find—" I looked around, on top of the desk, hoping to find anything to use as an excuse.

Aaron held out an envelope with my name on it.

"My check." I took it and slapped it on the palm of my hand.

Still staring at me, he raised an eyebrow. Okay, he didn't believe me. Why would he? No one hides under a desk for any good reason. Right, Mr. Clinton? My shoulders dropped, and I pushed my hair behind my ears. "I was hiding."

There. I admitted it.

Aaron looked around at the empty room. "From who?"

"Trey and Samantha."

"Ah," Aaron's eyes flicked to the ceiling, "you witnessed one of their famous spats." He pursed his lips.

I folded the envelope and tucked it in one of my back pockets. "So, they do that often?"

"Yes." He walked across the room toward the mayor's office. "More so recently."

Confused, I frowned. "They're about to get married. Shouldn't they be more—"

"In love?" Aaron interrupted as he sat down at his desk.

"Well …" I shrugged. I would think that a couple about to enter into a marriage would be … happier? I was far from an expert on the topic—the longest relationship I had been in lasted a whopping six months and I had been about fifteen. I wasn't relationship material. I was better at short-term, *hell*, even one-night stands. So, really, what did I know? Maybe misery started before the nuptials.

Aaron searched my face and his eyebrows lowered, creating creases in between. "You really are new here." His face relaxed, the tension leaving his shoulders, and he snorted. His lips turned upward as a smile formed. "Trey is a perpetual cheater." Aaron crossed his arms. "I think Samantha thought he would stop when they got engaged. Hell, she pushed it in hopes he would."

Oh, I mouthed the word. "Has he?" I had seen first-hand that Trey was flirtatious, but flirting didn't necessarily mean cheating. Did it? Again, not an expert.

With a quick laugh, he said, "Based on their arguments, Trey claims he's stopped." Aaron spread his arms out as he shrugged.

"She doesn't believe him?" I barely knew him and I'm not sure I would believe him, especially after the spectacle at the meeting hall.

He shook his head. "I don't believe him either." He went quiet, then said, "Their arguments got really bad about two months ago."

"What happened two months ago?" I asked, trying to re-call anything that stood out in my mind. The only thing I could think of was that it was about the same time he stopped coming into The Witches Brew.

"No idea," he said.

The phone on his desk rang. "I gotta take this." He waved at me.

Giving him a quick wave back, I turned to leave as he answered the phone, "Mayor Miller's office …"

A gust of wind hit me as I walked down the steps and I

pulled my jacket off from around my waist. There was no way Aaron didn't use hairspray, I thought as I slid my arms into the sleeves, the wind blowing my hair around my face. I saw Tessa and Leah walking down the sidewalk toward The Witches Brew. I picked up my pace, barely paying attention as I crossed the street, and thought about the last two months. What could have changed two months ago that caused more tension between Trey and Samantha?

A horn honked and I reached my arms out, my palms aimed at the car. A spell lingered at the tip of my tongue to stop the car when its brakes squealed. Clenching, I apologized and jogged to the other side of the road to the safety of the square. Sweat was in all the wrong places and my heart was pounding. Freaking pay attention, Riley! That had been too close. I had almost used my magic in a very public way.

Wrapping my arms around me as the chill in the air grew, I walked through the Town Square, passing by the large stage. It was almost complete. The festival crew was hanging the dark backdrop. As my adrenaline was calming down, I returned to my thoughts about Trey and Samantha. I couldn't think of anything that happened two months ago. Honestly, I probably had heard something but I barely paid attention to any gossip I overheard at the café. Now I wished I had.

Tessa spotted me and waved as I neared the café. "Missed you at the sale today!" she yelled.

This time, looking before I crossed the road, Tessa wrapped an arm around my shoulders to pull me in for a sideways hug.

"Madame Mayor requested the coffee cart," I explained.

Taking a look behind me at Leah, I saw her brows crease. "Where's Maisie?"

Wrinkling my nose, I said, "She took off."

40

Wait. I stopped walking. Maisie. Two months ago, I hired Maisie. Leah opened the door to the café and the two of them walked inside. I turned toward Town Hall, rubbing my arms. Two months ago, Trey stopped coming into the café.

Maybe Samantha hadn't set the fire after all. Maisie had been late this morning. She had cuts on her hands. Could she have cut her fingers on the glass from the bakery? Could Trey and Maisie be …

"Coming, Riley? I want to show you a necklace Leah found." Tessa tugged on my sleeve.

Chapter 7

Sitting next to Tessa at the counter, I stared at Leah's necklace. Attached to a thin silver chain was a large oval pendant with a silhouette of a woman's bust carved into the white pearl. She had tight ringlet curls falling to her shoulder and her lips were turned down. She looked sad as if she had lost something that could never be returned to her.

"She just found it at the bottom of an old trunk," Tessa's voice was high pitched. When she was excited, her face brightened and her voice rose a few octaves. "I had just put it in the back of the store and hadn't gone through it yet." She grinned resting her chin on one hand, looking at the necklace with dreamy eyes. "It's as if they were meant for each other." Tessa loved finding treasure and giving them new homes. Maybe the woman in the cameo was longing over a lost lover too.

"It's pretty," I said, watching Leah press it close to her chest, her finger rubbing over the intricate carving. The necklace was a good fit. Leah had broken up with her long-time boyfriend before coming to work for me and his absence still bothered her occasionally.

Playfully smacking my arm, Tessa corrected me, "It's beautiful. I wonder how old it is."

Without answering, I continued to stare at the necklace. Leah looked at her hand, the tip of her finger blackened. Her expression soured and she wiped her fingers on her apron. Getting up from the stool, I walked around to the other side of the counter, leaning my hip against it and handed Leah a cleaning rag. Old usually meant dirty in my experience.

"What's up with you?" Tessa asked, her voice returning to normal.

Taking a deep breath, I blinked. "Sorry, I guess I'm just deep in thought."

"About what?" Leah turned the sink on to wash the soot from her hands.

I blew out of my mouth in a raspberry noise. I didn't want to tell Leah about the altercation with Maisie. She already couldn't stand her to begin with. How could I put this delicately without giving Leah more of a reason to be annoyed with Maisie? I pushed away from the counter and the bell above the door chimed.

Saved by the bell.

Tessa took a quick look over her shoulder. Turning back, she wiggled her eyebrows up and down. "Look at the stud who just walked in."

Looking past Tessa, I watched Dimples from the meeting hall come toward the counter. His blue eyes were set on the menu board behind me. Oh, God. I could feel my pulse speeding up and my armpits were starting to sweat. I searched for Leah. She had disappeared across the café to wipe down a table.

"He's all yours." Tessa grinned, her long black waves bouncing around her as she busied herself staring in her coffee cup as if there was something more interesting inside than the puddle I was becoming.

Gritting my teeth in a smile, I whispered, "Shut up." I pulled the ticket book out of my apron pocket as he approached the counter.

His attention lowered until it landed on me and I sucked in a breath. He had the clearest blue eyes I had ever seen. Oh, frick, what was happening to me? I licked my lips. I guess it had been a while ...

"Welcome to The Witches Brew," I started. "Which—p—potion will you ch—choose?" Embarrassment crept onto my face. From this day forward, I vowed to never make anyone say that again.

His lips twitched. "I don't know," he began and a shiver ran down my spine, his voice smooth with a slight southern drawl. "I heard the Hocus Focus was pretty good." I stopped myself from leaning across the counter, he could talk to me all day.

He must be new in town. Everyone had tried the Hocus Focus. Hell, we had been open for six months. "It is, but—" I swallowed. "It's only served in the morning." It was not my goal to have everyone wide awake late at night.

He rapped his fingers on the counter. What large paws you have. I wonder what those hands could do. His head rose to read the menu board again. His tongue flicked out to lick his bottom lip then he lowered his head, making eye contact with me. Oh, God, take me now! My knees felt like they would buckle. Even from across the counter, I could smell his cologne. It was a sweet musky scent with a hint of vanilla.

The pool of sweat forming under my arms was too much. Did I put deodorant on this morning? Oh, shit! I can't remember. At least my flannel shirt was covering the sweat stains. Why was I having such an intense reaction to this man? I'd seen dimples before. I wasn't a stranger to men! But this felt like ... swooning. Was this what it felt like to swoon? I did *not* like it.

"I think a to-go cup of Midnight Brew will do fine," the corners of his mouth smirked. My face had to be the color of a tomato.

As I turned around to fetch his order, thankful to be out of his sight, I caught a glimpse of a huge grin plastered on Tessa's face. My eyes narrowed at her. She was getting a kick out of it. This was *not* funny.

"The red velvet cupcakes are to die for." I heard Tessa whisper. There was a tinge of humor in her voice. This really was not funny, Tessa. Nope. Not at all. Of all the men I had dated in my twenty-eight years, I had never felt starstruck. But those dimples … those bright blue eyes … the drawl … his hands …

"That sounds good."

His voice made me jump, which was probably for the best since my imagination began a not-so-work-appropriate daydream. I gave him his coffee.

Placing his cupcake in a box on the counter in front of him, I couldn't help noticing his smile. Our fingers touched as he took the box from me. Could my face get any redder? Forcing the smile on my lips not to get too big, I felt my heart drumming rapidly.

"Thanks." He pulled his hands away and I grabbed the counter, refusing to crumble.

What in the world was going on with me? I felt like a love-struck teeny-bopper who'd just met their celebrity crush.

Spotting Leah next to the register, I cleared my throat. "She'll check you out."

"Thanks," he said again.

As he moved to the other side of the counter, I turned away, let out a sigh, and pulled my shirt from my body to let in cool air.

45

"I think he was already checking you out." Tessa giggled into her coffee cup as she brought it up to her lips.

"Would you get out of here?" I stuck my tongue out at her.

She slid off the stool and blew a kiss to me, fluttering her lashes. "Are we still on for tonight?"

"Yep." I nodded and waved my fingers at her.

"Is Leah coming?" she asked, pulling her jacket on.

I shook my head, glancing at the man.

"Looks like it's just the two of us then." She took one last sip of her coffee. "Bye, Leah," Tessa called out.

Leah waved as the cash register dinged. Dimples followed Tessa out of the café a moment later and the tense muscles of my shoulders relaxed.

"You okay?" Leah asked as she came up beside me.

Nodding toward the door, I asked, "Who was that?"

"A walking heartbreak." She huffed.

Glancing sideways at her, I said, "Oh, come on."

"It's not worth it. It'll only lead to a broken heart." Leah scowled and grabbed a clean rag from under the counter.

I shook my head at her pessimism and crossed my arms. "They can't all be bad." I mean, he could be as bad as he wanted.

She exhaled sharply through her nose. "They are." She moved past me and out from behind the counter to wipe down tables and retrieve a stack of empty dishes.

Okay, Debbie Downer. I knew she was turned off from relationships right now. I suspected she was still pining for whoever broke her heart. She wouldn't talk about him; she wouldn't even tell us his name—except jackass. I watched her smile return as she mingled with the few remaining customers. At least I could count on her to keep her mood in check, unlike Maisie.

Five minutes until closing and the display case was mostly

empty. I pressed the power button on the coffee machine and it beeped off. Moving into the middle of the café with a wet rag, I began to clean as Leah cashed out the till.

The door chimed and I looked up from wiping down a table to see Alice walk in. She looked around, her arms wrapped around her torso. Her eyes didn't seem to focus on any one thing in particular. Leaving the rag, I waved and made my way toward her.

"Hey, Alice," my voice was a whisper. She looked like anything could spook her.

Her eyes finally focused on me. She pulled out the closest chair, with a slight tremor to her hand. Sitting down, she said, "The mayor's aid called."

I sat down across from her. She hadn't needed to come all the way to the café. It felt cruel to make her deal with a wedding cake the same day her business was set on fire. "I'm really sorry."

Alice shook her head, her silver hair loosening from its braid. "No, I'm not upset about that."

Lowering my eyes to her hands as she placed them on the table, I admitted, "I feel like I'm stealing business from you." I didn't even want the job in the first place, but still.

Alice's lips twitched into a weak smile and she reached across the table to pat my arm. "I know how Esther is. Don't you worry for a moment longer," she reassured me.

I wrung my hands together. "Esther said you have a binder with cake details—"

"Had," she corrected me. "It's missing from the bakery."

"Missing?" I repeated. Maybe she had misplaced it? I looked up at Alice and dismissed the idea. For a woman in her seventies, Alice's mind was sharp. She might be on edge right now, but Alice had a keen eye for details.

Alice chewed on her bottom lip and leaned closer, even though there was no one else around. "The police suspect it was burned on the stove, where the fire started. The binder rings were—" she clicked her tongue, gave her head a little shake, then pushed her hair behind her ears. "But, anyway, Trey and Samantha wanted devil's food cake with a chocolate ganache frosting."

"Thanks." I gave her a sympathetic smile. Devil's food cake was easy enough but I had never made a ganache frosting before.

"Good luck, Riley. I do not envy you right now." She reached across the table and patted my hands again.

Alice stood. She pushed her chair back underneath the table when I had a thought.

"Hey, Alice, when did you tell Esther about Samantha's cake?"

Alice flicked her eyes to the ceiling. "Riley, you will learn soon enough that Esther Miller knows everything, even before it happens."

What did that mean? How could Esther possibly know things before they happened? Was she psychic? I was a witch, so I felt I had to assume there were other *things* out in the world.

I watched Alice walk to the door and scrunched my brows. She had to be exaggerating. I'm sure she had someone at the police station in her pocket, giving her access to information before it leaked out to the public.

A gust of cold wind came through the door as Alice opened it. Leah slapped her hands down on top of the counter, receipts threatening to fly to the floor. I stood, picking my rag back up. Alice was exaggerating, right?

Chapter 8

Leah and I finished cleaning the café after closing. I waved goodbye to her as she walked outside, overlapping her unbuttoned coat tightly across her waist. The frigid wind sent a shiver down my spine as it poured in, replacing the warm air of the café. During the day the wind was bearable, once the sun went down it felt as if winter had already moved it. Snapping my fingers, the lights turned off around me, only the light from the lamp posts pouring through the window. I locked the door, thankful I had a thick jacket on.

Holding my bag against my chest, I ran down the street to Odds 'n' Ends. It was too damn cold. I pulled the door open and noticed Tessa was absent from her usual front desk post and the main lights were off.

"Tessa?" I called, taking a step inside. The store had the musty scent of an old book, reminding me of when I was a child and would flip the pages under my nose to breathe it in before consuming the words. Hell, who am I kidding, I still do that.

"Almost done!" Tessa yelled from the back. I heard something hit the floor and then a long chain of curse words that would make a sailor blush.

"Don't hurt yourself." I laughed and began looking around at the assortment of trinkets stacked to the ceiling on metal shelves around the store. Odds 'n' Ends was a treasure trove for the old and strange. Tessa accepted anything she found interesting, and that was just about everything. Your junk is another person's treasure, her motto not mine.

The bookshelves lining the middle were overflowing, forcing Tessa to pile stacks on the top. The clothing racks at the back were packed with fabrics from the last few decades. Bowls of potpourri were scattered throughout the store, but nothing could squash the smell of old. I personally loved the smell, but it could be overwhelming. Tessa had a tendency to keep the front door cracked open during business hours.

Wandering around, I weaved my way to the back, past the old porcelain dolls that watched me as I quickened my steps. "Creepy little shits …" I mumbled, frowning. Turning a corner around a bookshelf, I yelped as my shin collided with an old metal trunk.

"You okay?" I looked up to see Tessa poking her head out of the doorway to her office. She had a box under her chin and her arms barely fit around it.

Nodding, I waved my hand at her. "Yeah, just a bruise." I rubbed my shin, wincing. There would definitely be a bruise.

Tessa chuckled and disappeared back into the room. Another loud thud. More cursing. It sounded like she was rearranging her office and having a particularly hard time with it.

My shin throbbed and I looked down at the trunk. The brown leather was faded and flaking and the latch was broken off. I sat on my knees, ignoring the pain of my shin, and pushed the lid open to rest on its hinges. I rummaged around faded garments, then found a medium-sized, black leather box with its own smaller silver latches. The box was in pristine shape, no fading or flaking. It looked out of place. I pulled it out, sitting it on top of the clothes and saw a name printed in silver cursive on the side. Agatha. I traced the letters with my fingers, wondering what was inside. Maybe a hat with large feathers or one with many jewels. My heart skipped a beat as I tried to open it, but the latch was locked. Damn.

Not to worry. I touched the tip of my finger to the keyhole. "*Reserare.*" The latch clicked open and I pushed the lid up.

"Oh …" the disappointment slipped from my lips. It was nothing more than a wide-brimmed, pointed hat, resembling a fedora. The black wool was faded with patches of dark brown sewn on in a few places. Why would anyone put such a tired-looking hat inside a box to keep it safe?

I picked up the hat, expecting the fabric to be scratchy, but it was worn and soft. I looked around to see if Tessa had a mirror, spotting one next to a clothing rack. I took a few steps and placed the hat on my head, adjusting it. I scrunched my nose as I looked at it in the mirror. Maybe whoever it belonged to accidentally placed it in the box. I reached out to remove it when the pointed end stood straight up. My eyes widened and I felt a shock to my temple.

"Ouch!" I pulled it off quickly and dropped it. It landed on the ground before my feet.

You could say that again! a woman retorted.

Rubbing my forehead from the lingering pain, I glanced around Odds 'n' Ends to see where the voice had come from. I hadn't heard the door open and Tessa was still cursing away inside her office.

"Who's there?" I whispered.

I heard footsteps and grabbed the hat off of the floor.

"Did you say something?" Tessa walked toward me, pulling a large tote over her shoulder.

"No. Did you?" I asked.

Tessa raised a single eyebrow, "No—" she looked at the open trunk behind me. "That's the same box Leah found her necklace in. What did you find?"

Maybe I had imagined the voice? I rubbed my forehead; the shock had been very real though. I followed her closer to the trunk and kneeled to place the hat back in the box. "Just an old hat."

"It looks like a witch hat!" Tessa exclaimed. I looked up at her, her face flashing with excitement, before returning my gaze to the worn hat. I guess it did look like a witch hat—a really old, worn out, retired witch hat. "You should use it for your costume."

I pursed my lips and stared at it. I was going as a witch to the Halloween Festival. I know, I know. But this didn't really go with the costume and—"I think I want something not so …" I trailed off as I closed the lid to the hatbox and stood.

"Not so old?" Her lips turned upward with amusement.

"Exactly." The voice I heard lingered in my head, but I couldn't make sense of it, like trying to remember faces from a dream. Biting the inside of my mouth, I decided I'd imagined the response. Yep. That was it, and I was sticking to it.

"Well, it's yours if you change your mind." Tessa shifted the tote to her other shoulder.

I closed the lid to the trunk, not bothering with the latch since it was broken. I was still wondering why anyone would be keeping that hat safe. I'm sure it meant something to someone once upon a time, but now it belonged in the trash.

I heard that. The voice made me jump and I spun around, searching for the culprit. Tessa was pushing the trunk toward her office door. It had not been Tessa's voice. It belonged to someone older.

Tessa returned with a grin, her tote causing her to bend from its weight. "I need to go through that tomorrow."

Running my hand through my hair, I sucked in a deep breath, trying to suppress my nerves. I must be feeling off from all the excitement today. Yeah, that was it. I was tired, my nerves were shot, and I was hearing voices in my head. Oh, goody.

"Ready to go?" Tessa asked as she made her way past me to the storefront.

I trailed behind her and took one more look over my shoulder before following her out the door. It was all in my head. The voice wasn't real. I held my breath, waiting for a response but I was met with silence.

We crossed Main Street, the bright lights from the ice cream parlor lit up the dark surroundings. It was crowded inside, so I took a seat outside on one of the light blue benches, letting Tessa go in alone. I pulled my flannel jacket closer. Even though it was cold out, Frostbite served a peppermint hot chocolate flavored ice cream during the fall and winter months. It had become a quick favorite of mine and I tried to get it as often as possible before the season ended.

I watched visitors shuffling around Town Square as I waited. The pile of hay bales was now stacked high in a large square that took up one-fourth of the square. They must have finished the maze over the course of the day. At least two dozen small, rectangular folding tables were placed evenly through the grass on the side opposite of the maze. One of those would be for The Witches Brew cupcakes I had promised to bake.

"Here you go," Tessa pushed the door open with her back, handing me a large waffle cone overfilled with brown and white swirled ice cream. I took it from her and picked a piece of crushed peppermint from the top and popped it in my mouth. Heaven in a cone.

We were silent most of the way through town, our mouths too busy devouring the cold treat. It probably wasn't the wisest idea to eat ice cream in the freezing cold of late October, but we were and we did. I had no regrets, and I'd do it again. We crossed the road toward my cottage, and I decided to ask about Trey. They had all grown up in town together, Tessa was sure to know more about him than I did.

"Trey has always been a player," Tessa explained. "Since we were in high school. Ten years later and he's still the same." She shrugged, more focused on her ice cream.

I guess Aaron was right. Samantha was hoping he'd change if they got married, but so far it looked as if he'd remained the same. "If she knows how he is, then why is she marrying him?"

"Beats me." Her contempt was hot on her tongue, her ice cream was probably going to start melting.

That explained Samantha's disposition. It was possible she finally realized marriage was not going to change Trey the way she hoped it would. But it also made me think she was having second thoughts. Maybe Samantha was the perpetrator after all. Could she be trying to sabotage her own wedding so it would look like it wasn't her fault?

I felt something brush my leg. I stopped abruptly. "Oh, God, what was that?" I turned in a circle, trying to find what touched me. It was too dark to make out anything. The street lamps were few and far between in this area.

"What?" Tessa asked, turning around with me.

"I swear something just touched my leg," I whispered, the hairs on the back of my neck standing.

Tessa looked up and down the street. "It was probably just the wind."

Just the wind. Okay, she was probably right. I was still

freaked out over the voice I heard in her store. We began to walk again and a small, black figure ran past me. I yelped; my body froze in place. Tessa screamed and grabbed my arm. My ice cream slipped out of my hands and the cone fell to the ground, barely missing my boots.

"I told you something touched me!" I said through my teeth, trying to keep my voice down.

Tessa's grip on my arm tightened. I stepped over my ice cream, disappointed I wouldn't be able to finish it, as we began to walk in the direction it went—toward my house. My boots scraped the concrete as she dragged me with her. My eyes searched the ground. Whatever it was, it had been small. Oh. My. God. Was it a rat? How big could rats get? Please don't be a rodent. Please, don't be a rodent.

"Where the hell did it go?" I whispered.

"There, I think." Tessa pointed to a large oak tree resting between my house and my neighbor's.

I squinted. Where? My feet began to dig into the ground again. I couldn't see anything until a pair of yellow eyes blinked. I stopped, forcing Tessa to stop with me. Rats didn't have yellow eyes. Right? Red, I think, but not yellow.

I heard a quiet *meow*.

It was just a cat.

Leaves rustled nearby. Spooked, we ran up the three long steps attached to my porch and shoved our way inside. I bolted the door. I pressed my back against it and a laugh escaped me. I couldn't believe I was this freaked out over a little cat. Tessa threw her tote on the ground and bent over, putting her hands on her knees as she laughed with me.

After several deep breaths, we got busy finishing our costumes. Tessa only needed a few minor touches, but I was dragging my feet because of the changes we had recently made to mine. Or rather, Tessa had recently made.

It hadn't been my idea to go as a witch to the festival. When Tessa suggested it while hanging out at the café, I almost choked on my coffee. She thought it would be a fun costume to go with The Witches Brew theme. I tossed the idea around for a few days and then decided it *would* be fun to dress up like a witch—like myself, my *real* self.

I went into the bathroom to put on the costume and we continued with our conversation before the cat spooked us.

"How have you not heard the rumors?" she spoke through the bathroom door. "I wish Samantha would just call it off."

Tessa didn't realize someone was taking care of that for her—though that someone might very well be Samantha. This whole thing was making me feel more confident in being single. People who were supposed to love you had a tendency to disappoint.

Tessa pushed the door open to look at the costume. It was a long, black dress made out of a thin fabric that sparkled in the light. My breasts were pushed up and I had more cleavage than I thought I possessed. Thank you, push-up bra. I pinched the fabric together to cover myself up. This was way out of my comfort zone. I didn't even wear low cut shirts.

Tessa slapped my hand away, forcing me to stop messing with the fabric. She tapped her index finger on her lip and mumbled, "Something's missing."

"What?" I turned to look in the mirror as Tessa disappeared behind me.

Squirming, I fought with the elastic on my shoulders. I had wanted an upright collar—sort of like Maleficent, but Tessa insisted I go for a sexier look. What reason did I have to look sexy? Though, maybe Dimples would be at the festival. I sighed, who am I kidding? I looked at my reflection and noticed Tessa reappear behind me with a dark purple, waist-cinching belt.

"Oh, no!" I turned to her and backed away.

"Riley Jones." She crossed her arms, the belt dangling by her side.

"I look fine," I begged as she began to unlace the strings, ignoring my pleas.

"You look frumpy." She wrinkled her nose.

What? Frumpy! How rude. I didn't look frumpy. I looked … comfortable.

Tessa wrapped the belt around my waist, forcing my hands out of the way. Lacing it back up, she pulled the strings unnecessarily tight.

"Okay! I can't breathe!" I gasped.

"That's the point," she muttered and tied it. She took a step away from me and looked me over. A smile grew over her face and she whispered, "Perfect."

Oh, great. I was her little masterpiece. Her project to sex up. I didn't want to sex up—well, maybe if Dimples was involved. I had just wanted a simple witch costume, but with Tessa, nothing was simple. She had turned me into a vixen.

I looked in the mirror and took in a sight I barely recognized. The cincher made my waist look smaller and my hips wider. I saw Tessa tap a finger against her lips again and I recognized the look on her face.

"What now?" I asked, watching her in the mirror.

Tessa bounced to the kitchen table. I stepped into the doorway. She turned around with a pair of scissors in her hand.

"What are you doing?" I took a step back into the bathroom. Smart, Riley. Corner yourself.

Tessa narrowed her eyes, her focus on my dress. "Adding a

finishing touch." She glanced up at me as she knelt before me. "Don't move."

Gritting my teeth, I watched helplessly as Tessa took the end of my dress in between the blades of the scissors and began to slide upward. She moved past my ankle. The cold metal touched my knee. I held my breath. The only sound I could hear was the fabric being cut as she worked the shears further up my thigh.

Oh, God. I looked up at the ceiling.

Tessa stood, clasping the scissors in her hands.

With my mouth open, I glanced at Tessa. "You just—"

"Made it better." She put the scissors into her back pocket. "Now, take it off and I'll hem that up then we'll be done." She gently pushed me back into the bathroom and shut the door.

Chapter 9

Fumbling for the towel that hung outside of the shower, I wrapped it around myself before stepping out onto the plush green bath rug. The bathroom was hot from steam, the fan had burnt out months ago and I hadn't gotten around to getting it fixed. Wiping the fog off the mirror with my hand, I saw the dark circles underneath my eyes.

I had already been awake when my alarm clock started to scream at four in the morning. Tossing and turning all night. My dreams had been haunted by talking hats, black cats, and an employee who needed to be fired and to my disappointment, not once did Dimples make an appearance.

I was not looking forward to going into work. In fact, I was dreading it so much I was tempted to call in sick. Except, I was the boss and didn't have that luxury. Taking another look at the bags under my eyes before turning on the hairdryer, I took in a deep breath.

Through the loud hum, I heard a thud from outside the bathroom. I turned it off, setting it down gently on the counter and cracked the bathroom door open. Great, someone is breaking in and I'm naked. I pressed the towel closer to my chest, praying it wouldn't loosen and fall. The house was still dark, only the light above the kitchen sink on. Holding my breath, the only noise I heard was the pounding of my heart.

You're hearing things, Riley. I clenched my jaw and exhaled sharply. When did you turn into such a scaredy-cat?

I stood in the living room, holding my breath, trying to listen for any sound out of the ordinary. After what felt like an eternity—probably only about thirty seconds—I turned the living room light on. I closed my eyes as I took in a deep breath and adjusted the towel. I wasn't usually so jumpy. I had lived alone since I left the last foster home. But I had always lived in apartments and there was always some noise from my neighbors. I suppose I was still getting used to the silence of small-town living. Whatever was causing my newly found anxiety, it seemed to be sky-high.

Sky … high … Shit!

I had forgotten my broom! Panicking, I ran up the steps to the loft, my towel loosening from my movements. Giving it up, I threw it on the floor, and, as quick as I could, I pulled on a black pair of panties and matching bra. Shimmying into dark blue jeggings and a white crew-neck shirt, I grabbed a long-sleeved, black and red flannel shirt and my thick black jacket from the bed then ran back down the stairs. Finding my boots next to the front door, I shoved my feet into them as I pulled the jackets on.

Hoping my broom was still where I left it, I ran down the porch steps. Getting about halfway down the stone walkway that cut through the front yard, I stopped dead in my tracks. What in the freaking hell … I turned around. Sitting next to the welcome mat on the front porch was the black leather box from Tessa's antique store. It hadn't been my imagination. I had heard something.

Slowly walking back up the steps, I stood a short distance from the box. Taking a quick look at my watch, it was not yet five in the morning. A little early for anyone, even a best friend, to deliver a package. Especially a package I wasn't too fond of having—one that freaked me out quite a bit.

Biting my bottom lip, I stared at the box while I decided on my next move. Okay, it's just a hat. Just an old, possibly talking, hat. You got this, Riley. Kneeling, I hesitantly reached forward. It's just a hat. As my fingers got close enough to almost touch it, the latch clicked open. I yelped—not just a hat! I tumbled backward landing hard on my rear end.

"Nope!" I said out loud. "You're going back."

Reassuring myself—more like lying to myself—it was just a box, I stood then swooped an arm down to grab the handle tightly. Walking back down the stone path, my laces slapped the ground, the plastic tips making clip-clop sounds that were deafeningly loud in the otherwise quiet pre-dawn. I kept my eyes on the box as I turned onto the street, wary of what would happen if I looked away.

I collided with something solid.

"What the—" I screeched as the momentum sent me flying backward. I landed on my tailbone. The box flung out of my grip and I heard it land with a thud. Blinking up at the dark sky, splaying my arms out above my head on the cold asphalt, I could feel a bruise forming. Please let this be a dream. Please, *please*, be a dream.

"I am so sorry!" A hand reached out and grabbed my arm under my elbow. In one swift motion, I was yanked upright.

Stars danced in my eyes as I lifted my head and found myself in the rather sweaty arms of—"Dimples?"

"I am so sorry," he repeated, his eyes searching me.

Great. It wasn't the costume that was going to get me noticed.

I croaked out, "It's o—okay." Butterflies fluttered in my stomach and I was sure I looked like I had a serious sunburn on my face. Thank God it was still dark outside.

He bent to pick up the old hat. He stopped a moment to study it and his brows furrowed. As I had, he was surely wondering why it was in such a nice box. Beats me, buddy. After a quick glance at me, one brow raised, he placed it back inside. Securing the latch, he handed the box to me. Our fingers brushed as I took it from him.

"Sorry, again." He ran his hand through his caramel-colored hair, it fell to the side in a messy part.

"It's okay," I repeated. It seemed it was all I could say.

Lowering his gaze, his lips turned upward and the corner of his eyes creased. He turned away and continued his morning jog. I found myself staring after him as if he were a decadent slice of cake.

Focus, Riley!

I closed my eyes, reminding myself of my current predicament. I had a strange hat following me and a missing broom. Reopening one eye, I peeked at the enticing confection as he turned on to the next street and disappeared out of sight.

I huffed my way down the street until I reached Oak. The box hit my thigh with every step. It would definitely create a bruise right above my knee, or a friction burn. My watch said five thirty-five, which was later than I usually got into work and I still had one more stop to make. I stopped a few feet shy of Odds 'n' Ends and looked down at the box realizing there was no way I could explain to Tessa how I had this in my possession.

I moved out of the light of the lamp post and set the box down on the sidewalk. I knelt in front of it and unlatched its lock. A bright light flashed from inside as soon as I cracked the lid. What the—I whipped my head to the side but I hadn't been quick enough and was temporarily blinded. It felt like I had just stared into the sun. Blinking rapidly to clear the spots from my vision, I opened the lid again, this time squinting just in case it happened again.

But the box was empty.

The hat was gone.

What the hell just happened?

I heard movement coming from Tessa's shop and closed the box. Grabbing it by its handle, I hurried back down the street and decided to take the alley to The Witches Brew. I was certain by now that Tessa had not left the hat on my doorstep. If I didn't know any better, it seemed the hat had its own mind and was following me. Except now it was gone and there was no way I could explain that to Tessa without potentially giving away my secret.

Just imagine that conversation—Hey Tessa, somehow this hat walked out of your store all on its own. Yes, an inanimate object moved on its own. No, I don't know where it is now. It blinded me and ran away.

That would go over really well. Go ahead and lock me up in the looney bin and throw away the key.

Reaching the back door of the café, I sighed in relief as I caught sight of my broom unscathed, still leaning where I had left it the night before. Touching the wooden handle, I whispered an apology, even though I knew it couldn't hear me. It was, unlike the hat, an ordinary broom—until I spoke magic into it.

Chapter 10

I walked into the kitchen and dropped the hatbox near the door when I remembered Maisie was supposed to be working this morning. Both of my employees had a key to the café so they could get in without having to wait for me. Yet, here I stood in a dark kitchen. The ovens were cold. Everything was just as clean as I had left it the night before. Gritting my teeth, I could feel my blood pressure rising. I suppose when she had said "I'm done," what she meant was she quit. Well, if she dared to walk back through the door, she would be fired. I was done playing her games.

Snapping my fingers, the fluorescent tubes above me shook, the filaments threatening to burst. I closed my eyes and took in a deep breath, then exhaled slowly. The last thing I needed was to have to bake in the dark. Pushing down my irritation, I snapped my fingers again—this time calmer—and the ovens clicked on to begin preheating.

Okay, Maisie, since you didn't show up, I will bake my way.

I didn't need her. Nope, I'd worked in the café by myself for months and I could work by myself again. I began to fire off commands with a point of a finger or a snap. The top to the large bag of flour unfolded and opened up wide. A measuring cup buried itself in the white powder then floated out of the bag toward one of the empty chrome mixers, pouring its contents inside and creating a small plume. The measuring cup returned to the bag of flour and repeated the process. I could do this by myself as long as I had a little magical help.

The refrigerator door swung open and a carton of eggs bobbed toward the mixers. One egg at a time gently hit the rim of the large bowls and the two sides of the shell opened, the liquid dripped into the flour. The empty eggshells floated into the trashcan near the door. Okay. Flour, eggs, water … I snapped my fingers and the stove clicked a few times before the flame appeared. A small pan settled on top of the burner grate and a stick of butter unwrapped itself and plopped into it.

As I whisked the ground espresso beans into the butter myself, the measuring cup added the sugar into the mixers, as well as the remaining ingredients for each type of muffin. I moved the pan off the heat and pointed to the refrigerator. The container of blueberries floated, and one at a time the small berries jumped into one of the mixers. While I poured the espresso mixture into a separate mixer, a smaller measuring spoon scooped cinnamon into another. The aroma of espresso and cinnamon wafted through the air. Another snap of my fingers and the mixers locked their heads in place and began to whisk.

I grabbed three large muffin pans and with a few snaps, lined each hole with thin, white paper. All three mixers turned off, their heads leaned back and the wet batter dripped from the whisks. The large chrome bowls floated upward and with ease, they bobbed up and down as they filled their designated pans just enough to create the perfect muffin top.

Sliding the pans in the oven, I set a timer and walked into

the front of the café, the swinging doors hitting a little extra hard against the wall. I usually found baking therapeutic. It calmed me down—just not today. I took a deep breath; it was not going to do me any good to blow up. I snapped my finger and turned the lights on. This time, the bulbs didn't shake or threaten to burst. I was still feeling furious. Maybe cleaning would help. I grabbed a rag and some cleaner and began vigorously scrubbing the already clean tables while I waited on the muffins to bake.

I spent my whole life not being able to trust anyone. It was hard for me to rely on other people—it didn't come naturally to me. I felt like I had been fighting my whole life for what I needed or wanted. I never had anyone to turn to, to hold me when I was upset or to just tell me I was doing a good job. I had to be that person. Even now.

Don't get me wrong, not every home I lived in was terrible but they were full of other kids begging for attention just like me. Moving to Wildewood had been the best decision I had ever made. I finally had a place where I felt like I belonged, more or less. And this café … it was fully mine. I didn't have to fight over it. But eventually, I'd needed an extra set of hands. I had not expected the café to be so busy. So, when I put out a hiring sign, Leah had come in and saved the day.

Then I felt the need to hire a second employee. What a mistake. I should've just stuck with Leah and made it work. Or at least not hired the first person to apply. Maisie was slowly destroying any progress I had made relying on people.

I heard the lock on the front door turn and my body went rigid. I looked up and saw Maisie walk inside. Deep breaths, Riley. I felt my nostrils flare as I watched Maisie stroll into the café. That's right, *strolled*, like nothing was wrong.

"I wasn't expecting you," I said bluntly, clenching my jaw.

"Why not?" She stared straight ahead, not making eye contact, and walked behind the counter.

"What are you doing?" I followed, tossing the cleaning cloth on a table. Was she really acting like she hadn't walked off the job yesterday? I'm pretty sure her last words were, and I quote, "I'm done."

She finally looked at me as she put her bag underneath the counter. With a raised eyebrow, she said, "I'm going to start the coffee." Her voice held a question in it.

Okay, she *was* going to act like nothing happened. "No." I crossed my arms.

She stood from her bent position and repeated, "No?"

"I—" I pinched the bridge of my nose, closing my eyes for a moment. Stay calm, Riley. But my pulse was speeding up. Maybe I could turn her into a toad, or—Oh! A rat. I really didn't like rats. I looked at her, putting my hands back down to my sides. "I think you are done here." I had no idea how to turn something into another thing, just wishful thinking.

Her eyebrows raised, her mouth forming an *O*. Had she really not seen this coming? "Are you firing me?"

I licked my lips, my mouth suddenly dry. "Yes." She really hadn't seen it coming.

Maisie took a step backward, her mouth slack. "Why?"

I rubbed my forehead. Why hadn't I called in sick today? Better question, why did she come in? After the spectacle at Town Hall, she should've just kept on walking. "I think you know why."

Maisie walked around the counter to stand in front of me. Her lips were pressed firmly together and she held tight fists down by her sides. My knees locked and I wasn't sure if it was from panic or from standing my ground. I *was* feeling quite panicky. I did not like confrontation.

"This isn't fair," Maisie said.

This wasn't fair? Was she joking? I looked up at the ceiling for a moment. "Maisie—"

"I'm here, aren't I?" she interrupted, almost yelling.

"An hour and a half late," I responded, then added, "*Again.*"

Her mouth opened slightly. She stuttered but it was my turn to interrupt.

"You have no respect for this business." Oh, my God, why was my mouth so damn dry? I licked my lips again. "No respect for me. You are never on time. You're rude to the customers." I sucked in a deep breath. "It's time for you to go."

Tears welled in her eyes and I thought I saw her bottom lip twitch. She walked back behind the counter and grabbed her bag. "This is bull." She knocked over a sugar shaker as she slung her bag onto her shoulder. Walking past me, she muttered, "You have no idea …"

Turning on my heels, I followed. "I have no idea about what?" Riley, shut up! Just let her go.

She turned to face me and I almost ran into her. "You think it's so easy for everyone to be just like you." Tears were now streaming down her face. "You have no idea …" she couldn't finish the sentence. She adjusted the strap on her shoulder. "Not everyone has had a perfect life, Riley. Not everyone can be just like you."

It was my turn to open my mouth. I had no idea how to respond. Maisie turned and rushed out the door, the little bell chiming loudly in the quiet café. I stared after her, stunned and confused. She had no idea what type of life I had and honestly, why the hell did it matter? This was a business. My business.

I had the right to expect certain things from my employees. Right?

I stomped over to the coffee machine. Was I expecting too much? To be on time, to be friendly … that wasn't too much, was it? Though—I poured coffee grounds into three separate filters—Leah did seem to be run-down recently. Grouchier. Maybe I was putting too much on her shoulders and the stress was finally getting to her. After pouring water into the back of the machine, I heard the oven timer go off. She deserved some time off and she would get it. After this one last favor …

Chapter 11

The coffee maker beeped as it finished. Oh, shit! I stood quickly from my bent position, remembering I'd forgotten to add the most important ingredient in the coffee and banged the back of my head on the top of the large display case. The empty metal pan clattered on the floor and I grabbed the back of my head. Ow! Ow! Ow! Damn, that hurt! I had already unlocked the front door, the closed sign had been turned to open. I shook my head, trying to shake the pain off and placed my hands on the carafes. It wouldn't be a huge deal if I had forgotten. It was still coffee. It would still taste good—it just wouldn't be *as* good.

With a headache forming, I closed my eyes and repeated the spell I had said every morning for months. The magic that normally flowed through my fingertips barely dripped out. I huffed. Come on, Riley. I needed to ground myself. To focus. I stomped my foot, even though it didn't help. The tips of my fingers tingled, but it quickly vanished. The Hocus Focus would be Hocus Not-So Focus this morning. I just couldn't get it up.

Something made a loud thud behind me. I jumped and turned, making a rather terrible noise: *iiiieee*. I hadn't heard the door chime. I had been too deep in my concentration, not that it

70

had done any good. I pressed my hand against my chest, trying to slow my heart and met Aaron's eyes as he sat on the other side of the counter.

"You scared the sh—" I looked down at the counter and saw what had probably caused the thud. "What is that?" A one-inch binder with colorful tabs sticking out sat in front of him. I wiped my palms on my apron, they were sweaty from the heat of the coffee machine, or my sudden rush of adrenaline.

"That," he poked the top of it with a finger, "is a copy of the binder for the wedding cake." His voice was flat. His eyes flicked down at the binder and he scrunched his nose.

"Why is it so thick?" I cocked my head.

"Esther is very thorough." He pulled the black cashmere scarf off from around his neck and mumbled, "And apparently made duplicates of everything."

"You seem positively thrilled to be delivering this to me," I joked.

Aaron took a breath through his nose, his eyes slanted as he continued to stare at the binder. "I didn't realize when I took this job as assistant to the mayor, that one of the duties was going to be *wedding planner*," he said the last two words through gritted teeth.

I pulled a blueberry muffin from the display case and set it on a plate in front of him in hopes of cheering him up. I studied him as he pulled the plate closer and inspected the brown and purple pastry. His scowl never dissipated as he pulled the thin white paper off from around it. Well, I tried. The door chimed and I looked up to see Leah scurry in. She ran behind the counter, panting as she came to a stop beside me.

She took a deep breath. Had she run the whole way here? "I came as soon as I got your message." She pulled her jacket off and pushed her bag under the counter. Running her fingers through her hair to fix it and said, "It's about time you fired that ungrateful—" Her eyes landed on the white binder and she froze. "What's that?" She tilted her head just like I had.

I saw Aaron roll his eyes as he took a bite of the muffin.

Placing my hand on top of the binder, I responded, "Wedding cake details."

Her mouth formed an *O*.

The pendant light above Aaron flickered. I glanced up at all the string lights across the ceiling as they blinked and grabbed the binder off the counter. That's weird. "We will need to look through it and make sure we have everything for the cake."

As I handed the binder to Leah, the light above us burst in a loud shatter. Glass from the bulb flew around us. The binder hit the ground as Leah screamed. Aaron covered his head with his arms and I jumped back making another *iiieee* noise.

Backing off of the stool, Aaron stood and shook his scarf free from the glass. "What the hell was *that*?"

I grabbed his plate and threw the muffin into the trash. "A power surge?" I took a rag and ran it across the counter to remove the glass. It hadn't been me. I hadn't used any magic. I looked up at the remains of the pendant and groaned. The bulb hadn't been the only thing to explode, the whole glass covering was gone. That had been one serious power surge. Except, only the one light exploded. I bit the inside of my mouth, that was strange.

Leah tiptoed to the kitchen door, glass crunching under her shoes as she grabbed the broom sitting behind it. She swept up a pile of the shattered bulb and bent to push it into the dustpan. Her necklace fell into it. She picked it up and mumbled about needing to fix the latch as she shoved it in her pocket.

"Could this day get any worse?"

I heard Aaron mutter to himself. He bent over and ran his hand through his hair but stopped and dusted off his shoulders. Little flecks of glass sprinkled to the floor.

Possibly, I thought.

After we cleaned up all the glass, I gave Aaron a new muffin and flipped open the binder to the first page where a picture of a large cake had been put in a clear cover sheet. Oh, crap. I flicked my eyes to Aaron and tried to hide the discomfort from my face. "Esther knows I won't be making the same cake as Alice, right?"

Aaron smoothed his hair down. Looks like all that hairspray he used had created a barrier and no glass from the bulb had penetrated it. "I was afraid you were going to say that."

Trying to put a little smile on my lips, I responded through gritted teeth, "I just don't have the time."

His shoulders sagged. "Can you give me some idea as to what you can do so I can at least tell Esther something?"

Something was better than nothing, I suppose. I was going to need to give him a whole box of muffins to make this better for him. I tapped my finger on my lip, trying to come up with something quick. "I can make a smaller cake for the bride and groom and—" Good grief, I still had to make enough for the town. "A few larger sheet cakes for the guests."

Aaron inhaled audibly. "I guess that'll have to do. This whole wedding is a joke, anyway."

Leah piped in, "Aren't they all?" She pulled the necklace from her pocket and placed it back around her neck.

I pressed my lips together and placed Aaron's muffin into a to-go box. I wasn't sure why either of them cared one way or another. If Samantha wanted to marry someone who would probably never stay faithful to her, that was her business. I'm sure Tessa had warned her numerous times and she was still going through with it. I wonder if Dimples was a two-timing, son of a bi—

"Esther wants you to bring a sample of the cake by Town Hall tomorrow for them to taste," Aaron interrupted my thought. He hung his scarf around his shoulders.

I stared at him. Excuse me? She wanted me to do what? Hadn't they already gone through this with Alice? "Why?" is all I could say.

"Because that's what Esther wants." He shrugged. "And what she wants, she gets."

The door chimed a few times as other customers walked in and took their seats. Leah left my side to tend to them. "What Esther wants, Esther gets," Aaron had said that to me multiple times. I suppose that's how he excused her demands. Leah and I had enough to do with all the cupcakes I had promised for the festival. Now I had to make a tasting cake on top of that? This day *could* get worse.

Aaron took another glance up at the shattered bulb and retrieved his to-go box. "I've got another errand to run before I need to be back to Town Hall." He picked up his satchel from the neighboring stool and swung it over a shoulder.

I carried the binder to my office and flipped through the pages of clear view sheets. Esther was going to have to accept what I could do in the short time frame she was giving me. I could've said no, right? I didn't, but I could've. Except, maybe there was some truth to her getting what she wants. Why hadn't I said no? I closed the binder and a yellow piece of paper fluttered to the floor. I picked it up: a dry-cleaning ticket. It must've accidentally hitched a ride in the binder. I poked my head out of my office to look out of the large front window but saw no sign of Aaron. Folding it, I placed it in the pocket of my jacket hanging on the back of my office chair. I would give it to him later.

Chapter 12

I scribbled down a list of ingredients we needed to finish icing the cupcakes for the festival and for the tasting cake I was now going to be making. I called Fletcher's Hardware down the street to order a replacement pendant, which hopefully wouldn't take too long to come in. It wasn't a normal thing for Eugene Fletcher to keep in stock. I left Leah in charge of baking more of the cupcakes and headed to Wildewood's only grocery store, The Stop and Shop, owned by Ben and Eliza Davis. Most people just referred to it as Eliza's because Ben was never around much.

The shelves in the baking aisle were looking especially empty today. Hopefully, Eliza would restock soon so I didn't have to drive out of town. Specifically, because I didn't have a working car. The Davis' always made sure to take care of the restaurants in town but the festival must be clearing out the shelves quicker than they could keep them stocked. At least it wasn't toilet paper they were running out of. That would be a particularly shitty disaster.

The metal wire basket dug into my arm. The handles bowed under the weight of the groceries as I added another bag of powdered sugar precariously to the top. One sudden move and it was sure to fall to the floor. I wished I had grabbed a cart instead. But I was almost done and refused to admit defeat against a wire basket. Turning out of the baking aisle, I headed, as quickly as the basket would allow me, to the dairy section against the back wall of the store. Cream cheese was the last ingredient on my list.

I grabbed as many boxes as they had on the shelf and held them close to my chest, balancing them under my chin as I turned toward the register and ran straight into something solid.

The sound of air being forced out of the person in front of me was loud.

The boxes of cream cheese fell from my arms, landing with soft thuds on the ground. The arm of the basket broke, pouring bags of sugar on to the ground: *splat, splat, splat*. My mouth gaped open. I took a look at the mess of groceries on the ground before peeking up at the person in front of me.

Dimples.

"I am so sorry." I blinked, closing my lips tight. Why? Why did it have to be him? Of all the people in this town, why did it have to be him, *again*.

He put a hand to his stomach where the basket had probably hit him. He snorted a quiet laugh as he kneeled down and picked up a box of cream cheese. He was wearing light blue scrubs. Was he a doctor? A surgeon? He looked up at me for a split second. "It seems we are just meant to bump into each other."

Literally.

I placed the broken basket on the floor, my arm crying with relief as it quickly regained feeling in a thousand little pinpricks. I squeezed my hand into a fist a few times. "It seems like it."

Kneeling beside him, I began to place the groceries back into the basket. He glanced at me through the hair falling into his eyes—his beautiful, baby blues …

"My name's Ethan Mitchell, by the way. Not Dimples."

Oh, my God. Had I said that out loud? I wanted to sink into the floor and hide, but instead, I said, "Riley Jones." I stood, holding the basket with my arms wrapped around it in front of me. "Wait, Mitchell? Are you related to Jennifer?"

Ethan pushed himself up from the ground and nodded. "That would be my baby sister."

"I had no idea she had a brother." I shifted on my feet, the basket feeling heavier. "How is she doing?"

He placed the last package of cream cheese on top of the basket. "She's pretty upset."

We walked away from the dairy section and I noticed he had no groceries of his own. Maybe he just wanted to walk me to the register. Oh, Dimples—I mean, Ethan—how gentlemanly and … strange. Knots were forming in my stomach. I didn't need to be escorted. I could handle this. The same package of cream cheese slipped back onto the floor.

Ethan reached to pick it up. He held it out above the basket and his forehead creased. "How about I carry these for you?"

I shook my head. "You don't have to do that." I can handle this. Another package of cream cheese slipped to the floor and I looked up at the ceiling. Thanks for making me a liar.

"I don't think you're going to make it to the register if I don't." He picked the package off the floor. I should've just waved the white flag and gone back to get a cart. "In fact," he took the basket out of my arms, "let me just carry all of this for you."

"Oh. You really don't have to do that." I shook my head but my arms sighed with relief as the weight of the basket was lifted from them.

Ethan held out a few boxes of cream cheese. "Here, you carry these." His lips turned upward and that beautiful dimple that made my knees go weak formed. He walked to the front of the grocery store and I followed, feeling a mixture of embarrassment and contentment.

Well, since I was here … my eyes roamed his backside. He sure did look nice in a pair of scrubs. The sleeves clung tightly to his biceps. My eyes traveled further down and I felt my cheeks flush. He could handle my groceries any day. I know, I know. I said I could handle it. So, sue me. It wouldn't be right to let a good view go to waste.

Ethan set the basket on the belt and turned to grab the cream cheese boxes from me. "I'll see you later." He smiled, his eyes roaming over my face.

I met his eyes and stuttered a goodbye.

I stared after him as he turned into the animal aisle before I refocused on my basket. I took the groceries and placed them in a single file on the belt before looking up to see Connie Fields, Wildewood's florist, with Eliza Davis.

Eliza had a white apron tied loosely around her voluptuous waist. Her thin, graying brown hair was cut short, curling just under her earlobes. Her hands shook slightly as she helped Connie place small bouquets of yellow gerbera daisies, orange chrysanthemums, and red carnations wrapped in clear plastic into a large plastic vase attached to the end of her register.

Connie, who was at least a half-foot taller than Eliza, pushed her circular black-rimmed glasses up her nose and leaned closer to her friend and whispered, "I heard they found fabric on the broken glass of the door." She placed another bouquet into the vase.

I raised an eyebrow, most definitely not eavesdropping, and grabbed a pack of gum. Tearing the plastic wrapping from around it, I popped a piece into my mouth while I waited. I glanced at the tabloids in front of me and picked one at random. Pretending to read about how to drop ten pounds in a week on a cabbage diet. I glanced at Eliza as she clicked her tongue.

"Ben's friend who works at the station told him they found blood on the broken glass," she whispered back.

I sucked in a breath, the gum lodging itself in my windpipe then began to cough. I bent over, holding onto my knees as I coughed the gum up. Eliza and Connie went silent, both staring at me. Connie crossed her arms and raised an eyebrow.

"Hello, ladies." I cleared my throat and wrapped the gum back into the paper it came from.

Connie pushed a strand of her silver hair behind her ears. She grabbed her flower cart and pushed it to the next register. "Everyone is looking forward to your cupcakes, dear," she spoke to me as she began to place more of the same bouquets in an empty vase.

I swallowed, my throat hurting from all the coughing. "I hope they meet everyone's expectations."

Connie chuckled. "I'm sure they will."

Eliza scanned my groceries, placing the items in a large brown paper bag. I glanced at Connie. "Just curious, do you guys know what color the fabric was on the broken glass?"

Eliza shook her head. "Riley. You shouldn't gossip."

Connie pushed her cart back to the register. She looked at her friend, bemused. "Eliza, you're one to talk." She rolled her eyes in a dramatic way, winking at me when she was through. "No one has mentioned the color, but I imagine they have a pretty big cut."

I paid for the groceries and said my goodbyes as they continued to *not* gossip. With the large bag held tightly against me with one arm, and the other holding the bottom, I walked across

Town Square. I knew of two people so far who had their fingers bandaged. The mayor's had been a small enough cut for a single band-aid to cover while Maisie's had been more severe-looking. Maisie had been late to work that morning, she had a pretty bad cut on her hand, and Trey stopped coming into the café around the same time she was hired. Things were starting to add up and I was feeling more confident that I knew who the arsonist was.

Chapter 13

Later that evening, once the café was closed for the night, Leah and I got to work baking the remaining cupcakes. We would frost them another night. I was looking forward to having this task off my shoulders now that I had a wedding cake to start working on. I wasn't sure how Esther would act toward me if I fell short. No pressure or anything.

The four mixers were coated in sticky cupcake batter. A thick dusting of flour covered the counters and the black and white checkered tile floor underneath. All of the cupcake pans were soaking in water in the deep basin of the farmhouse style sink. I looked around at the mess we had made during our baking session. This was going to take a while to clean up, but as much as I was dreading it, the evening had been a success. Every single cupcake I had promised was baked.

"See you tomorrow!" Leah yelled from the front of the dark café.

"Bye!" I yelled in response, hearing the door chime. Turning the faucet on, I grabbed a sponge. There was a mountain of pans that needed to be washed before I could leave. I would regret it in the morning if I didn't do it now.

The door chimed again. I set the sponge down and walked to the swinging doors, standing on my toes to look over them. "Did you forget something?"

I looked around but saw no one. Leah hadn't come back in. Wiping my wet hands on my apron, I pushed the doors open and walked through the dark café. That was strange. Maybe the wind had pushed it open a little before it closed all the way. I flipped the open sign around to closed and put my hand on the lock when I saw something out of the corner of my eye skittering across the floor. Sucking in a breath, I turned and pressed my back against the door. My eyes scanned the floor. Something small shot from under a table toward the counter.

"What the—"

My heart started to race. I took a step forward. I could hear scratching sounds from behind the counter. Oh, God. There's a rat in here. I don't like rodents. My head swam. Queasiness flooded my system. It's okay, Riley. You're a witch. You can handle a measly little rodent. The scratching continued then I heard the sound of something ripping. Then something spilling to the ground like marbles. Cringing, I wished I had my broom. Not only was it a tool for travel, but it also packed a punch. It had multiple uses. A multi-broom.

The skittering sound started back up. The creature bolted under the swinging doors. I took a deep breath—all right, Riley, you can do this. You can do this! I sucked down any courage I still had and screamed, *Sparta!* as I chased after it through the doors. Okay, I didn't really scream Sparta ... out loud.

The moment I stepped foot into the kitchen, I yelled, "*Veni,*" with my hand outstretched toward the creature, hoping to bring it into sight. Instantly, I regretted it. The spell bounced off of the black creature as it continued to run and a bag of flour flung itself at me instead.

"Oh, shit!" I ducked.

The bag burst as it hit the doors. In a white cloud, the flour rained down all over the floor and covered me from head to toe. It created a thick haze in the air. Swatting at the cloud, I searched for the creature. I'd never had a spell bounce off something before. My eyes swept back and forth, trying to catch a glimpse of it. I saw something thin and black disappear inside an open cabinet. A tail, maybe?

I wanted to try the spell again, to make it come to me, but I wasn't sure what was in the cabinet with it and didn't want anything hard or sharp flying toward me. Nor did I want a rabid rodent to fly at me. I really should've thought that through.

I took a few steps toward the cabinet and spotted the bakery's broom. Whispering, I motioned for the broom with a curl of my fingers. It shook as if waking from a slumber. I caught its plastic handle in my hand and turned it upside down, holding it like a bat ready to strike.

Clicking my tongue a few times, I tried to coax whatever hid inside the cabinet out. "Come here, little rat."

I could hear it rustling around, then a quiet mew. A mew? What a minute—I lowered the broom and laid it against the island. Crouching, I clicked my tongue again. "Here, kitty," I spoke softly.

It quietly meowed. But something about it didn't seem right. Crawling on my hands and knees, I moved closer to the cabinet. A small, black cat was curled up, its tail flicking back and forth. Was this the same cat from last night?

"Come here," I begged, snapping my fingers in hopes to catch its interest. Instead, it laid its head down, making a weak noise.

"What did you get into?" I asked, pushing myself up from the floor.

In the front of the café, I snapped my finger and the overhead lights came on. Behind the bar, I saw little black balls all over the floor. I bent down and picked one up, bringing it to my nose and sniffed. Chocolate covered espresso beans. I wasn't an expert on cats, but I was pretty sure they shouldn't be eating these things.

Going back to the cat, I sat down. "Please, do not attack me," I begged, reaching into the cabinet. Gently, I wrapped my two hands around the feline's midsection then drug the cat out to rest in my lap.

"Are you following me?" I asked, petting its soft black fur. There was a little patch of white fur between its eyes in the shape of a crescent moon. That was unique. I turned my arm over, exposing a small, pink crescent moon birthmark on my wrist. "We have matching birthmarks."

The cat mewed again as if answering.

Rubbing behind its ear, I stood and held the cat against me. "I think I need to get you to a vet." The cat nuzzled into the bend of my arm while I walked into the dark alley. I pointed to my broom with my index and thumb. I brought the two fingers together as I spoke a transforming spell. Three times, I repeated the spell and hand motion.

The broom shook, moving away from the wall. It stood upright on its bristles and as it shook it began to shrink. Only a few inches long, the broom floated in the air. I whispered again and a small chain with a circular ring appeared at the tip of the handle. Snatching it, I secured it on to the café key ring. It was a neat trick I learned when I needed to hide my mode of transportation. I didn't want to draw too much attention if I carried around a broom with me from work at night. Oh, it's just me,

Riley Jones. I definitely do not ride on this … I just enjoy sweeping the sidewalks.

Quickening my pace, I took a shortcut through the broken gate behind the café and reached the next street in seconds. The animal clinic looked dark but I could just barely make out a light in the back. It was after hours, but what would it hurt to check. Rapping my knuckles on the glass door, I caught my reflection. Flour covered me from head to toe. I looked like a ghost. The black cat was spotted with white dust, too. I looked past my reflection and became mortified as I stared into the eyes of none other than Dimples.

Are you freaking kidding me? This cannot be happening! I groaned. What had I done to deserve this continuous embarrassment around this man?

He unlocked the door. "Riley?" His eyes wandered over me and he raised an eyebrow.

I took a step back and flour drifted off my clothes like snow. This cannot be happening. I wanted to click my heels together. There's no place like home.

"Everything okay?" he asked, totally ignoring the white powder covering every crease and cranny it could find. I appreciated it, I really did. But we both knew the truth.

Looking down at the cat, I licked my lips and tasted flour. "I think he's sick. He … or she … got into a bag of chocolate-covered espresso beans."

"I can keep it overnight if you'd like." Ethan reached for the cat.

It hissed as the tip of Ethan's fingers touched its fur. Claws sank into my arm, through my shirt, and the feline pushed out of my embrace. Wincing, I let go and watched it land upright on the sidewalk. Another plum of flour wafted off me.

"Looks like he's okay," Ethan commented as the cat bound down the road.

He? I stared after the cat. Yep. Definitely a he.

"Are you okay?" Ethan turned his attention to me.

A nervous snort came out of me and I clapped my hands over my mouth in an explosion of flour. My cheeks flushed and I began to sweat, despite the chill in the air. A smile crept over his face and the heat in my cheeks deepened.

"I have to go," I squeaked through my hand then raced off in the direction the cat went, leaving a white trail behind me.

Heaving as I reached my street, I slowed to a stop to catch my breath. I hadn't run like that since gym in high school. Though, I bet, had I been running from my own embarrassment, I would've made better time on the mile. I walked up the stone path to the front door of my house and saw the black cat lying on the doormat.

"What are you doing here?" I crouched to pet him. "You're a little troublemaker, aren't you?"

The cat leaned into my hand as I rubbed its soft fur, his purrs becoming loud.

"Where did you come from?" I asked, not expecting an answer, and how did you know where I live?

Opening the front door, the cat rushed past me. It was cold outside and maybe it only wanted a warm place to sleep. I didn't see the harm in it for one night, but I was not going to become the town's crazy cat lady. I was already single, the first step. One night, Mister, just one night. I pulled my jacket off, flour raining on to the floor. Groaning, I walked to the refrigerator and pulled out leftover chicken wings from Mike's.

The cat rubbed its side against my leg as I opened the container. I pulled a piece of meat off a bone and dropped it to the ground. I watched him turn his nose up into the air, uninterested in the fried chicken.

"Beggars can't be choosers," I muttered as it pushed the food around on the floor.

Okay, maybe cats didn't enjoy buffalo wings. I imagine it probably wasn't good for their stomach anyway. I opened a cabinet and started to search for anything he might want to eat—or could eat. In the very back, I found a few cans of tuna. They must have been left by my dad. His cabinets had been pretty bare near the end and I hadn't cared to clean them out. I basically lived off of cereal. Peeling the lid off, the cat jumped onto the counter as the fishy aroma flooded the room. I set it down and watched the cat's pink little tongue lick the wet fish.

"Tuna good, buffalo chicken bad." I placed the leftover wings in the microwave.

I leaned against the counter and glanced at him as he lapped up the tuna. I decided to use him as a sounding board since I had no one else to talk to. Things were already strange in Wildewood, how could this be any worse? Step two in becoming a crazy cat lady: Speak to your cat like they're human. Check.

Oh, well. "Okay, little cat, help me figure this one out."

He looked up at me for a moment before returning to his tuna. Good, he was listening.

"Samantha's wedding is only a few days away. The fire at Just Treats could have been accidental, except the glass on the back door was broken and only Samantha's cakes were destroyed."

The cat made a slurping sound.

I grimaced. Manners, please? "Sam is acting really strange about the whole situation, but there are too many coincidences surrounding Maisie. If I didn't think Maisie was causing all of this—but I do—I would guess Samantha was trying to sabotage her own wedding. So, why doesn't she just call the whole thing off? Why go to all this trouble?"

The cat meowed and turned away, its rear now facing me.

Okay, fine. I get it. He didn't want to help me after all. Leaving the cat to his own devices, I went to the bathroom and washed the flour off. I was ready for this night to be over. I had been embarrassed too many times today and I was exhausted. From the upcoming festival, not to mention the wedding cake I was now supposed to bake. I really needed to learn how to say no, but I found it so hard to disappoint people. That's probably why I let Maisie stick around a lot longer than she deserved.

Slinking up the steps in my towel, I heard the cat jump from the counter and pad up the stairs behind me. My pajamas were warm and smelled like fresh linen, much better than the smell of flour. I climbed into bed, the cat jumping up after me. He curled into a ball on the pillow next to mine. I watched him for a moment, deciding if I should force him back outside. He looked so warm and I swear I could hear him purring as he slept.

I didn't have the heart to make the cat leave, so I laid down beside him.

"Good night, kitty," I whispered and I could have sworn I heard a quiet *Goodnight* in response.

Chapter 14

The blaring sound of the alarm startled me out of deep sleep. My heartbeat was quick and sweat beaded my brow. I blinked up at the ceiling, taking a deep breath to calm my nerves and wondered if I'd actually heard a goodnight response. I had been so exhausted, maybe I had just imagined it. Then again, I swear a hat had talked to me. I rubbed the sleep from my eyes and looked over to the pillow next to mine. The cat was gone. Did I dream the cat also? I pictured Ethan trying not to laugh at my flour-covered self. Nope. As much as I wished that had been a dream, it had been very real.

I put my feet on the floor and groaned as I hobbled my way to the wardrobe. My legs were stiff from running all the way home. I groaned again when I came to the top of the stairs. When the house had been built, it only had one room which was downstairs off the kitchen. My father had added the loft many years ago before his health had taken a turn for the worse. I loved the openness of the room, it's narrow walls, and the exposed wooden beams. The only downside to staying in the loft was that the only bathroom was downstairs. Normally, this wasn't a problem. Today, the muscles in my calves and thighs did not want to

89

take the stairs. Sideways, walking down the stairs, I held on to the banister as if my life depended on it.

Heading to the shower through the dark living room, I heard a low, guttural sound behind me.

Snapping my fingers, the lights turned on, flooding the open space of the living room and kitchen in a warm, golden glow. The black cat stood next to the last step of the stairs. Its fur raised, back arched, making the deep, throaty sound.

"What the—" My steps faltered.

The old hat was sitting on the island counter.

I dropped my clothes on the ground and extended my arm toward the kitchen, calling the broom that sat behind the trash can to come to me. Its hard, wooden handle slammed into the palm of my hand and my fingers curled around it. Holding it like a bat, I walked slowly toward the hat.

"How did you get in here?" I whispered, looking to the front door. It was still locked. There was something preternatural about this hat. I could handle that—I wasn't normal myself. But what I didn't understand was why it was following me.

I inched toward the counter and the hat moved, a slight shake to its floppy brim. I froze. Okay. Maybe I couldn't handle this. I swung the broom. The bristles barely touched the black wool. A bright light flashed, blinding me. The broom hit the ground and I covered my eyes. It was too late. With bright spots in my vision, everything that had been on the counter was now on the floor. I spun around to scan the living room, but the hat was gone.

"What do you want from me?" I yelled and pounded balled fists on the counter, feeling frustrated over the game it was playing. I leaned against the counter, my knuckles turning white as I gripped the edge. Closing my eyes momentarily, I took in a breath and loosened my grip. I picked up the paper towels and salt and pepper shakers off the floor then set them back on the island. Rubbing my hands over my face, I just wanted to know what it wanted. What could a hat possibly want? Seriously—since when did inanimate objects start having wants and needs? Did it actually want me or was it just screwing with me because I was the one who found it? I looked at the cat and I swore he shrugged.

"Don't you start with me either." I pointed at the cat before shutting the bathroom door.

As I brushed my hair, I rolled my eyes at my reflection. Step three in becoming a crazy cat lady: treat your cat like a human. I was well on my way to becoming the town's crazy cat lady after all. Great.

Checking my watch, I was barely on time. I threw my flannel jacket on, having left the heavier one in my office and burst through the front door. The black cat right beside me.

"Whoa!" a voice came from the darkness as I stepped on to the sidewalk.

A scream escaped my lips as I put the brakes on. Ethan came jogging up the sidewalk, panting. He waved, giving me a smile.

"You seem to be in a big rush these days," he said in a breathy voice, continuing to run in place.

"Ah—yeah, just really busy," I responded.

"At least we didn't run into each other." He winked.

Oh, God. Please don't wink at me. It was too much. I glanced down at my boots. "I don't think my tailbone could take another fall." A foreign noise escaped my lips. Oh. My. God. Did I just giggle?

Chuckling, he said, "See you later, Riley." He jogged away and turned on to the next street.

Wait—why was *I* running? I crossed the street, this time at a slower pace. Rushing wasn't going to help me figure anything out in regards to that damn hat. I wasn't late for work yet. All running would do was put me out of breath and make me sweaty. Not to mention, my legs were still groaning. Maybe if I stretched them out … I took longer strides, trying to stretch out the muscles in my thighs. Thank goodness no one was looking, it probably looked like I had forgotten how to walk altogether.

I came to a halt in the alley behind The Witches Brew. The café's back door was wide open. What the hell? Fear crept up my legs. I tried to swallow but it felt as if something was lodged in my throat. I looked down the alley in both directions. I was alone. I didn't own a cellphone to call for help, each one I had after moving to Wildewood had fried. I assumed it had something to do with my magic. The only phone I could use was inside the café but I didn't want to go in there alone. And right now, I was all alone.

I took a deep breath and crept toward the door. Of all the witchcraft I knew, I wasn't immersed in defensive magic. I poked my head into the doorway and saw the lights in the kitchen all the way into the café were off. I snapped my fingers and the lights flicked on.

With my fingertips, I pushed the door open wider. Crap, I shouldn't have touched it. I pulled my hand back to my side in a fist. Scanning the room, it was still caked in flour from the night before. It looked like a flour bomb went off. I held my breath, listening, but I couldn't hear any noise coming from the café area. It was completely silent. Even still, I was scared to walk in. All right, I'm just going to go around to the front and—the cat ran past me. Flour swirled on the floor in little tornadoes from his paws.

"No!" I screeched. "Come here!"

He jumped onto the counter and sat down, tail swishing.

That's when I noticed all four mixers were missing.

I had been robbed.

Chapter 15

I had gone into the café through the front door to call nine-one-one, afraid of possibly contaminating any evidence the police could use to find who had robbed me. The cat had done enough damage to any shoe prints that might have been left in the flour, though the kitchen had been left in such disarray I couldn't tell one footprint from another.

It was still dark and quite chilly as I waited outside the café on one of the black chairs. The cat laid next to my feet under the chair, its tail swishing back and forth, hitting my boot with each swing. His ears stood straight up, moving with every little noise. He looked sphinx-like, but he was on high alert.

A nagging thought kept replaying in my mind. No matter how hard I tried, I couldn't remember if I had locked the café the night before. I had rushed out so quickly I could not recall. Let's say I had forgotten to lock the door, why would anyone take only the mixers? There was a safe in my office with cash in it. The till still had money inside. Yet, none of that was missing—just the mixers. It wasn't as if these mixers were hard to come by, sure they weren't cheap, but you could order them online easily. This didn't feel like the run of the mill burglary. No, this felt more intentional, as if someone was trying to send a message.

But what was the message? Was the robber the same person who had set fire to Just Treats? My stomach knotted. Was I now being targeted because I was making the new cake?

I looked down at the cat. He had crawled out from under the chair to sit in front of my shoes. He stared catty-corner down the street. I followed his line of sight; a police car was driving toward us. Finally. Though I had only been waiting a few minutes, it felt like an eternity. Time felt frozen and a new fear was sinking in. The car parked in front of the café and heaved as Pete Kelley emerged from the driver's side. He was a welcome sight this morning. He waddled around the front of the car and took his hat off his head.

"Hey, Riley." He stopped in front of me as his partner shut his door. Pete looked at me with a thoughtful expression, he gave me a small smile and I appreciated it. This was the last thing I wanted to have called Pete for. I enjoyed our small talk in the café, his deep Santa-like laugh when I gave him extra muffins. I knew he thought of me as a niece and I didn't like worrying him.

I stood as the other man came near us. The cat jumped into the chair I had been in and climbed onto the table as if he needed to be a part of the conversation.

"This is Officer John Russell. He will be leading the investigation. Time for us geezers to let the young guys take over." Pete winked at me.

John Russell reached his large hand out to shake mine. He was a tall, fit-looking man, unlike his counterpart. I bet he just graduated from the academy. The blue uniform hugged him nicely. There probably wasn't even a bald spot under that hat he was wearing. *Boy*, were these two men quite the opposites.

I led them into the café, retelling the events of the morning. But there wasn't much to tell. I walked to work, like I always did, and noticed the back door was open and the mixers were missing. Russell produced a small digital camera from his pocket and went into the kitchen to look around. Pete found his usual stool and took a seat while we waited.

"Would you like me to make some coffee?" I asked Pete, beginning to feel restless. I needed to fill the silence; I was starting to feel claustrophobic.

"That would be great." His eyes lit up. Pete was not one to resist a free coffee or a muffin, but I couldn't offer him one this morning.

I looked past Pete and saw the cat still sitting on top of the table, watching us. Did he think he was a guard dog? I shook my head and prepped one side of the large coffee machine. Pressing start, I placed three to-go cups on the counter. The kitchen doors swung open and I jumped. My nerves were shot. I hated to admit this, but I wanted to get out of the café as soon as possible. My favorite place was currently the one place I did not want to be. I felt violated and I just wanted to crawl back into bed and pretend this had all been a terrible dream. I'd wake up and forget about it soon enough.

Unfortunately, this wasn't a dream and I wouldn't be waking up from it soon.

Russell apologized for startling me. Without sitting, he replaced his camera with a small notebook and flipped it open to a clean page. "Can you tell me anything out of the ordinary from the day before?"

I blinked, staring at him. He was standing near the kitchen doors, a short pencil in his hands ready to scribble something down. He glanced up at me when I didn't answer. How far out of the ordinary should I go? I wrapped my arms around me and raised my shoulders in a shrug. "I can't think of anything." Which was a lie, but I was pretty sure the black cat outside and the hat following me had nothing to do with the break-in.

He scribbled on the pad. What he could've possibly written down was beyond me. "There's no *obvious* signs of forced entry. Though it's quite a mess in there." He flipped to a clean page. "Is that how you left it?"

I cleared my throat and bobbed my head. "Not usually but I did leave in a hurry last night." I glanced at the cat who was still staring at us.

"Any reason why you left in such a hurry?" he asked.

I glanced at Pete. He was staring at the empty to-go cup. I turned to grab the carafe and filled the cups. "I had to take my cat to the animal clinic. He—well—ate some chocolate."

More scribbling. Pete's face lit up and he prepared his coffee. I'm surprised the man didn't have diabetes with the amount of sugar he poured into the hot liquid.

I offered Russell a cup but he shook his head. I guess he didn't drink on the job. "Who all has keys to the café?" he asked.

I set his cup back down on the counter and picked up the carafe to return it. "My assistant Leah Crane and—" The carafe hit the warmer with a loud thud.

"What?" Russell asked.

"I just fired my other employee." I mentally kicked myself. "She has a set of keys also." I had forgotten to collect them. Maisie rarely used her key, one of us was always here before her. Dammit! I hadn't even thought about the key. Is that why there were no signs of *obvious* forced entry? Maisie had used her key to get into the café.

Russell tucked his notebook inside the small pocket of his

shirt. I walked him down the hallway toward my office to make sure nothing had been removed. Everything was just as I left it. I had locked the office, but only I had a key to that room. He asked me a few more questions about Maisie and Leah, mostly where to locate them for questioning.

Another pair of men walked into the café as we emerged from the hallway. They wore cloth booties over their shoes and gloves as they made their way into the kitchen with Pete standing watch at the swinging doors while sipping on his coffee. I could hear them talking from my perch at the counter. They had found sets of fingerprints near the backdoor, but most likely they would be mine. Leah and Maisie always used the front door. One of the men took an impression of my fingerprints to rule me out. I wonder if Maisie would do the same without a fight. If she was smart, she would've worn gloves when she robbed me.

It took them about an hour to collect any evidence they believed would be helpful, which wasn't much. They took pictures of the readable shoe prints in the flour mess, but those too would probably be mine. The cat had trailed through the flour, smearing most of the footprints in his path. But even without him doing that, when I first looked into the kitchen, I hadn't noticed a clear impression of a shoe. It was as if the flour had been purposely skewed during the thief's departure.

I walked to the kitchen and pushed the doors open. My eyes scanned the mess until I noticed the kitchen broom sitting near the back door. Wait a minute—that's not where I left it. Should I call Pete? Then I noticed the hatbox was missing. Oh, shit. Did they take the box as well? They'd be truly disappointed when they opened it. Serves them right!

I rubbed my temple at the onset of a headache as I walked

back into the café and sat on a stool. I believed Maisie was involved. In both crimes. There were just too many coincidences. She was hired two months ago and then Trey stopped coming into The Witches Brew because of *ulcers*. Yeah, I knew what that ulcer was now. Maisie had a pretty bad cut on her hand that could have been caused by breaking the glass on the back door at Just Treats. She wouldn't have needed to break my door because she had a key.

I tapped my fingers on the cold granite, staring into the kitchen above the doors. The details for the wedding cake had most likely been the cause of the fire at the bakery and the wedding cake was destroyed. Setting Just Treats on fire should have been a complete deal-breaker for having a wedding cake on time for Samantha's and Trey's wedding, but she hadn't considered me as a replacement. I didn't bake cakes, so why would anyone suspect me? Esther was a stickler for tradition, so it made sense—in a psychotic type of way—for the wedding to come to a halt, at least temporarily. But then Esther hired little 'ol' me. Stealing the mixers wasn't a deal-breaker to make the cake, it would just make it more difficult, which is why I believed this was her way of telling me to back out of it. What would happen if I followed through with baking the cake? Would The Witches Brew be set on fire, too?

Feeling like I was being watched, I swiveled around to see the cat sitting outside the front door. He mewed and scratched at the glass. I could use some company. I walked to the door and pulled it open, the little bell chiming. I needed to invest in more security. Maybe a camera in the alley, though it wouldn't do me any good right now.

I crouched down to rub his head between his ears. "I think I know who is trying to stop this wedding."

He meowed, leaning into my hand as I scratched under his chin.

Taking the noise as a sign of interest, I whispered, "Maisie Law is the saboteur."

The cat nipped at my finger. Ouch! I shook my hand. "I'm not a big fan of hers either, but that's no reason to bite."

I stood and crossed my arms, narrowing my eyes at the kitchen. Okay, Maisie. I hear you loud and clear. However, I have my own personal mixer at home. I was going to bake this cake and it would be the best damn wedding cake ever made. But first, I needed to change the locks to the café.

Chapter 16

I stopped at the door to Fletcher's Hardware and looked past it toward Just Treats. Crime scene tape still blocked the doorway. Usually, in this spot, you could smell the bakery. Not today. It would be a while before the wonderful aroma of Alice's business enveloped us again. I hope they caught the son of a bitch who took that away from all of us. If I had any real proof, I'd lead them straight to Maisie. But currently, all I had was a whole bunch of presumptions.

The door made a deep single chime as I pushed it open and the smell of sawdust filled my nose. The front of the store was empty. Usually, he or his son, Michael, was at the register. I noticed the large rolling service door in the back was open. Perhaps they were both busy with a delivery. I made my way to the far end of the store past rows of shelves, following the signs to where I assumed door knobs would be.

I was planning on replacing the two locks at the café instead of getting them rekeyed. Wildewood didn't have a locksmith, though the neighboring town of Twin Falls did. They had everything we didn't. I would not be surprised if the town's slogan was, "We have everything Wildewood doesn't." I'm kidding, I think.

Anyway, I'm sure Tessa would let me borrow her car to go to Twin Falls, but I didn't feel comfortable leaving the café completely defenseless.

I walked into the door hardware aisle and stared at all the options. I didn't realize just how many there would be to choose from. I just wanted the exact same knobs, or something very similar.

"Can I help you?" a gruff voice asked from behind me.

Startled, I spun around. I hadn't heard anyone coming. Eugene stood behind me with his large arms crossed over his chest and I relaxed. For a big guy, he was light on his feet. He was an older man, in his late sixties but he was built like an ox. There were scars covering his hands and arms from years of manual labor and a few on his cheeks. His thinning white hair was combed over, trying to hide the balding taking place on the very top. His arms unfolded as recognition relaxed his squared shoulders.

Pressing a hand to my racing heart, I said, "You scared me!"

"I'm sorry." He held his hands up, palms facing outward in disarming surrender. "I just heard about what happened."

"Word travels fast," I started, pushing hair behind my ears. I wonder if that's how Esther found out about Samantha's cakes. It sounded more reasonable than her being a psychic—or the culprit.

Eugene's eyes softened. "Can I help you find anything?"

I looked back down the aisle and finally spotted the locks I had in mind. Pointing toward them, I said, "I need to replace all the locks to the café." All two locks. Maybe The Witches Brew wasn't all that secure after all. I had grown too content in this little town where crime rarely happened to stop and think about extra precautions, until now.

We each grabbed a package of the new locks. They were the

exact round shape and bronze finish as the ones already on the doors. There was nothing special about them, I just liked them. Walking to the register, I handed the one in my hand to Eugene and without scanning them he placed both in a large paper bag. I raised an eyebrow at his actions and pulled cash out of my pocket and handed it to him.

Eugene shook his head.

"Come on." I placed the money on the counter, my voice pleading against his generosity.

"I won't take your money for this, Riley Jones," his voice was firm and he pushed the money back toward me.

"Eugene, I can't accept this." I looked at him, the creases between my eyebrows deepening.

He walked around the counter and handed me the bag. "Your business was robbed. It could've been any one of us. It's the least I can do."

I shoved the cash back into my pocket and thanked him. Taking the bag out of his arm, I headed to the door. He was wrong, though. It couldn't have been "any one of us," because not everyone was involved in the wedding of Samantha and Trey.

Before I stepped out of the hardware store, I turned back around. "Eugene, I have a broken bathroom fan. Do you think you guys could help me with that?"

"You know we can." He smiled; his chest filled with pride. "Just call me when you're ready."

Good. I could over tip to pay him back for the locks and he'd be none the wiser.

I walked back to the café and a cold dread washed over me the closer I got. The police hadn't said much when I told them about Maisie. She was the only person I could think of to have broken in without having to actually *break* in. I wish I could prove she and

Trey were having an affair, maybe then I could talk to Pete and he or Officer Russell would look further into it.

Passing by Odds 'n' Ends, Tessa flung her door open and called my name. She shoved a pencil behind her ear as she stepped out onto the sidewalk in a pair of tight-fitting overalls with a white shirt underneath and an oversized flannel shirt unbuttoned above it. Rubbing her hands together, dust wafted off and dissipated into the crisp air. She must've been watching for me.

"Are you okay?" She wrapped her arms tightly around my neck, the large bag crinkling as she pressed it into my chest.

"I'm fine," I reassured her with a lie, trying to wriggle out of her embrace. The bag was digging into my throat. Tessa had no sense of personal space. She was as touchy-feely as one could get and sometimes, like now, I forgot just how suffocating it could be. But I wouldn't change her for the world. I always knew where to go when I needed a hug.

"I can't believe these things are happening in Wildewood." She took a step back from me, her arms falling to her side. A frown deepened among her feminine features and I could see tears beginning to form, making her eyes glisten.

"I'm sure the police will figure it out soon." I shifted the bag to rest on my hip. I looked down the street to the café and felt antsy. I loved being around Tessa, but right now all I wanted to do was change the locks and go home. "I gotta go, Tessa. I'll see you later?"

"Please be careful, Riley," she called after me then I heard the chime on her door.

News really did travel fast in a small town.

Unlocking the front door, I realized how silly it was to try to keep the café safe with the same locks. Though, I didn't think Maisie was brave enough to try to rob the same place again without the dark of night to hide in. What else could she possibly take that would help sabotage the wedding? There was no point in taking the binder because the mayor probably had a backup. Come to think of it, I don't think Maisie even knew about Aaron delivering the binder to me. But it didn't matter. This had been a message, plain and clear. I was being bullied to back out of making the cake, but I wasn't going to play.

I placed the new locks on one of the tables closest to the front door and cut the packages open. I had never changed a lock and after inspecting it, I realized I didn't have the tools to even take the old ones out. I leaned back in the chair and stared at the ceiling, my arms dangling by my sides. My frustration level was on the rise. I suppose I would need to go back to Fletcher's for a screwdriver. All I wanted to do was change the damn locks and go the hell home! I wanted to curl up under my blankets and pretend this day never happened.

Oh, shit. I still had to pick up the grocery order at The Stop and Shop to make the tasting cake for Samantha and Trey. *This evening.* I was never going to go home. At least not any time soon. I laid my head on the cold table, staring out the big window toward Town Square. The festival looked almost ready. Rows of white canopies were pitched and tables placed underneath. Soon, this week would be over and I was going on a week-long staycation.

I breathed out a frustrated sigh as I stood to leave, *again.* Closing the door behind me, I spotted Ethan coming down the street. He wasn't in scrubs this time. He had a gray, long-sleeved shirt on with the sleeves pushed up around his elbows and a pair of tight-fitting blue jeans. I was not disappointed, but he sure did look scrumptious in those scrubs. He put his hand up to wave, the skin of his hip slightly exposed. Jogging, he reached the fence around the patio and wrapped his fingers around the cast iron as he leaned on it.

"You okay?" His eyes searched over me.

I felt a twist in my stomach and flutters of butterflies.

"Yeah." I shrugged. Why wouldn't I be? A laugh bubbled up in my chest at the sarcastic thought but it died before reaching my mouth. "My café is down a few mixers and my dignity has another ding in it but other than that, yeah."

He shifted his weight and looked past me into the café. "Changing the locks?"

Glancing behind me to see them sitting on the table, I said, "I was. I don't have a screwdriver."

"Give me a minute." He backed away from the fence. "I'll go grab one." He turned and before I could stop him, he jogged away, back down the street.

I looked up at the gray-covered sky and took in a deep breath before going back inside the café to wait for him. I made a tired effort to clean up the flour all over the floor in the kitchen but ultimately decided to do it later. I leaned against the coffee bar and stared at the locks on the table. I wondered if I could figure out a spell to keep intruders out. Too bad I didn't have a grimoire to help me out.

I poured myself a new cup of coffee and stared into the dark liquid. With a gentle wave of my index finger, a ceramic cow filled with cream floated toward it. I lowered my finger and it tipped over, cream pouring from its mouth creating swirls in the coffee. The cow lowered to the counter. Leaning on an elbow on the bar, I made a circular motion with the same finger and the stirrer rotated around the inside of the cup. The front door opened and I sprung up. I grabbed the stirrer but hit the cup too aggressively and it tipped over, spilling over the counter in the process.

"Whoa." Ethan dropped a faded red toolbox on the table and held his palms up. "I didn't mean to startle you."

I felt like a deer caught in the middle of a busy highway. Every little noise was spooking me. Grabbing a clean rag, I covered the spill. "It's okay. I'm just feeling anxious."

"Rightly so." He walked over to the counter and wiped the rest of the spill. He looked up at me with deep worry on his face and I cast my eyes to the counter. I was holding it together pretty well, but if he kept looking at me with sympathy in his eyes, I was liable to lose it.

While Ethan got to work removing the old doorknobs and deadbolts, I ran to pick up my grocery order for the tasting cake. Eliza had been kind enough to keep the pity off her face, instead, reassuring me the Wildewood police would find "the sucker who thinks they can terrorize the town."

When I got back, Ethan was kneeling in the doorway, twisting a screwdriver. He looked up and spotted me. The smile that flashed across his face stopped me in my tracks. Was that really for me? I don't think I had ever caused someone to smile just by coming into view. I kind of liked the idea.

"How's it going?" I asked as I walked into the gated area of the patio and set the groceries on one of the black tables.

"Just about done." He pushed himself up and rolled his shoulders back. I tried not to stare, but … I did. "I think you should consider getting a security system."

I couldn't agree more. I twisted my hands taking a seat in one of the chairs.

He walked to the chair across from me and sat down. The sweet scent of vanilla from his cologne wafted to me on a cool breeze. He smelled so good. I closed my eyes tight, trying to dislodge the carnal ideas trickling into my head. Now was not the time, Riley.

"You okay?"

His voice did not help.

Looking down at my hands in my lap, I felt silly. Weak, to be exact. I didn't want to be alone like I thought I had. The more I thought about it, the more I realized I didn't know what Maisie was capable of. I felt vulnerable and it was a feeling I despised. I had been alone most of my life and I had never felt like this. I did not like it one bit.

Nodding again, my voice was quiet, shaky, "Yeah. I just have a lot of baking to do."

Ethan looked into the café. "How are you going to do that?"

"I'm going to do it at my house," I answered. I couldn't crawl into my bed just yet, but at least I'd be at home.

I could feel him looking at me. A part of me wished he would excuse himself and leave, yet another part of me wished ... I didn't dare finish that thought. He wiped his hands on his jeans and stood.

"I suppose I should get back to the clinic," he began, pushing the chair back underneath the table.

"Thank you for helping me." I stood also. I'd be lying if I said I wasn't a little disappointed that he was leaving.

"Anytime." Ethan retrieved his toolbox from the table inside. He hesitated for a moment as he walked past me, but continued until he was outside the fence. He stopped and turned around. He pushed his hair back away from his forehead, his eyes looking at the ground. "Would you like some company?" He peeked at me from his downcast eyes. "My mom taught my sister and me how to bake. I could help."

My heart fluttered and I found myself sitting up a little straighter. Oh, Mister Mitchell, where have you been all my life?

Chapter 17

Ethan carried the grocery bags for me but I had the hardest job—carrying the eggs and not tripping over myself. My shoelaces slapped the sidewalk. I kept my eyes on the ground, making sure, with each step, there wasn't a lace under my foot. Moments like this I wished I didn't dress like a toddler and remembered to tie my boots. But they were just so easy to slip on and off. Sometimes, I tucked the laces into the sides but not this time. I could hear them the whole way as we walked down Cattail Road and I knew Ethan could too. Each time one of the laces hit the ground, I swear the noise grew louder.

I glanced at Ethan. He was standing tall with the two bags in front of him as if they were weightless. I wondered what type of woman he liked. I couldn't imagine I had made that great of an impression. I know I had made an impression, just not the one I wanted. I suppose after physically colliding with him numerous times, I was hard to forget. But what could he possibly see in me? I stammered. I stuttered. I tripped. I fell.

I lifted my chin to see him better and he smiled at me. My eyes darted away to focus on the ground in front of me. Perhaps he liked walking disasters? Well buddy, if that's the case, I'm all yours.

We made it to the stone steps that led to my porch and the black cat ran past me. The toe of my shoe caught the edge of one of the stones and I stumbled. Ethan grabbed my arm, holding one of the bags against his hip as he helped steady me. My grip on the eggs became unstable and I fumbled with the carton as it tried its best to open. I glared at the cat and I swore he shrugged his shoulders as he sat in front of the door, licking his paw as he waited.

"He seems to be in a rush to get inside," Ethan remarked. He shifted the bag back into a natural position in his arm.

"I'm not sure why," I mumbled as I unlocked the door and held it open for Ethan. "He doesn't live here." Though, it seemed like he thought he did now.

Ethan walked to the kitchen and placed the bags on the island. The cat jumped on to one of the two stools and his eyes followed Ethan's movements. I guess I did have a guard dog—er—a guard cat. Ethan reached out to pet him but was greeted with a swat. He tucked his arm back to his side. "He's not too fond of me." Ethan chuckled.

Setting the egg carton on the counter, I leaned against it and studied the cat with crossed arms. Something clicked. Was this cat my familiar? The only knowledge I had about them was from what T.V. had taught me. Could they really exist? I shook my head. There was no way this cat was a familiar. If anything in pop fiction was true, familiars were supposed to talk; they were supposed to be helpful.

This cat did neither.

Pushing away from the counter, I pulled groceries out of the big brown bags and placed them on the island. I arranged them in two categories: the sponge for the cake and the icing. I could feel the heat from Ethan's stare and motioned to the pantry door. "Could you grab the aprons?"

Really, I just wanted him to stop staring at me for a moment. Ethan quickly retrieved the white, stained aprons that hung on the inside of the door and handed one to me. Taking it, I watched him slip one over his head and tie it tight around his waist. Pressing my lips together, I tried not to laugh. The apron was meant for a woman, with its ruffles on the bottom edges. But he wore it without any shame or embarrassment. This was definitely not the first time he'd worn an apron like that. I tied mine, having to fold it so it didn't hang too low.

"What temperature does the oven need to be?" he asked, his body bobbing slightly as he waited for instructions.

"Three-hundred-and-fifty-degrees," I muttered, pinching my bottom lip with my fingers.

I swiveled around and opened a thin cabinet next to the refrigerator. I grabbed a one-subject notebook, its spiral spine uniquely messed up. The notebook was filled with hand-written recipes I had collected over the years. When I became an adult and was kicked out of the system, I spent my free time baking when I wasn't working. I knew I had a devil's food cake recipe but not one for the ganache. Thankfully, the mayor had put one in the binder. Though, I felt that was a little rude since, originally, the job had been for Alice. I'm sure Alice knew how to make it without the mayor's help.

Flipping through the old book, I found the cake recipe. The familiar cursive was slightly smudged with dried batter that looked eerily like blood. I placed it open on the island. "The mayor wants me to get a cake to her today. But," I checked the clock on the oven, "I don't have enough time to let the cake cool. So, we are going to make cupcakes."

When Ethan didn't respond, I looked up to see him watching me. The corners of his mouth were slightly turned up.

"What?" I glanced around.

Ethan rubbed his hand over his mouth. "Nothing. You just look cute when you're in the zone."

Cute? Me? I could feel my face turn the color of a boiled lobster. I looked back down at the recipe and cleared my throat. Trying to take the attention off me, I said, "If you prep the pans," I shuffled past him to the oven and pulled two cupcake pans from the cabinet beside it, "I'll start sifting."

I prided myself on being a great multitasker, but I was having trouble concentrating with him so close. The musky scent of his cologne was all I could smell. When his body accidentally brushed against mine, my pulse sped up. My kitchen all of a sudden felt too small. One wrong step and I'd be in his arms. But, would that be such a terrible thing?

I slid the cupcake pans into the oven and set the timer above the stove. Wiping my hands on my apron, I took a step back and turned around. Ethan placed his hands below my shoulders, stopping me from bumping into him. I looked up. His Adam's apple bobbed as he swallowed. He wet his bottom lip. I looked further up, into his blue eyes, my chest heaving just barely brushing against his. His hands slid down my forearms and his fingers caressed mine for a second and for the first time in a very long time, I didn't know what to do.

My mind scrambled for words and I blurted out, "Ganache."

"Ganache?" A grin spread across his face, his dimples forming.

Really, Riley? I closed my eyes briefly. "I mean, we need to make the ganache."

Ethan stepped away, grabbed the dirty mixing bowl and laid it in the sink. As he was washing it, I realized I had never grabbed the binder from my office. Unlike Alice, I did not know how to make a ganache frosting and was relying on that recipe from the mayor. Crap.

Drying the mixing bowl, Ethan studied my face. "What's wrong?"

"I forgot the recipe at the café." I didn't own a computer. I didn't have a smartphone or a tablet. And, believe it or not, I didn't own any recipe books.

Ethan's shoulder rose and fell in a quick gesture. "No problem. I know how to make a ganache."

My mouth opened in awe. "Really?"

Wiping down the counter with a sponge, Ethan glanced at me. "I told you, my mom taught my sister and me how to bake." His dimples reappeared and I couldn't help but smile in return.

While Ethan made the ganache, I tried to scribble down every step of his recipe in my notebook. It was not a hard recipe by any means, but truth be told, I found myself watching his movements more than anything. Ethan wasn't a small man. He was tall and his shoulders were broad but the gentle way he whisked the cream as the chocolate melted on the stove without slinging a single drop was mesmerizing.

He poured the ganache into the mixing bowl and placed the pan in the sink to soak. I dipped the tip of my pinky into the almost-finished product—we still had to whip it—and squealed. It was perfect. Delicious. Decadent. Ethan took a taste but a small droplet of the chocolate landed on his beard, right under his lip. Without thinking, I grabbed one of the rags from the island and reached to wipe it from him.

"You have icing—" I pointed to my own mouth.

He ran his finger under his lip, smearing it further.

"Here, let me help." I dampened the rag and as I turned around, Ethan was standing right behind me. So close that it startled me. I hadn't heard him move. My hand shook as I brought the rag to his lip, trying to gently rub the frosting from the short coarse hair. My finger traced his plump lip, then ran down the length of his chin. He wrapped his hand around my wrist, lowering it to his chest. I took a step backward, hitting the sink. Closing the space between us, his lips brushed mine.

I dropped the rag as his hand circled the back of my neck, deepening our kiss as his tongue ran against the parting of my mouth. He wrapped his hands around my waist and picked me up, as if I weighed nothing, and set me on the counter. Pressed between my legs, he held me steady with his arms around me. I relaxed knowing I wasn't going to fall into the sink and became okay with wherever this was headed. Then the timer went off.

His shoulders sagged and I heard him sigh. He pulled away from me, setting me back on my feet. I touched my mouth, my chin slightly burned from his beard. The timer went off again. Squeezing past him, I slid my hands into a pair of oven mitts and pulled the cupcakes from the oven. Ethan placed the mixing bowl into the refrigerator to chill the ganache. The rich smell of the burgundy cake wafted through the room. Poking a toothpick into the center of one of the cupcakes, I inspected it. They were perfect.

I set cooling racks along the counter and popped the cupcakes out. While everything cooled, Ethan and I cleaned the kitchen, making small talk. Ethan was six-years older than his sister, Jennifer. He had moved away after high school to attend veterinary school in Atlanta, to follow in the footsteps of his father but had recently had a change of heart. His true passion was photography, which was a drastic change in careers. He was working part-time at his father's clinic while he got back on his feet in Wildewood.

Ethan whipped the ganache in the mixer and I cored a small hole in the center of each cupcake. He handed me a piping bag. I could feel his eyes on me as I piped the frosting out into thick layers. My movements felt stiff. Awkward. Act natural, Riley. Unfortunately, the more *natural* I tried to act, the worse it got. I wasn't used to someone staring at me.

Setting the bag down, I wiped my hands on my apron. I took a small plate from the cabinet and placed a finished cupcake on it. With two forks, I turned to Ethan. "Want a taste?"

Ethan took a fork and we both cut into the cupcake. Placing the fork into my mouth, I watched his reaction. His eyes fluttered closed as he slowly pulled the prongs of the fork from his mouth.

He shook the fork at the cupcake. "Riley, you might put Alice out of business."

My laughter turned nervous. Someone was already doing that. I swallowed a second bite and changed the subject, "Thank you for everything today." I pushed the crumbs on the plate around with my fork.

His silence caused me to look at him. He untied his frilly apron and draped it over the counter.

"Do you have a date to the wedding?" he asked.

I shook my head. The whole town had been invited but until this week, I hadn't planned on going. I didn't much care for weddings. They were sappy and I knew I'd cry. It was almost impossible not to cry at a wedding. Well, I might not cry at this particular wedding now that I knew what I knew about the groom.

"Do you?" I asked. I didn't want to know the answer. If he was seeing someone, I would be crushed.

Ethan moved around the corner of the island to stand in front of me. His hands rested on my hips and he pulled me against his body. "That depends." He lowered his head, his lips brushing against the delicate skin of my neck.

I closed my eyes, my breathing shallow.

My voice shook as I responded, "Depends on what?"

He pressed his lips right below my ear and whispered, "If you will go with me or not."

My eyes popped open. How could he not already have a date? He was—well—he was gorgeous. I raised my chin to look into his eyes. Was he playing with me? "You don't already have a date?" I just couldn't believe it.

He shook his head. "Nope."

My brows furrowed. "And you want to go with *me*?"

His lips twitched and the skin around his eyes creased. "Riley, I want to do a lot of things with you, but," he tucked a piece of hair behind my ear, "I'd like to take you on a date first."

"O—okay." I stuttered.

Ethan had to get back to the clinic before they closed for the week. He kissed me goodbye, this time, a sweet, delicate kiss. I watched as he walked down the stone path. He turned to look back at me, raising his hand. I stood a little straighter and wiggled my fingers in return. Feeling warm fuzzies race through every inch of my body, I walked back into the house.

I don't like him, a gruff voice resonated in my head.

"I don't care," I replied, shutting the door.

Wait. Who said that? I crept back toward the kitchen. The black cat sat in front of the island. His tail swished back and forth as he tilted his head up to look at me.

I swallowed. The warm fuzzies vanished. "Did you just speak?"

The cat meowed and licked his paw to rub behind his ear.

Okay—I was imagining things again. I kept my eye on him

as he moved to lie on the couch. I loaded the cupcakes into a carrier. The sooner I got these to Samantha and Trey, the sooner I could start making the actual cake.

Movement out of the corner of my eye caused me to tense. The cat stretched then curled back up. There's no way he had spoken to me. Except, it had been clear as day. For shit's sake, I didn't have time to deal with any more talking things. Hats. Cats. What next? My broom? Was it going to tell me just how uncomfortable it was when I rode it?

Clicking my tongue, the cat opened its eyes. "Come on."

Waiting impatiently as he stretched again, I held the door open as he padded out onto the porch. He jumped in one of the chairs and curled back up. Maybe he had spoken to me, he certainly understood me.

Chapter 18

With the carrier in my hands, I stood on the steps of Town Hall and stared at the door. The cat sat to the right of me. I glanced at him. I could hear a commotion inside and was deciding if I should come back later when the door opened. A hand poked out and wrapped around my wrist.

"Thank goodness you're here," Esther exclaimed, pulling me inside.

Fumbling with the box in my hand, my shoes slipped on the hardwood. Esther grabbed the carrier from me, leaving me to catch my balance as she walked toward the sitting area.

Aaron was sitting behind his desk, looking contempt as ever. His eyes were cast to the ceiling, his fingers tapping on the arms of his chair. It seemed he was tired of the "famous spats" Samantha and Trey had been having. I don't blame him. I wasn't too thrilled to be standing in the room with them myself. If I was quiet, maybe I could back out and no one would notice.

"The cake is here!" Esther held the box up in front of her face. Her smile was forced and … was that desperation? Had she been hoping my arrival would break up the tension in the room?

Samantha stood to the side of the glass coffee table. She

was in a pair of black jeggings and a long mustard-colored tunic sweater. Her hair was down, falling around her shoulders. Besides the scowl on her face, she looked more like herself than yesterday. Her arms were crossed and her lips pursed. Her chest was moving up and down and her nostrils were flared. Trey was sitting on a dark blue couch against the wall. His elbows resting on his knees and he had his head in his hands, looking down at the ground.

"Trey." Esther snapped her fingers. "Samantha. Come taste."

Esther placed the box on the table and lifted the lid open. I opened my mouth to explain why there were cupcakes instead of a cake, but Esther picked one up without questioning. She licked the icing off of her finger as she switched hands.

"Here." She handed one to Samantha.

Samantha turned away from it. Esther scowled and handed it to Trey. Cake could fix a lot of emotional issues, but I don't think this was the band-aid these people needed. Trey stood, taking the cupcake from her. He peeled the paper off and took a bite. I shuffled back and forth on my feet, trying to decide if anyone would notice if I ran out. I didn't want to be in the middle of this. The tension in the room could be cut with a knife and to say I was uncomfortable would be an understatement.

Esther picked up another. "Aaron, would you like a taste?"

Aaron sat up at the sound of her voice and waved a hand in the air. "I'll pass."

"It's good," Trey muttered through a mouth full. "Very good," he added as he took another bite.

I saw Aaron glance at Trey, his eyes little slits. Yikes. If looks could kill and all that.

Esther took a small bite. "Oh, Riley." She licked her lips. "These are almost seductive."

I wondered if that was why Ethan and I had almost—

"I knew we could count on you."

I watched Samantha turn toward the table. She unfolded her arms and picked up one of the cupcakes. Okay, good. Maybe she had calmed down. She held the cupcake in front of her, staring at it, then her eyes darted toward Trey. Her frown deepened, creases forming on her forehead. Her voice was low and angry as she spoke through her teeth, "Do you think your girlfriend will like it?"

Trey squeezed his eyes shut as he released a sigh. His hand pinched the bridge of his nose. "Samantha, I've already told you—"

As if his voice was a trigger, Samantha's back straightened. Her nostrils flared. The cupcake in her hand sailed over the table and hit Trey square in the chest. The light brown frosting smeared down Trey's white and blue checkered button-down shirt as it slid down to the floor. My mouth fell open. I heard Esther gasp.

Samantha picked up another cupcake. "Ask her if they're good enough for *our* wedding!" her voice was loud and wild. Whatever Trey had done, or was doing, Samantha had had enough. She was unhinged.

Could I leave now?

Trey only blinked at her, his mouth forming an *O*. His arms were outstretched as he looked at the mess on his chest. My own eyes were wide. I covered my gaping mouth with a hand and took a step back, hoping no one would notice. Time to go, Riley. Just very slowly, one step at a time, walk backward to the door—no tripping. Trey flung the icing off his chest with a swipe of his hand, it landed on the wooden floor. At least it wasn't carpet.

I yelped as another cupcake went flying. Trey ducked. It smashed against the wall behind him. Slowly it slid down the wall onto the couch he had been sitting on. Trey rolled his shoulders back and licked his lips. Oh, shit. Time to go, time to go!

He held his hands up in front of him, palms open and flat. "Samantha, I'm not seeing anyone."

Not believing what he was saying, Samantha picked up a third cupcake. Thank God I had only brought a half dozen with me. Motion behind Samantha drew my attention. Aaron rose to his feet, going around his desk. Samantha reared her arm back again and Trey held his hands up, covering his face.

"Samantha, that's enough," Aaron whispered behind her.

Thank goodness someone was finally trying to stop this madness. I looked at the cupcake on the couch, on the floor. What a waste of a perfectly good cake.

Tears were running down Samantha's cheeks. She lowered herself into a chair, dropping the cupcake on the table. It landed sideways, the icing sliding off. I jumped when Esther turned to look at me. Her expression was confused as if she had forgotten I had been standing near her. She spun me around with a yank of my arm. Pressing an envelope into my hands, she forced me to walk with her to the door.

"They tasted perfect. Do that again but bigger." She made a big gesture with her arms out wide.

"But—" I started.

She forced me out the door, slamming it in my face as I stood with my nose almost touching it. My mouth hanging open.

Why was this wedding even happening? I could not help the question echoing around in my mind. How could I after the show I'd just been forced to watch? Was I the only person who thought this wedding should just be canceled?

I looked down at the envelope in my hand. Peeking into it, my eyes widened. It was a check for a lot more money than I had expected. Should I keep it? Give it back? A pit formed in the bottom of my stomach. No, I couldn't. It didn't feel right to help. Samantha was obviously uninterested in this marriage. Did I want to play a part in a marriage doomed for failure? Why was she being so stubborn about going through with it? I thought back to the last fight I had walked in on—I remember hearing Samantha imply that she couldn't call the wedding off because of Esther. Why would Esther want her daughter to be miserable? What was she gaining from this marriage?

Okay, I just needed to walk back into that building with my head held high and hand the check back. Simple as that. I wasn't going to play a part in this circus. My conscience couldn't handle it.

The door flung open and Trey almost walked into me.

I moved out of the way. His lips were pressed firmly together as he walked down the porch steps without a word. His steps slowed and he glanced at me.

Trey stopped after a few more steps. I watched as his shoulders rose slowly. "Riley—" but he shook his head and continued to walk away.

I watched him for a moment, wondering if he'd stop again and tell me what was on his mind but then I saw a police car pull up to the front of the station next door. Officer Russel unfolded out of the driver seat and opened the back passenger door. My mouth fell open again as Maisie climbed out uncuffed. They disappeared into the building.

Holy shit. My pulse sped up. Was the crime spree finally over? Were they going to sit her down for questioning and find out all the juicy details about her and Trey's two-month-long affair and her unwillingness to accept he was marrying someone else?

Even so, I was going to return the check. I wanted out of this. The mayor would just have to accept my resignation. I pulled the door to Town Hall open and stepped into the short hallway before the main room. I could hear heels hitting the ground, getting louder as I moved further into the building.

"Samantha," Esther's voice was rigid. The hair on my arms stood.

The footsteps stopped. The silence was eerie. Everything in my being told me to get out *now*. I'd come back later. I looked around and saw the opening for the staircase that led to the basement. I ducked behind the wall and took slow breaths, hoping they hadn't heard me.

"This nonsense must stop." I heard Esther hiss and the footsteps begin again.

"I don't want anything to do with this anymore." Samantha sniffled loud enough for me to hear. Her voice was shaky, filled with sadness. I stifled a groan; I really couldn't bake this cake.

"I know you're hurt, but you're not innocent here either," Esther retorted.

What the hell did that mean? I pressed my lips together. Was Samantha—

I could feel the two of them directly behind the wall I was pressed against. I held my breath until I heard the click of their heels move away. Light from the front door spilled into the hallway. Leaning slightly into the doorway, I saw a shadow fall onto the ground. My eyes rose to see Esther standing in the hallway with her eyes closed. She took in a deep breath and began to walk, her heels quieter than before. As I sucked in a much-needed breath, the noise stopped. I froze with my hands clasped over my mouth, pressing myself against the wall again until I heard a door shut from the back of the building.

I scampered as quickly as I could out of Town Hall.

I walked quickly, as fast as my short legs could take me until I stepped on to the grass of Town Square. I shoved the envelope into my back pocket. I guess I was still making the cake after all. The conversation between Esther and Samantha had been revealing. Samantha obviously no longer wanted to marry Trey. Rubbing my temples, I was now wondering if maybe Maisie was innocent in all of this. Well, mostly innocent. I still had my suspicions that she was the other woman Samantha kept referring to, but with Samantha losing control of her usually-cool demeanor, I was beginning to wonder if she was the one sabotaging her wedding. Perhaps that's what Esther meant by "you're not innocent here either."

Remembering to check both ways before I crossed the street, I hurried to get back to The Witches Brew. Leah was sitting outside on one of the little black chairs waiting for me. I hadn't had a chance to give her a new key to the café. Running my hand through my hair, I pushed all thoughts of Town Hall aside. We had work to do. Hundreds of cupcakes to frost, and though the task ahead was daunting, at least it would take my mind off of everything for a while.

Chapter 19

"Done." I dropped the last piping bag of white frosting onto the counter and slumped into a stool, my back aching from being hunched over for hours.

Emptied bags stained with red, black, white, and green frosting layered one side of the sink. Finished cupcakes lined the counters and refrigerator shelves. I glanced at Leah. The corners of her lips twitched into a smile. This was the first time we had taken on such a big feat together. I could see she was proud. I was too, especially after our mixers had been stolen and we had to use hand mixers.

"If we can do this in just a few hours, I know we can make Samantha's and Trey's wedding cake in the time frame Esther has given us." I wiped icing from my palm on to the white apron. I still didn't want to participate, but I hadn't yet given the check back. And even if I did make the cake, I was just a hired hand. It didn't matter if I agreed with it or not, right? Well, that's what I was telling myself anyway.

The lights above us flickered.

"We better get these covered before another bulb blows." Leah placed the cupcakes, each topped with white frosting and two edible chocolate chip eyes, into a large box. They were supposed to be mummies, with the frosting layered in flat strips and the eyes looking through, but I suppose they could also be ghosts.

The cameo necklace she wore slipped from around her neck and fell to the floor. Picking it up, she cursed and mumbled, "The damn clasp."

My body groaned as I stood, I took the necklace from her. It was heavier than I expected. She turned around and I helped secure it back around her neck. My fingers felt cold after I linked the two sides of the clasp, making sure it wouldn't fall back off. I rubbed my hands to warm them. Whatever the chain was made of it didn't seem to stay warm long. Maybe that's why Leah's attitude had been icier.

Leah placed her hand on the cameo as she turned to me. The flickering subsided. I decided to err on the side of caution and grabbed another box to place black rose-shaped cupcakes in, careful not to get icing on my fingers—only an optimistic thought; it was impossible not to. I cast my eyes to the long fluorescent bulbs for a moment. We never had issues with the electricity until Town Square had begun transformation for the festival. All the electricity being used for it must be overloading the circuits.

Continuing to load cupcakes into boxes, I heard a tapping coming from the front of the café. Peeking over the swinging door, Tessa stood outside bundled from head to toe holding the mysterious hatbox in one hand, the other vigorously waving at me. A smile was plastered on her face and she rocked on her heels as she waited.

So, that's where that damn box vanished to. For an inanimate object, it sure did get around. I stifled a groan, forced a smile of my own, and unlocked the door for her.

"Hey." Tessa stepped into the café, bringing the cold night air in with her. She shivered once more, her jaw chattering before the door closed behind her. Stripping off her black scarf and thick black pea coat, she dropped them on a chair and followed me into the kitchen with the hatbox in her hands.

"Here to help with cupcakes?" I asked, giggling.

Tessa responded with a loud laugh. "You know I'm not a baker."

The last time I had asked for her help, before Leah came into the picture, it had been a disaster. Her baking skills were equal to my carving skills. The only thing Tessa was good at in the kitchen was eating.

"Actually, I figured you hadn't had time to find a hat for your costume with all the—" her hand fluttered in the air and her voice trailed off as she put the box on the stool I had been sitting on and opened it. Reacting quickly this time, I closed my eyes expecting a flash of light then felt the hat being placed on my head.

"I think it has a bit of authenticity to it." She straightened the point at the top.

She's not wrong. I heard the disgruntled voice of a woman.

Trying to hide my reaction to the voice, I opened my eyes one at a time. I struggled to smile, wanting nothing more than to take the hat off but not wanting to hurt Tessa's feelings. At least this time I hadn't been shocked when the hat was put on my head. I was just hearing voices. Definitely nothing out of the ordinary here.

Stop being such a wuss, the voice scolded me.

"I'm not," I snapped.

"You're not what?" Tessa's brows furrowed as she searched my face.

Shit. I removed the hat and heard it arguing as I placed it back in the box. "Nothing." I glanced around at Tessa and Leah, wondering if they had heard anything. No one else was reacting to the other voice in the room. Was I losing my mind? No—no I wasn't. This hat was actually speaking to me—just me. It wasn't an imaginary voice in my head, even though I was the only one who could hear it. I clicked the latches shut on the box and the voice disappeared but not before it called me a few choice words. How rude.

I saw Tessa looking toward the back door. "What's wrong?"

"Have the police figured out who broke in?" all of the pep had gone from her voice.

Shaking my head, I took the box and set it near the swinging doors. "No, but I saw Maisie being brought into the station this afternoon when I was at Town Hall."

Tessa walked to the door and placed her palm against it and whispered, "Do you really think she's capable?"

Leah sneered with a curl to her lips. "It's pretty obvious she did it."

Shrugging, I went back to placing cupcakes into boxes. "I have no idea what she's capable of."

"I'm just not sure she did this …" Tessa mumbled.

It didn't matter what any of us thought until I had real proof. But all I had was conjecture. However, my café being robbed right after I was hired to make the wedding cake and Maisie being fired made me lean more toward Maisie. I glanced back at Tessa, her face had gone solemn. Was it possible she knew Maisie better than I realized? Besides Tessa being an openly friendly person, they both had a tendency to frequent Mike's.

"Do *you* think Maisie is capable?" I questioned, raising an eyebrow. My hands slowed as I watched her.

Tessa sat down on the stool. She leaned on her elbows on the counter, her eyes going back to the door. "I really don't think so." She looked at me, a small smile forming. She shrugged and pushed her hair behind her shoulders. "But I'm not a detective, so what do I know?" Though her smile had returned, a pit was forming in my stomach. Was she hiding something?

No, not Tessa. She was as honest as they came.

With Tessa's help, we finished packing up the cupcakes quickly. The refrigerator doors fought with me to close, but this time I won. With three sets of hands, the kitchen was cleaned in record time. I said goodbye to both women as I locked the front door with the new locks Ethan had installed. I was feeling confident Maisie wouldn't be breaking in tonight—not easily at least. I hadn't seen her again after she went to the police station and I was hoping they were holding her overnight. I wasn't convinced she wasn't involved, even if Tessa didn't agree. But, just as a precaution, I lowered the hatbox to the ground and pressed my hand against the door. Closing my eyes, I pictured myself as a tree, my legs as the trunk, I dug deep into the earth searching for a word to further secure my business.

My voice barely above a whisper, I said, "*Custodio.*"

My hand tingled, heating up as magic poured from my palm into the wood of the door. I pressed my other hand on the opposite side of the door and whispered the word again. Slowly opening my eyes, I saw a shimmering veil of gold covering the door. I blinked and the veil disappeared from sight but I could feel its presence. I walked around the building into the alley and performed the same spell on the back door.

Double-checking the physical lock, I grabbed the keys out of my pocket, noting the little broom dangling from the keyring. It was a lot later than I usually left and though I didn't think I was in any true danger, I still had this nagging feeling I couldn't shake. I didn't want to walk home alone in the dark. This would be a great time for Ethan to bump into me.

I glanced around the alley.

Taking the broom off the keychain, I held it in my palm. "*Crescere*," I spoke normally, not worried about anyone hearing me and blew on it as if it were a dandelion. The miniature broom began to shake and wobble. I laid it on the ground and took a step back. The handle grew. The bristles fluffed like a bird shaking its feathers. Straddling it, I hooked the handle of the hatbox on to the handle of the broom and saw a shadow. My heart began to race. I dropped the broom to the ground with a loud clunk that echoed in the deafening silence of the dark street. This was it. I had been caught. It had finally happened. I closed my eyes, exhaling deeply. When I reopened them, the black cat sauntered up to me. I felt as if I would throw up.

"You are really beginning to bother me," I hissed, picking up the broom then shimmied the box back in place.

Keeping an eye on the cat as he sat watching me, I gripped the handle tightly. "*Subvolare*," I spoke the word that gave the broom the ability to rise into the air. The cat walked toward me as my feet started to dangle. He rose on his hind legs, swatting at my boot.

"Want to come with me?" I asked.

He meowed in response.

I forced the broom back down and the cat jumped into my arms. I pulled my jacket around him and buttoned a few of the buttons to keep him secure as we rose above the top of the buildings then into the night sky. The clouds hid most of the light from the moon as we soared over Wildewood to get to Cattail Road. The town was dark with only the dim yellow glow from the street lamps. The lights from the square were out, except for the little tea lights in the pumpkins. I guess a fuse had blown after all.

In less than three minutes, my boots gently touched the soft ground of my backyard next to the porch. There was a tall, wooden fence that circled the property offering more coverage than landing in the front yard. The cat wiggled out of my jacket and jumped to the ground. I expected some agitation as we made our way home, but he'd stayed perfectly calm the whole time. Perhaps this wasn't the first time he had ridden on a broom …

"You are a strange cat," I said as I unlocked the door.

With the broom in one hand and the hatbox in the other, I walked into the back hallway. The hairs on my arms stood. Something wasn't right. I looked around in the dark, scanning as much as I could of the living room. There was someone inside. I snapped my fingers and the lights flashed on. I dropped what I was carrying to the floor.

Chapter 20

Maisie stared at me from the living room.

"What the fuck are you doing here?" I screamed, pushing the door closed with my foot. It slammed behind me. Adrenaline raced through my body as my pulse quickened. Not only had she broken into my business, but now my home? Oh, hell no.

Maisie winced at my words. She rubbed her palms against the side of her thighs and licked her lips. "I'm sorry. I—"

"You what?" What could she possibly say to make this situation any better?

The cat meandered past me to go further into the room—near Maisie. No, run! Shoo! Save yourself! What the hell was he doing? Didn't he understand she was the bad guy?

"I—" her eyes darted from her shoes to me. Her voice was quiet, without the attitude I had become accustomed to. "I need to talk to you."

"So ..." I crossed my arms. "You decided breaking into my house was the way to go about it?"

The hatbox fell on to its side making a loud thud. I jumped. I glanced at Maisie who was looking down at the cat. I ran past

132

the two of them, reaching for the phone that hung on the wall between the kitchen and living room. I wasn't playing this game. The police could handle it. This was harassment. Maisie caught on quick and rushed over, pressing her hand against the phone to force it back into the mount.

"I'm sorry," she whispered.

I jerked away. "Get off me." It was taking everything in me to resist the urge to use magic. I just wasn't ready to expose myself. Not to her, of all people. She seemed to not realize I had snapped to turn the lights on, but I wasn't going to take another chance.

I stepped away from her. "What do you want?" I pointed to the kitchen island. "Do you want to rob me again? The mixer is in the cabinet."

A deep crease formed between her eyes. "You think that was me?" She shook her head. "I didn't steal from you!"

I didn't believe her. What criminal admits to their crimes? "Just take what you came here for and leave before I run outside and start screaming."

Her shoulders sagged. "I came here to talk to you. That's it."

The cat rubbed its body against her leg, purring loudly. I studied him, wondering why he was so willing to be near her. The last time we talked about Maisie, he bit me. I flicked my eyes to the ceiling. I can't believe I was even playing with the idea of a talking cat. *We* didn't talk. I had talked about Maisie and he bit me.

Maisie bent to pet him and he leaned into her touch. Okay, you traitorous son of a bitch. I squinted at the cat, feeling betrayed. The last thing I said about her was that she was the one sabotaging the wedding. Maybe the cat had been trying to tell me something I just didn't want to hear. I sucked in a breath, trying to push down the anger I was feeling and decided to listen. Yes, listen to what the cat had been telling me.

"What do you need to say?" I looked from the feline traitor up to Maisie.

Her eyes got big. I guess she hadn't expected me to listen after all. "I—" She shifted her weight on her feet, her forehead lined with deep thought-wrinkles. I watched as she swallowed, bobbing her head as if she was preparing to bare her soul to me.

"You what?" I didn't want a soul-baring moment with her though.

"I'm—" she took in a deep breath. I saw a tear roll down her cheek.

What could she possibly have to tell me that was this incredibly difficult for her? She was twisting her hands and licking her lips. Spit it out, Maisie. Was she about to apologize? Finally, her lips parted.

Then I understood.

Maisie's voice entered one ear and ping-ponged around my brain as I tried to comprehend what she had said.

"I'm your sister."

Time seemed to stand still. I couldn't believe it. There was no way. No way she would even know. I was abandoned as an infant. There was no one else with me when I was found at the fire station. I was alone—all alone.

I shook my head, my mouth open, then quickly snapped my jaw closed. I was speechless. Blinking slowly, I said, "Why are you saying that?" Maybe she had found out about my inheritance and wanted a part of it.

Maisie took a step toward me. I moved a step away. She held her hands up and her eyes were desperate. "It's true," she whispered.

Narrowing my eyes, I shook my head. No. This wasn't true. My whole life I had been alone. Hot tears streamed down my face, there was nothing I could do to stop them. Why was she lying? I unclenched my jaw and demanded, "You need to leave." Just get out of my house. Go away!

Taking another step closer to me, Maisie's voice shook. Her tears were pooling around her eyes. "Riley. I am your sister."

As she reached out to me, I yanked away, stumbling back a few steps. "I don't have a sister. I'm alone. I have always been alone."

She lowered her head, her hand falling to her side. "I know we haven't gotten off on the right foot. I was just—"

"There's no feet." I raised my voice and swung my arms in front of me in a crisscross. "We are not sisters."

The cat ran to me. I expected him to rub against my leg, to comfort me. Instead, he made a B-line past me and jumped on to the hatbox as the latch clicked open. No, no, no! I ran to the box, sliding on my knees, and latched it before it had a chance to escape again. Now was not the time for your shit, I thought as I set the box upright.

I turned back to Maisie. "You need to leave. Now."

Without argument, Maisie turned and walked to the front door. She paused with her hand on the doorknob. Raising her head she said, "We are sisters."

I stayed on the floor for a moment, just breathing and staring at the door. I could feel the mix of anger and sadness bubbling up in my throat, or maybe it was stomach acid. I picked up the hatbox and shoved it into the coat closet near the front door. I snapped my fingers and the door locked. Standing on my toes, I looked out the small windows at the top of the door. I could see Maisie's dark silhouette as she walked down the street. Could she really be my sister? Was it possible?

No. There was no way. My bottom lip quivered and my chest felt heavy. My stomach was in knots. Tears burned in my eyes and clouded my vision as I walked up the stairs to the loft. If I had a sister, I wasn't alone anymore. But if it was true, then why did I feel such terrible pain in my heart? I kicked my shoes off and crawled under the soft comforter. I buried my face into my pillow and screamed. My body rocked as my screams were replaced with sobs. I poured out three decades of heartache.

Chapter 21

It was Halloween, my favorite holiday, and yet, I woke with a heavy heart. My throat was coarse from crying and I was dehydrated. I turned my head, blinking the sleep away, and saw the cat sleeping next to me. Maisie's voice echoed in my head, *"I'm your sister."* Did I really have a sister—a sibling I never knew? Was this some ploy to get me to believe she was innocent of the recent crimes? That seemed drastic, even for her. If it was true, why hadn't she told me months ago? There had been so many opportunities for her to tell me. Hell, she could've written me a letter.

Sitting up, I watched the cat stretch on the bed and open his mouth in a big yawn. He rolled on to his back then on to his belly, stretching once more before jumping to the floor. The pads of his feet made soft pitter-patter noises as he walked down the steps of the loft. At least he seemed to have slept well.

It was kind of comforting knowing he had slept next to me after I had cried myself to sleep last night. Maybe he really was my familiar. My familiar. It had a nice ring to it, even if he liked Maisie. Perhaps he was trying to tell me to accept her, but right now all I could think about was that I had been alone for twenty-eight years and now I possibly had a sister who seemed to have been just as alone. That made my heart ached, knowing we both had felt the same pain throughout our entire childhood.

I remembered what she yelled when I fired her, "*Not everyone had a perfect life like you.*" Now I understood what she meant. She thought I'd had a different life than her. She probably thought I had been adopted and raised by a loving family. I often dreamed about it, but it never happened.

How had she found out about me? Andrew had never mentioned two children, though he hadn't mentioned much about anything. Talking had been a chore and he hadn't been too forthcoming about who my—our mom had been. He kept brushing it off and telling me we'd, "Talk about it later." Later never came. He took that secret to his grave.

I changed into a clean outfit and sat back down on the bed to tie my boots. I was feeling confused. Hell, I was feeling a lot of things but confusion was pushing everything else to the side. In one week the most bizarre occurrences of my life had all combined, one right after the other. Something strange was going on in Wildewood and I felt like the epicenter of it all.

Hearing the cat scratch at something, I stomped down the stairs. He probably wanted to go outside. As I got to the bottom of the steps, I saw that he was raised on his hind legs swatting at the doorknob of the closet door. This wasn't peculiar at all, I snorted a laugh and opened it.

"What do you want?" I asked.

The cat rubbed his side against the hatbox. Stifling a groan, I pulled it out of the closet surprised it was still where I had left it. I'd forgotten I had stuffed it in there until this moment. Picking it up, I set it on the kitchen island. I took my chances unlatching it.

When nothing happened, I shrugged and decided to deal with the major headache I woke up with. I went to the sink and filled a glass of water to the brim. Sucking it down as if it was oxygen, I turned my attention back to the box. The lid flung open and the hat jumped. The glass slipped from my hand, shattering on the floor, and I began to choke. Struggling for a breath, I watched as the hat bounced, its brim bending to give it leverage. What the fu—

Put me on, the woman's voice demanded.

No, thank you. But my fingers twitched as if it had been a command I couldn't ignore. Um, no! Hello, I was in control here. I grabbed a rag to clean up the broken glass on the floor, trying to ignore the urge I was feeling to place the damn hat on my head.

Now, she demanded again.

Nope. Not going to do it. Even though I was refusing, I found myself inching toward the hat, my arms outstretched. Oh, what the hell—I picked it up and placed it on my head, closing my eyes.

I opened my eyes and stared into a black void. My kitchen had been replaced with nothingness. Then a tall, thin woman flickered into view before me. She looked like me as if we could be related. We had the same square jaw and small nose. She had long, reddish-brown hair that fell to her hips. It was wavier than mine but the same color. Her arms were crossed over a white, daisy-print blouse tucked into a pair of high-waisted jeans. Her narrow waist was accentuated by a thin, black belt. She looked at me and my mouth opened at the sight of her eyes—hazel.

"Hello, Riley," the woman spoke. Her lips twitched into a smile. Was this my mother? Is that why she had been following me?

"You're—" I was dumbfounded, recognizing her voice as the one coming from the hat.

She shook her head at the statement I hadn't said. "My soul is attached to that tired old hat," she explained with a flitter of her hand. "It's how I'm able to stick around."

Oh, that makes perfect sense—except nothing made sense anymore. Not this, not the cat, and not Maisie. Was I experiencing a mental breakdown of some kind? Had I gone into a psychosis?

The woman chuckled and as if she could hear my thoughts, she answered them, "You're perfectly sane, Riley, and Maisie is your sister."

Oh, yeah, I was totally sane listening to a woman possessing a hat. My brows creased and I crossed my arms over my chest. "How do you know?"

"We'll talk about that later. For now, just have faith. She *is* your sister."

Those words sounded familiar. No one was or had been, willing to tell me the straight truth. I started to question her when the void began to disappear and I was back in my kitchen with broken glass on the floor, the cat staring at me. I sighed, at least a dead woman couldn't die again without explaining things to me. I took the hat off my head and heard the word 'twin.'

Twin? I shoved the hat back on my head, pulling it over my eyes with such force I thought I might break its seams, but nothing happened. The void didn't return, the woman wasn't there. It was just me standing in my kitchen with a floppy old hat covering half my face. I threw the hat back into its box and felt hot tears rise again. So, not only was Maisie my long-lost sister but she was also my twin.

I had always felt something was missing, even after finding

my father. There was always this piece of me that felt empty. This was it. I had a twin. It made sense now why I never felt whole. I choked back my tears and wondered who had separated us and, more importantly, why. Why would someone keep us apart? The heavy feeling in my chest returned, but this time it was anger.

The cat meowed at me and I looked down at it. "You both know more than you're letting on. I know it." I slammed the lid to the box shut. Snapping my finger, the latch locked. She wasn't going anywhere until I got some answers.

Chapter 22

The sun was already up by the time I left the house. The muscles in my calves and the bottom of my feet were sore as I pounded the concrete to the café. The cat kept up with my pace, though he was careful to stay a good distance from me. That was probably smart of him. My jaw was clenched and it was beginning to hurt. I wanted to know who separated us. Why weren't we found at the same location? Even if we hadn't been placed in the same home, there was a chance I still would've known about her. Right? The woman in the hat, whoever she was, knew more about me than I did, perhaps she knew who was behind it. Would our mother have done that? She gave us up, but would she have been so cruel to make sure we never found each other?

Then there was Maisie. Did she know the whole time we'd worked together? Is that why she came to Wildewood? I had spent the last two months feeling nothing but irritation with her and now I'm told she is my sister. Not just my sister, but my twin. I needed to find her… but I didn't know where to look.

Unlocking the café, the cat ran inside before I slammed the door. I walked to the counter and grabbed on to the edge. Closing my eyes, I forced myself to take a deep breath. The Witches Brew was closed for the day to prepare for the Halloween Festival later this evening. I had work to do and I needed to push aside the problems in my personal life to focus on my professional one. Easier said than done since they seemed to be weaving together, but I was trying.

After a few deep breaths, and not feeling much better, I concocted a plan. If I couldn't get any concrete information about my personal life, I could at least try to get some about the recent crimes. While the coffee was brewing, I busied myself making a fresh batch of blueberry muffins for the Wildewood police station. There were only a handful of officers and someone was keeping them quite busy. So, my plan consisted of bringing them coffee and muffins in hopes someone was feeling chatty. Okay, I was hoping Pete was there.

I filled a large, disposable coffee thermos box, securing the cap tightly. I flicked my wrist and the muffins floated into a white to-go box that sat open on the counter. Grabbing my jacket out of the office, I slipped it on over the flannel shirt. I hoped this worked, assuming they had something to divulge. I walked out of the café, setting the boxes on a table to lock the door. Crossing the street, I walked through Town Square, past the hay maze, the dozens of canopies, and the stage. Maisie walked out of the police station. I froze, guilt filling my chest. Did they think she had something to do with the recent crimes? I mean, I did—or rather, I had. I tried to shake the guilt. Trying to convince myself I had nothing to feel guilty about. At the time of the robbery, I had no idea who she was to me.

I straightened my posture, taking in a shaky breath, then made my way to the station. Maisie sat on the steps, her arms draped over a large blue duffle bag in her lap. Her eyes were focused on the ground. I stepped onto the sidewalk in front of her. She raised her head, squinting up at me.

My stomach flipped as I looked at *my* twin. I studied her features. Our hair was the same color, our eyes hazel, and the same small nose. Her face was more of an oval-shape, while mine was square. Her lips were thinner and she had freckles across her nose. We might be twins, but we were not identical. I cleared my throat, realizing I had just been staring at her. "What are you doing?"

She shrugged and leaned back to prop herself up with her elbows. "I ran out of money."

"What does that mean?" The carafe was beginning to feel heavy. Her running out of money didn't explain why she was sitting outside the police station.

Maisie stood, throwing her duffle bag over her shoulder. "It means I can't afford to stay at the Bed and Breakfast anymore." She glanced at me. "I'm leaving."

She took a few steps past me and I reached out to stop her. Her body stilled as my hand gripped her arm. I looked down and saw a familiar mark on her skin, right below her thumb. My chest heaved as I pushed my jacket sleeve up and held my arm out to show her my wrist.

"We aren't just sisters." The crescent moon birthmarks matched.

Maisie shuffled on her feet, her hand circling her wrist to hide the mark. She sniffled, and I saw her jaw clench and her lips turn down. She ran a finger under her eyes and whispered, "I've got to go." She began to walk away, her pace quick.

"Wait!" I tried to catch up with her but the items I carried slowed me down. I stood in the middle of the sidewalk and screamed, "You can't leave!" Not now.

She kept walking. She didn't even turn around. A man and woman with two little girls walked past me. The girls, with their long blonde pigtails in matching Halloween outfits, held hands as they jumped over the cracks in the sidewalk. I felt like I had just been punched in the stomach. I wanted to drop everything and run. That could've been us.

The cat rushed past me and caught up with Maisie before she was out of sight. My vision clouded as tears formed. The heaviness in the pit of my stomach returned as I faced the station. The recent crimes in Wildewood seemed nothing in comparison to letting the only family I had walk away. I wasn't alone anymore, and yet, I felt more alone than ever. I readjusted the thermos, took in a deep breath, and pulled the station door open.

The building was small and in need of an update. The walls were gray, peeling in spots, and the furniture was brown and worn. Susan Byrnes sat at her circular desk at the front. She was a middle-aged woman with bottle-red curly hair falling past her shoulders. Her job consisted of being the receptionist and nine-one-one operator. I glanced around the quiet room and immediately spotted Pete Kelly sitting at one of the few desks.

Pete looked up from his computer and grinned with rosy cheeks. "Riley!" He stood, pulling his pants up by his belt. "What brings you here?"

I placed the thermos box and muffins on Susan's desk. "Just stopped by to say thank you. I know you all have your hands full this week."

Susan lifted out of her chair just enough to reach for a muffin. Her brown eyes grew large as she picked the one she wanted. "Thank you," she said and sat back down, pinching a chunk of the muffin top off and placing it in her mouth.

Pete grabbed his coffee cup that read, "World's Greatest Police Officer" in bold blue letters from his desk. He took a few steps toward us then stopped. "Oh! Suz, let me go get you a cup!" He turned on his heels and shuffled to the break room.

While Pete was away, I leaned on an elbow and whispered to Susan, "Have you guys found anything out about the fire or burglary?"

"Riley." Susan waved a hand at me and took another bite from her muffin. I hadn't enchanted them like I did the other day with Pete but I was hoping it wouldn't matter. "You know they don't tell me anything."

Raising an eyebrow, I said, "I know you hear things." The station was tiny and Pete was rarely quiet about anything.

Her cheeks grew red and she swatted at me again. "The only thing I've heard is that they found some type of orange fiber on the glass at the Bakery. They think it's from a jacket or a shirt. It seems to be their only clue until the results for the blood come back from Twin Falls."

"I wish I had some good news to tell you," Pete said, breathless as he came to Susan's desk. He poured coffee into both mugs. Pete grabbed a packet of creamer and sugar from the breakroom and ripped them open. He poured the contents into his coffee and used a small wooden stick to stir. "We have no leads on the burglary at the moment."

"What about Maisie?" I pried, wanting to know what he thought of her involvement.

Pete brought his mug to his lips. "She has an alibi who checked out," taking a sip, he paused. "Your coffee is so much better than anything we make here."

I caught sight of Suzie glaring at Pete. She must make the coffee at the station. Tread lightly, Pete.

"What was she doing here, then?" I asked, nodding toward the door.

"She was letting us know she was leaving town. She didn't want us to think she was fleeing. Ya know, she's really not a bad kid." He returned to his desk. "I never noticed before, but she looks an awful lot like you." He held his cup toward me before sitting. "Thanks for this, Riley. I promise to let you know if we find anything out." He leaned back in his chair, the frame groaning. "This is a strange time in Wildewood."

He had no idea just how strange. I left the station feeling like I had accomplished something. I finally had a color for the fibers the police found on the broken glass of the bakery. Come to think about it, what an odd color to wear to break into a store. If it had been me, I would've been dressed from head to toe in black—blend into the darkness—not orange. Unless … unless this had been a spontaneous crime—a crime of passion.

I wasn't sure the police were connecting the two crimes like I was. But I knew they were connected. They both pointed to the upcoming wedding of Samantha and Trey. Someone was sending a message: they did not want this marriage to happen. But at what cost? How far would they go? I didn't want to wait for the DNA results to come back from Twin Falls to find out.

Wrapping my jacket tight around me as the wind began to blow, I shoved my hands into the insulated pockets and felt something crinkled. Pulling it out, I inspected it. The dry-cleaning ticket Aaron had left in the cake binder he had dropped off. I had completely forgotten.

Chapter 23

Trampling through the grass between the police station and Town Hall, I was going to pop in real quick, give a little apology, then be on my way. Hopefully, Samantha and Trey weren't in and I wouldn't find myself in the middle of another spat. I pulled the door open and walked down the short hallway, but Aaron wasn't at his desk. It was eerily silent as if the entire building was empty.

Okay. Plan-B. I would just go pick up his dry-cleaning for him. I shoved the ticket back in my pocket before sprinting across Town Square to the alley beside The Witches Brew. The scent of clean linen from the laundromat attached to Phelps Alterations and Dry Cleaning became strong as I walked out of the gate and onto the street behind the café.

The door to the dry-cleaners opened and, to my surprise, Aaron stepped out and yelled into the building as the door began to close, "I'll be back."

His jaw was clenched tight and he closed his eyes as he rubbed his temple. I had a feeling I had played a part in his irritation. I pulled the ticket out of my pocket. Aaron visibly took in a deep breath, his chest rising and falling, before he rushed down the street.

Waving the ticket in the air, I called out his name, my shoe-laces slapping the sidewalk as I tried to catch up with him. He pulled his cell phone out of his pocket and placed it to his ear, his long legs allowing him to move much faster.

I slowed as he turned a corner, catching my breath. Well, since I was already here … I looked up to see the bold white letters above the black awning that read, Phelps Dry Cleaning. Plan-B continued. Hopefully, it would be as easy as handing over the ticket. I had never used a dry cleaner before.

"Good morning," I was greeted by a woman standing behind the counter. Her name tag read Sylvia Phelps. Her dark brown hair was pulled up into a tight bun except for a single short curl near her temple. The wrinkles on her hands were noticeably deep as she laid them on the counter.

I slid the ticket to her. "I need to pick up this item." Please let it be this easy.

She placed the glasses that hung around her neck on a gold chain on to the tip of her nose. Her eyes scanned the large number on the bottom of the paper. She turned to the rack of clothes that spun on the ceiling behind her. Pressing a button, the clothing began to move. She climbed on to a stool and still had to stand on her toes to grab a hanger covered in plastic. As she came back to the counter, I saw a rust-colored jacket.

"Here you go. The elbow should be good as new." She handed it to me and gave me a receipt.

"Elbow?" I muttered.

"Yes, the elbow that needed to be patched." She raised an eyebrow, because, *duh*, I should've already known this. "The stain is barely noticeable. Unfortunately, we couldn't remove it completely. Next time I suggest—"

I stared at the jacket in my hands, unaware of her still talking and left the dry-cleaners. Pushing the plastic up I draped it over the hanger to look at the sleeves, running a finger over the fabric in search of a seam that shouldn't be. It was almost impossible to tell; Sylvia had done an exceptional job. Bringing the sleeve closer, there was a brown stain in the fold of the seam. It was barely noticeable, but it was there.

Pulling the plastic back over the jacket, I swallowed realizing I might have evidence in my hands. Oh, fuck. Was Aaron Hall sabotaging Samantha's wedding? I stared down at the jacket and chewed on the inside of my cheek. What the hell was I supposed to do with this? I couldn't give it back to him, could I? Should I? Oh, fuck me. Just fuck—

"Hey, Riley!"

I jerked my head up to see Ethan standing outside the animal clinic, waving his hand.

This really was not a good time. I tried to hide the jacket behind my back. A gust of wind whipped the plastic around, the sound of it rustling was thundering. Very discrete, Riley.

Coming to stand in front of me, Ethan pulled a pair of thin, plastic gloves from his hands and shoved them in a pocket of his dark blue scrubs. The shirt he had on was printed with sloths hanging lazily from limbs. Was there anything he didn't look like a Greek God in? He took my head in his hands and pressed his lips to mine. Oh, who was I kidding ... maybe it was always a good time. His arms circled my waist and he pulled me close to him.

"I've been thinking about you all day," he whispered as our lips parted.

I licked my lips, stunned.

"I'll see you at the festival?" he asked. "I was going to help Jennifer at the Just Treats booth but since there won't be one ..."

his voice trailed off. He kissed me once more. "I'll find you when I get there."

Nodding, I watched him hustle back into the clinic. There was something irresistible about him ... something unnatural. I couldn't put my finger on it. I had never, in my life, reacted to someone the way I did to him. I power-walked back to Oak Avenue through the alley, the wind rustling the bag, reminding me about that predicament I was in.

Okay. I had to get rid of this jacket. I should take it to the police. Yeah, that's what I was going to do. I stepped out of the alley. There was no way in hell I was giving it back to Aaron. I stopped. He was sitting at one of the tables in front of the café. Taking a step back, I decided I would take a longer route to the station. He raised his head from his phone, his eyes widened. He'd spotted me.

Having no other choice, I let out a defeated breath. What was I supposed to do now?

"That's mine." Aaron stood, pointing at the jacket.

I reluctantly handed it to him, my pulse speeding up. This was a bad idea. A really bad idea. "You left the dry-cleaning ticket at the café."

He yanked the jacket from my hands as he left the patio area. "You need to get a cell phone, Riley."

If only they worked for me. "They patched the elbow nicely," I said, just loud enough for him to hear, immediately realizing that had been a mistake.

His eyes narrowed at me. He turned and crossed the street toward Town Square. With the sound of my heart pounding hard in my ears, I rushed inside the café, locking the door behind me. I watched Aaron weave through the festival area. Why did I say that? Why, why, why? Was I now in more danger than before?

I paced in front of the door for a few minutes, keeping my eyes toward Town Hall. Had Aaron been the one who had set Just Treats on fire? I started adding things up. Susan said they'd found orange fibers on the broken glass. Aaron's jacket was orange-ish. And that look he had given me ... was this all just coincidence? The pit in my stomach was telling me that, no, it was not a coincidence at all. I had accidentally uncovered the person behind the arson. But why was he doing this? Why did he care if Samantha and Trey got married? I ran a hand over my face, stopping in front of the door. If Aaron knew I was on to him, would he try to scare me off, again?

Stomping my feet in place, I balled my hands into fists by my side and decided I was not going to let him scare me. I looked at the large window in the front of the café. I had sealed the doors, but was it enough? I would be devastated if I came to work to find the café burned to the ground. It was not enough, I had to seal the entire building.

I pulled the blinds, something I never did. I stood in the middle of the floor and held my arms out, my eyes closed. I wasn't going to let this son of a bitch destroy me the way he did Alice. I took in a deep breath, grounding myself to call forth the knowledge I had tucked inside. "*Custodio,*" the word slipped from my tongue. My fingers tingled, but it wasn't enough. I needed more power to seal the whole building. "*Custodio,*" I said louder, my palms began to burn.

My hands were glowing like golden orbs, so bright I could barely see my fingers. I had never harnessed this much magic before. I took another deep breath. I opened my eyes wide then slapped my hands together and screamed, "*Custodio!*"

The two orbs exploded, sending thousands of golden splinters into the air all around me. I shoved my hands out in front of

152

me, pushing the suspended splinters toward the wall. Pivoting, I did the same in each direction. The four walls shimmered, the golden color creating a chainmail design, then it sunk into the walls, disappearing.

Let him try.

Chapter 24

After hours of piddling around the café, cleaning and catching up on dreaded paperwork, I couldn't take it anymore. I was unable to focus on any one particular thing for too long. My thoughts kept going back to Aaron and the orange jacket. I needed to find a way to get it back and bring it to the police. Would they even believe me? Probably not. I should just stay out of it. I had no idea what lengths he would go to to keep from getting caught. What the hell was I thinking? I should've just made a run for it, straight to the station, when Aaron spotted me. But let's be realistic, I knew I wouldn't be able to outrun him.

Checking the time, I realized I needed to get home to change into my costume. I power-walked, though my thighs were still unhappy from the other day. I managed to avoid running into anyone, including Tessa. I wish I could share what I knew with her. I suppose there was no reason I couldn't … unless it put her in harm's way. Crap, I hadn't thought of that. Okay, looks like I was on my own again. That was short-lived.

Walking into the house huffing and puffing, I noticed the hatbox lying on the floor beside the kitchen island. The salt and pepper shakers were next to it, turned on their sides. I picked the box up and placed it on the kitchen table, where there was nothing for it to knock over. I snapped my finger, the latch unlocked and the lid to the box flung open. The hat jumped. I'm not sure I'd ever get used to that.

I picked it up and placed it on top of my head. Closing my eyes, the image of the woman returned. She was wearing the same daisy-print shirt and blue jeans. Had she died in those clothes? Is that what happened? We were stuck forever in the same clothes we died wearing? Yikes. I needed to keep that in mind when I picked out my outfits.

The sound of her foot tapping stopped my thoughts and pulled me attention.

"It's about time." She placed her hands on her hips.

"What are you talking about?" I asked. Seriously, what was she in such a rush for?

She dismissed my question with a wave of her hand and began to pace. "Did you find your sister?"

"I did." Though I wasn't sure why she cared so much.

"And?" She faced me, her eyebrows raised.

"And nothing. She is leaving town." I gave a slight shrug.

The woman shook her head. Her hands waved in front of her frantically. "No, no! She can't leave. You two must be together."

"Why?" I wasn't disagreeing but why was this so important to her?

"Because—" She glanced around the void then held up her hands. "Sisters should be together."

Whoever separated us to begin with obviously did not agree with that. I ignored her, because I didn't know what to say. I wanted Maisie to stay but I couldn't force her. Hell, I didn't even know how to find her again. I changed the subject, "I am going to wear you tonight at the Halloween Festival. Can you behave?"

I didn't want to regret this decision. But what was a witch without her hat?

She opened her mouth and placed her hands back on her hips. "Of course!"

Good. I guess we would see just how well she could behave in public. I pulled the hat off, still able to hear her, *Can I behave? Who do you think you're talking to? I'll show you just how well I can behave.*

"We'll see," I mumbled. Leaving the hat on the counter as a test, I went upstairs to the loft to change into my costume. I tightened the corset as best as I could but I knew the moment Tessa saw it she would want it tighter. I, however, enjoyed breathing. Since she wasn't here to argue with me, I compromised, it was only sort-of tight. Just enough so it wouldn't fall down.

I slipped my feet into a new pair of knee-high black boots careful not to snag the black fishnet tights and found it difficult to bend as I zipped them up. I felt light-headed. I stood and sucked in a deep breath, or as deep as the corset would allow. Looks like I wouldn't be doing much sitting tonight.

I stepped out onto the front porch. Pointy-ish hat, wooden broom, black cat—wherever he was. I was becoming a true story-book witch, with a smidge sex appeal, thanks to Tessa.

I bet it feels refreshing to dress as you really are, the woman's voice vibrated in my head.

"Be quiet," I hushed, but she wasn't wrong. It felt freeing to be dressed as a witch. I closed my eyes, the breeze billowing my dress. Here I am. Riley Jones, friendly neighborhood witch. Opening my eyes, I raised my hand to snap my fingers making the hat stand tall when I heard someone clear their throat.

"Who are you talking to?"

Spinning, the broom raised to strike, I saw Maisie sitting on one of the wicker chairs on the front porch. Her duffle bag was next to her feet and the cat was lying in front of it. My mouth opened. I didn't think I would see her again.

"What are you doing here?"

Maisie stood and I lowered the broom. The cat meandered toward the front door and sat on the doormat. "I couldn't leave."

A small smile formed on my lips. Without thinking, I dropped the broom and took a quick step forward, my arms wrapped around her. Her body tensed and I buried my head into her hair. I felt her arms struggle, then slide around me. Tears welled in my eyes and I felt her tears on my bare shoulder. I had always wanted a sister.

"I'm glad you changed your mind," I whispered. I pulled away, searching her face. She wiped tears from her cheek. "Where will you stay?"

Maisie shuffled her feet and took a long look at her bag before returning to meet my stare. "I haven't figured that out yet. I just wanted to let you know I'd be around."

The cat meowed from behind me. I glanced at the front door. Okay, kitty. I'm going to trust you on this one. "Why don't you stay with me? I have an extra room."

Maisie's face lit up, she was clearly taken by surprise. "Really?"

My smile widened. This was the right thing to do. Now that I knew who she was, I couldn't just let her leave. I wanted to get to know her. I wanted to know *my* twin. Just being near her, I could feel the emptiness I had felt my whole life being filled.

"Yes. Really." I opened the front door. "Let me show you to your room."

Chapter 25

Clear lights strung from the tree in the center of the square flickered, threatening to go out. They wrapped around its trunk up to the first layer of limbs and were carried out with the branches over the festival, creating a soft golden glow. The pumpkins that were carved by the townspeople cast ominous yellow faces helping to contain the foot traffic. I hadn't been able to pinpoint mine ever since I had *fixed* it, but I was slightly relieved about that.

The band on the stage was a group of high school seniors chosen to play updated covers of classic Halloween songs. The music floated across the entire town. I would probably be able to hear it from my house if I wasn't sitting underneath a canopy with a few hundred cupcakes surrounding me.

My stomach growled at the smell of fried dough from the funnel cake booth nearby. The scent overpowered the sweet smell of the cupcakes. As soon as Maisie came back to the booth, I was going to indulge. Who didn't love delicious fried dough topped with powdered sugar? Heathens, that's who.

In the center of the table behind me was a large cast-iron cauldron Tessa had helped me find. She always knew where to find strange items. I had placed dry ice in the bottom then poured on water, the smoke cascaded out around the cupcakes stacked beside it. Flashing green lights behind the cauldron made the smoke glow and helped create the look of a real witch's brew.

The wind was calm, thankfully, unlike earlier in the day but there was an unmistakable chill in the air. The three sides of the canopy we had lowered helped block some of the chill, but with so much exposed skin from the changes to my costume, I was on the verge of becoming a sexy popsicle.

I spotted Maisie as she walked through the grass back to the booth. She was wearing a tight, fuzzy black sweater with a black skirt made of tulle that fell to the middle of her thighs. Her legs were covered with thick black tights and a pair of black combat books. Black cat ears adorned the top of her head and she had painted whiskers on her cheeks.

Maisie held up a plate in her hand as she neared the booth. She'd brought funnel cake. Hell, yes! We really were twins. You know, same thoughts and all that.

Handing me the plate, she held up a small pumpkin with her other hand. "They have a pumpkin booth near the stage!" She set it down on the table in front of me. On it, she had painted the face of a classic jack-o-lantern. "That was much more enjoyable than trying to carve a pumpkin. I hate carving pumpkins," she mumbled that last bit.

Chuckling at the lopsided eyes, it reminded me of the one I had carved. It seemed we both had trouble with pumpkin carving. "Me too," I agreed.

Sitting down in one of the two folding chairs we'd brought, Maisie held her still-bandaged fingers up. "I gave myself a serious injury trying to carve one for the festival. I had to get stitches and everything."

She snuck a piece of the funnel cake and sank back into her chair. I no longer thought she was the person who had burglarized The Witches Brew or caused the fire at Just Treats, but I was still curious.

"When did you get stitches?" I asked, trying to sound casual but my hand was shaking when I went for the funnel cake. I wanted to believe she was innocent and everything had just been a coincidence.

Maisie opened her mouth to answer when a group of young children walked up to the booth. Each held out a plastic, orange pumpkin. "Trick or Treat!"

"What scary costumes!" I quickly shifted gears and grabbed the large candy bowl we had filled with a variety of chocolates and dropped a few pieces into each basket.

A blonde-headed princess turned her nose up. She had a sparkly tiara on her head. Her pink dress puffed out and reminded me of the Good Witch from The Wizard of Oz. "I'm not scary."

Sneaking an extra piece of candy into her bucket, I whispered, "You're right. You're beautiful."

She grinned a big snaggle tooth smile and pulled on the sleeve of her mom's jean jacket. "Can we get a cupcake?"

The woman pulled a few dollars out of her pocket and told them they could pick out one each. Watching them as they made their decision, Maisie handed out four ghost cupcakes. The woman placed four dollars into the jar sitting at the back of the table and thanked us as her children walked away playing with their edible ghosts. Or mummies. Really, it could go either way.

Looking past the children, I watched a tall man steer around them. He wore a thick, brown sweater with tan slacks and a full-face mask of a werewolf. He raised his arms in the air, his furry, gloved hands had long nails. He growled, getting a squeal out of the princess. Pulling the mask off, he approached the table. Ethan's smile reached his eyes as he looked at me. His eyes trailed down my body and his stare deepened, his smile fading into something more carnal.

Maybe I should thank Tessa for turning me into a vixen after all.

"Hey." His voice was almost a growl. He placed a dollar into the jar and scooped up one of the green cupcakes. "Can you leave for a moment?"

I looked at Maisie. She nodded. "Go. I've got this covered."

It was strange seeing this side of her. All her anger toward me had faded within moments of her telling me the secret she had been keeping for months. Our instant connection felt like we hadn't missed twenty-eight years of each other's lives. Well, almost.

Ethan finished the small cake in about three bites then took my hand in his paw, the plastic from his glove was cold against my palm, and we weaved through the crowd.

I don't like him, the hat whispered in a matter of fact tone. I could picture her with her arms crossed and her eyes narrowed. Damn, I had almost forgotten she was around.

Faking a cough, I said, "Behave."

Fine. Suit yourself.

Ethan led me toward Tessa's booth. I had been so busy setting up my own that I hadn't had a chance to see her all evening. I was excited to see what she had done with hers. Tessa had a tendency to go over the top. Take my costume for instance. The slit in the dress ran up my thigh to right below my hip. Even with the fishnet tights, it would only take one strong gust of wind for everyone to find out I was wearing a thong. I couldn't blame Tessa for the fishnets, though. Those had been my idea.

"Do you want to get your fortune read?" Ethan pulled his gloves off and slipped an arm around my waist as we approached Tessa's booth.

The black canopy had all four sides rolled down. She had a sign outside the entrance that had a hand-drawn crystal ball with stars all around. "*Come in and find out what your future holds,*" the sign read. Ethan pulled one side of the entrance aside and let me in before him. What a gentleman, I thought until his hand trailed down my back and rested on the top of my butt. Hey, I wasn't angry about it.

It was incredibly dark once the curtain was closed except for a large, glowing ball in the center of a small, round table. Tessa sat behind it; the glow cast onto her as if she was holding up a flashlight getting ready to tell a scary story. Her eyes lit up once she recognized me. "Welcome!" She winked. "Sit, sit!"

Sitting opposite her on the only two chairs available, Ethan rested his hand on my leg above my knee. His fingers moved in circles, sending shivers down my spine. So focused on his touch, I didn't notice Tessa reaching her hand out toward me until she cleared her throat. Pressing my hand over Ethan's to stop him from moving further up my thigh, I handed Tessa my free hand. She took it and turned it over, palm up. Her smile vanished as she returned to the character she was dressed as: Tessa the Fortune Teller.

She looked like a natural-born gypsy. Her hair was wavy, pulled away from her face with a purple scarf wrapped around the crown of her head. Little gold trinkets rested on her forehead, hanging from the fabric. Her lips were bright red and large gold hoops hung from the lobes of her ears. Gold bangles were on each wrist.

She ran a finger over one of the larger lines on my palm and her features creased, creating deep lines between her brows. The orb in the center of the table flickered and she dropped my hand with a little yelp.

"The power is going crazy tonight." She picked my hand back up and cleared her throat, trying to get back in character.

She closed her eyes, running her fingertips gently across my palm. Her brows furrowed. Her voice was barely above a whisper, "I see heartbreak in your future, Riley Jones."

Opening her eyes, I watched as her pupils grew larger and focused on me. She swallowed and licked her lips, looking almost disturbed. Wow, she was really in character. I glanced at Ethan. Tessa let go of my hand and motioned for his.

Heartbreak? Ethan met my eyes for a split second before Tessa began to read his palm. What heartbreak could she be talking about? Why would she even say that? Was it to scare me? Or was Tessa really—who would be breaking my heart? Ethan? What if it was Maisie ... my mind went down a rabbit hole. I needed to find solid proof we were sisters. As much as I felt it to be true, I needed more than just feelings. After the festival, I was going to do some investigating. If I could find our original birth records ...

The orb's light pulsed again. Tessa sighed. "Esther needs to figure out what is causing that. It's messing with my vibe," she whispered as she ran her index finger over the lines on Ethan's palm.

Tessa closed her eyes, her brows creasing again. "I see romance in your future."

Tessa opened one eye and peeked at me. My face heated and

she winked at me, a smile forming on her lips. Okay, so Ethan wouldn't be the cause of my heartbreak.

I shook my head, why was I even running with these thoughts? Tessa wasn't a fortune teller, it was just pretend. There wasn't going to be any heartache in my future, not from Ethan and not from Maisie. I wish she would've created a happier future in her pretend reading of my palm. Thanks a lot, Tessa.

Outside the tent, I heard a shriek about the flickering lights. Ethan pulled the curtain open from where he sat and Esther stomped passed. She was dressed in a crisp, white pantsuit. Her white jacket flew open as she stopped and turned. The black camisole pulled from her white pants. Her gray curls were bouncing freely around her face.

"Where is Aaron? He was supposed to have dealt with this." Her lips became thin as she walked out of view then Samantha scurried after her in a long, white dress with large wings attached to her back. Trey, with a red-painted face, was right at her heels dressed as a devil in a pair of black slacks, red vest, and devil horns on top of his head.

"It's weird to see her frazzled," I whispered, returning to my chair.

"I would be too if the power kept trying to blow." Tessa shrugged, leaning back in her chair.

"I need to get back to my booth." I stood, leaning over the table to give her a hug. "I'll see you later?"

"Have fun." She smiled and straightened the black table cloth. "Not too much though." She winked. The lights flickered again and Tessa slapped her hands down. "Okay, this is getting ridiculous. I'm going to go see if I can help."

She stood; her waist cinched by a black corset similar to mine. I wondered if she got a two for one deal on them. Her skirt was layered with purple and red fabric, the gold trinkets were also sewn on to the top layer, creating a musical sound as she moved. She scooted past us, waving her hand in the air and calling for Esther.

I stood, straightening out my dress and started toward the opening.

Ethan's hands caught my waist. "Where do you think you're going?" He pulled me onto his lap and a little yelp escaped me. His hand trailed up to where the slit in my dress ended and he pressed his lips against my collar bone, sending shivers to trail down my spine.

I looked into his dreamy blue eyes. My arms went around his shoulders and my fingers buried in his hair at the base of his neck. He stole a kiss, his mouth hungry for more. About to give in, his hand crept further up, his fingers resting on the thin fabric of my thong. I groaned and pressed my hand against his chest as I pulled back.

Begrudgingly, I said, "Tessa said not to have too much fun."

He smiled, his hand ran down to my knee, leaving my hip cold without his touch. "I suppose it wouldn't be fair to leave Maisie by herself for too long." He stood, setting me on my feet. His hands found my waist again and he pulled me against his sturdy frame. I could tell he was going to have a hard time waiting until after our first date. I stifled a moan as he pressed even closer, his hands cupping my rear. Really hard. His lips found mine and I almost changed my mind. If Tessa was a fortune teller, she'd know not to come into the tent …

He pulled away and took in a deep breath.

It might be wise to avoid him until our date. I'm not sure how much more of this I could take. Ethan took my hand and led me out of the tent, making note of how he was holding the wolf mask right below his belt line. I couldn't help but feel a little satisfaction. I had been the cause of that.

I rubbed my other hand along my opposite arm as a gust of cool wind whipped around us. Ethan wrapped his arm around my shoulder and the warmth from his body caused me to melt against him. The string lights overhead flickered.

"I hope they figure out what's going on before we have a blackout." I pulled the hat off my head to lean against his chest and vaguely heard the hat complain about being squished. I ignored it, not wanting to ruin the sweet moment between me and Ethan.

"I'm sure she will. Esther knows everything." He kissed the top of my head.

Ethan removed his arm from around me and pulled his wolf gloves back on. I replaced the hat and found she was still mumbling, *She's never going to figure it out.*

Ethan took my hand and weaved me back through the crowd toward The Witches Brew booth.

Chapter 26

"Leah stopped by." Maisie looked up from the chair she was sitting in. She had a thick, fleece blanket wrapped around her. "She brought blankets."

"Oh, yeah?" That was awfully nice of her. She probably knew I'd forget a jacket. I had given Leah the night off to enjoy the festivities as my way of saying thanks for all the work she had put in at the café. But really, I was hoping it would help get rid of some of the crankiness she'd been carrying around recently.

As I craned my neck to see past Ethan, hoping to catch a glimpse of her, I saw him pull something out of his pocket. It jingled as he handed it to me. "I almost forgot. I had this made for your cat since he seems to wander." He placed a black collar in my hand.

"He's not my—" I held it up to see a silver bell dangling from it with a small, metal circle behind it. The name "*Bean*" was engraved on its surface.

"Bean?" I questioned, looking up at him.

Ethan ran his paw over the top of his head, pushing his hair back. "It seemed like a fitting name."

I stared at the four-letter word, thinking how silly a name

Bean was but how sweet it was of Ethan to make him a collar. Running my finger over the engraving, I whispered, "It's perfect."

As if he heard his name, the black cat ... *er* ... Bean poked his head out from under the blanket near Maisie's feet. His yellow eyes blinked at me and I bent to secure the collar around his neck. I flicked the little bell to hear it jingle.

Maisie rubbed behind his ears and he leaned into it and began to purr. "Hear that kitty, you now have a name."

"I'm glad you like it." Ethan leaned toward me and pressed his lips quickly against mine. I stood on my toes, thinking how I could get used to this. He pulled his mask over his head. "I gotta go scare some more kids. I'll see you later."

My heart skipped a beat as I watched Ethan walk back into the crowd. Would it really be so terrible to give this dating thing a real shot? Most of my *dates* ended with the walk of shame and me vanishing in order to never get close to another person. Mind you, I was not the one doing the walk of shame, it was more of a run and instead of shame, I felt panic and anxiety. People had a tendency to leave. It was best if I did the running instead of someone doing it to me ... *again*. Maybe this time, I wouldn't run away.

Ethan raised his arms in the air and howled as he walked past the few remaining trick or treaters. Little girls dressed as princesses and fairies squealed as he stomped by. A brave knight held out his sword to protect the fair maidens. The same princess who had visited the booth earlier stuck her foot out and kicked Ethan. I heard him yelp and grab his shin as he hopped away on one leg. I giggled but it was cut short at the sound of the woman in the hat mumbling obscenities about my fondness for a "*beast.*"

"Which beast?" I mumbled under my breath. She didn't seem to like anything or anyone.

I bent to scratch under Bean's chin and he purred louder. I pulled him into my arms and nuzzled his neck. I had never had a pet, but I wasn't sure he was an average house pet. Most pets don't speak. I set him back down and chewed on the inside of my mouth, staring at him. I think he spoke ... but maybe I had imagined it.

You certainly did not, the woman retorted.

Oh, would you just shut up. I pulled the hat off my head and placed it under the table near Maisie. She raised an eyebrow as I pushed it further underneath with the tip of my shoe. "The fabric is irritating me." It wasn't entirely a lie.

Maisie gazed past me and I saw her body tense. "Leah's coming back this way." She looked around the small booth then bundled the blanket up into a ball. Standing abruptly, she laid the blanket behind her on a chair. "I think I'll go get some hot cocoa. Want any?"

"Sure." I pulled a few dollars from the jar sitting on the table at the front of the booth but she was gone before I turned around to hand it to her. She hurried in a different direction than the one Leah was coming from.

Ah. I think I know what's going on. Maisie was probably feeling a bit on the nervous side around her. Leah had not been good at hiding her feelings toward Maisie. I wonder what she would think when she found out we were not only sisters but twins. I was planning on giving Maisie a fresh start, a second chance, and I didn't want anyone interfering. Hopefully, Leah would understand.

Leah had her arm hooked through Jack Hanson's, the photographer for the Wildewood Tribune. He had a black camera with a long lens hanging from around his neck. I finally understood why she never came to our costume-making nights. They were dressed as a dead bride and groom. Jack wore a large top hat, Abe Lincoln style, and his face was painted with gray paint making him look like the undead. He wore a tuxedo covered in a mix of cobwebs, dirt stains, and splotches of the same gray paint used on his face.

Leah waved as she spotted me. She was in a long, white dress that flowed around her legs as she moved. The train was attached to her wrist by a string so it wouldn't drag on the ground. Just like Jack's costume, hers was painted with splotches of gray and cobwebs hung off of the folds of the fabric. Her hair was pulled into a tight bun and a small veil was pinned into her hair and hung over her gray-painted face. The cameo necklace that she had found at Odds 'n' Ends laid between her breasts, matching her costume perfectly.

"You two look amazing!" I clapped my hands in front of me, grinning from ear to ear at the two of them. I had no idea what she would be dressing up as. She and Jack looked perfect together. Did this mean they were dating? With Leah being so bent out of shape about men, it would be nice to see the carefree Leah again.

I leaned into her, nudging her with my elbow and whispered, "I didn't know you guys were a thing."

Leah scrunched her nose and with a roll of her eyes, she responded, "We aren't. I'm never dating again."

Well, damn.

"Hey, Riley." Jack looked down at his shoes and I thought I saw his cheeks redden a bit. "Your costume is great."

Jack had asked me out a few times since I'd moved to Wildewood but I had turned him down each time. Don't get me wrong, he was a good guy. He was handsome. But until recently, I hadn't been interested in a relationship. Jack didn't seem like the kind of guy who could deal with a fling and I wasn't so desperate that I wanted to crush his heart, so it was better to just say no. Then there was the issue with me being a witch … Even with Ethan, I wasn't sure how to get around that long term. That was a problem for later.

"Thanks, Jack." I turned my attention away from him as he did an awkward shuffle. "Do you guys want a cupcake, on the house?"

Leah grabbed two of the midnight black ones and handed one to Jack. "These are my favorite."

He took the chocolate cupcake and began to pull the paper off when the band began to play their rendition of Bobby Picket and The Crypt-Kicker Five's, *Monster Mash*. "Oh!" He put the cupcake down on the table. "I've gotta get some shots of the band." He took Leah's free hand. "Come on. I promised them."

Pulling her behind him, Leah waved goodbye over her shoulder as they disappeared into the crowd. Her lips were curved upward into a smile. Maybe Jack had won her over after all. After a moment, I lost them in the crowd dancing around the stage.

"Is she gone?"

I jumped, spinning to see Maisie slinking back into the tent. I might have to put a bell on her, too. Smiling at the thought, I stated, "You know you won't be able to hide from her forever." I crossed my arms, rubbing my hands along my bare skin.

"I know." She held out a cup of hot cocoa to me.

Taking the cup, my sight drifted up at the canopy of lights beginning to flicker. It seems Esther still hadn't figured out the cause of the power surge. The festival only had one more hour until it was over so it just needed to hold on a little longer. I looked at the few remaining cupcakes on the table. Even with the power threatening to blow, the festival had been a success. I was happy about it. The jar in front of me was filled to the brim with one-dollar bills. The Witches Brew would be donating it to Just Treats to help Alice get back on her feet.

I heard a stream of muffled, angry words and looked down as Bean poked his head under the table. The chatter grew more explicit as Bean swatted at it then pulled the hat out by his teeth. The hat bounced on its brim. Yikes! I grabbed it before Maisie noticed and placed it in the chair.

"Leave her alone." I scratched Bean on top of his head.

"Her?" Maisie looked at me with a raised eyebrow.

I pushed my hair behind my ears. "It, I mean." Good grief, these two were going to get me in trouble.

Bean jumped into the chair and I swore I heard more than one voice bickering, this time a man's and woman's. Taking a quick peek at Maisie, she bobbed her head to Marilyn Manson's cover of *I Put a Spell on You*. Maisie was staring out into the crowd, completely unaware of the voices. Bean grabbed the pointy end of the hat between his teeth and jumped to the ground. He turned his head toward me and, as if baiting me, he took off.

"Bean!" I shouted. I placed the cup of hot cocoa on the table, hitched up my dress, and chased after him.

I could hear the woman's voice yelling at Bean as she was dragged along the ground. I rushed past people trying to be careful not to knock anyone over, wishing I wasn't in heels. My ankles felt like they were going to collapse at any moment. Turning to slip past a couple of superheroes, I tripped over one of the pumpkins lining the walkway and my heel got stuck in the mouth.

"Mother f—" my voice trailed off as I stumbled and shook my foot. The pumpkin flung into the air. It landed a few feet away and busted into several large, orange chucks. "Sorry, sorry!" I grimaced at the sight of a woman dressed as Cleopatra whose white dress was now speckled with orange bits. Shit, these two really were going to get me in trouble.

Get this rodent off of me! the hat screamed.

I ran past the orange explosion, a little faster than before. "Excuse me," I mumbled, sliding around a man in a large sumo costume.

Bean moved quickly, zooming around the feet of the crowd. I tried my best to keep track of him but the crowd got too dense near the music stage. Losing sight of him, I squirmed through the mass of people as it moved to the beat of the music.

Thinking I heard the little bell on his collar, I pushed past the dancers and found myself in the middle of a group of high school kids. They were jumping, bumping their bodies together. I felt a jab to my ribs as I forced my way through. Stumbling out of the mosh pit, I inhaled deeply and rubbed what would definitely be a bruise on my side. Why hadn't I just walked around? Don't go through a mosh pit, Riley, go around it. Good grief.

I hurried to the side of the stage, searching. Bean was nowhere in sight. Dammit. Where did that little shit go?

I peeked around the stage. The black backdrop made the area darker, harder to see as I moved behind it. It was blocking out most of the light from the canopy above the festival.

As the song ended, I heard his bell at the other end. Quickening my pace to catch him before the next song, I tripped over a wire and went down. My hands went out. I caught myself before I busted my nose on the ground.

Catching my breath, I groaned as I pushed myself up. The little bit of light I had to guide me vanished. The music stopped.

I froze. Shit, had I pulled a wire out? I could hear the drummer and the *plink plink* noise an electric guitar makes when not plugged in. My eyes widened, trying to find my bearings. There wasn't anything to hold onto to guide me.

If I ever get out of this hat, you're—

A piercing scream rang in my ears. The hair on my arms stood. The air around me got colder. What the hell was going on? I rubbed my arms and moved with a bit more caution over the wires until I had almost reached the end of the stage.

The lights came back on. The microphones on the stage screeched. My heart was pounding in my ears. I wasn't usually scared of the dark but that scream … I was spooked. Something brushed against my leg. I jumped, screeching. Peering down with wide eyes, I saw him. Bean. I gathered him into my arms. I pulled the hat from his mouth and placed it on my head.

You're mine, you filthy beast! her voice rattled in my head until I couldn't take it anymore.

"*Silentium!*" I opened and closed my hand, performing a quick silencing spell. Her voice muffled, but she was trying to overpower it. Just be quiet! I could feel a headache forming.

"That was a bad thing to do, Bean." I ran my hand over his fur.

Another scream blared. Then another.

The band stopped playing. This time not from a power outage. I heard a loud hush and, like an idiot, I ran toward the noise. The toes of my boots hit something hard. I held Bean tighter as my balance rocked. I looked down at my feet. A pair of men's black boots. I cocked my head. They were pointed upward. My eyes traveled up a pair of black slacks, to a deep-red vest. I stopped at the hilt of a large knife.

Oh. My. God.

174

I took a step backward. Bean fell from my arms. I clamped a hand over my mouth as I gasped. My eyes widened at the sight of blood pooling on the man's shirt.

Could this be a prank? Some elaborate Halloween decoration?

The hat's muffled voice ceased.

I looked past the hilt. I hoped to see the face of a dummy. The devil horns made my stomach drop.

I turned around, not wanting to see anymore. I had seen enough.

Trey Brewer was dead.

Chapter 27

Lights from the police cars flashed around the streets surrounding Town Square. Whispers from people standing around me faded away. I stood a short distance from the stage and held Bean against my chest tighter than he was happy with. Pete Kelley placed his hand on my shoulder as I finished giving him my statement. Blinking at him, I tried to understand what he was saying but my ears were ringing and I was having trouble focusing. I hadn't been able to tell him much. I was chasing a cat because he'd run off with my hat. The lights went out. A woman screamed—I think it was a woman—then I almost fell on to Trey's ... body.

Hearing a gruff voice, a man nearby grunted. I watched the black body bag that held Trey being lifted from the ground up onto a gurney. The hilt of the knife was sticking out of the bag with a separate evidence bag around it. Weird, black goo covered the hilt. It sparkled and shimmered as the blue lights from the police cars hit it. What the hell was that?

Realizing what I was staring at, I looked down at the ground, not wanting to watch anymore. Bean had finally had enough of me squeezing him, he used his claws to get his point across. His

176

bell rang as he landed on the ground, leaving me to stand by myself. Another officer walked past me wrapping another layer of crime scene tape on to whatever he could find to rope off the scene.

I heard my name and looked up to see Ethan, Tessa, and Maisie pushing their way through the crowd. Tessa's mascara ran down her cheeks. Her eyes were red. She wiped at them with the purple wrap that had been holding her hair back.

"There you are!" Tessa sucked in a breath and ran past Ethan to throw her arms over my shoulders and cried, "I just can't believe this …"

Maisie looked small next to Ethan. Her eyes shifted to the body bag then back to the ground. I saw the corners of her lips twitch and her frown deepened as she wrapped her arms tight around her torso. A tear ran down her cheek. She sniffled and brushed her sleeve under her nose.

"Are you okay?" Tessa cupped my face in her hands, forcing me to look her in the eyes.

I gave her a small nod and felt Ethan's large hand on the small of my back. His face was rigid, there was no dimple to be found.

Tessa surveyed the crowd and whispered, "Has anyone seen Samantha?"

I shook my head. I hadn't seen her since she walked past Tessa's booth. That was also the last time I had seen—I swallowed, my mouth feeling dry. I glanced around and caught sight of Aaron, his arms were wrapped around Samantha's small frame, her head buried into his chest. Her shoulders shook and the angel wings she'd been wearing were on the ground beside her. Aaron was focused on the gurney as the police rolled it to the ambulance. I noticed his arms tightened around her. Then our eyes met.

Sucking in a breath, I took a step toward Ethan, hoping his body would hide me from Aaron's sight. Goosebumps formed on my skin. Crossing my arms, it felt much colder out, though it wasn't. Ethan placed his arms over mine as I pressed my back against him. This time it didn't chase away the cold. The chill around me felt permanent.

We were moved by the crowd parting. Esther made her way through with her husband and Sheriff Vargas. She grabbed the railing on the steps of the stage and climbed on. She then proceeded to take a microphone out of its stand. The sheriff had his back to the stage, staring out into the crowd, his head moving slowly back and forth.

Esther tapped a finger on the head of the microphone, the crowd quieted. "Wildewood and visitors," Esther's voice rattled out of the speaker I was standing next to, "I have an unfortunate announcement to make." Esther wiped her nose with a handkerchief. "I cannot go into details, but I regretfully ask that everyone return to their homes and hotels. The Halloween Festival is over."

Ethan's hands went to my hips and I felt him pull me closer, protectively. Esther placed the microphone back into the stand and climbed off the stage, using her husband's hand for support. They walked through the crowd toward another officer standing with Samantha. She looked frail, with one arm wrapped around her own torso, her back curved, and her other hand holding a tissue to her nose.

Where was Aaron? He had just been next to her. Panicking, I pried my way out of Ethan's hold and looked around, turning in a small circle. Where did he slip away to?

"Who are you looking for?" Maisie asked as she came to stand next to me.

I shook my head. I hadn't told anyone about my suspicions

or about the evidence I had found. Surrounded by a lot of strangers was not the time, and with Trey's body too close, it was not the place. The police started shuffling people away from the stage.

"Come on." Ethan took my hand and guided me back to The Witches Brew booth. The further away I got from the crime scene tape, I felt like I could take a deep breath.

Maisie grabbed a few paper boxes and handed them around to the three of us. There were only a couple dozen cupcakes left. I took the box from her and picked up a cupcake but froze before I set it down and stared at the black icing.

Could the weird black goo be black icing? I don't remember Aaron coming to the booth to get a cupcake this evening. In fact, I hadn't seen him at all during the entire festival as if he was avoiding me, which I wasn't upset about in the slightest.

"Riley," Ethan's voice pulled me out of my trance.

I dropped the cupcake and it landed sideways. I looked up at him, blinking my eyes into focus and wiped the icing on my fingers on my dress.

He took the box from me. "I'm going to walk you home. We can get everything else tomorrow."

He filled the rest of the box with the remaining cupcakes and helped me place them into a small, foldable wagon. Maisie took the handle and I grabbed the jar full of dollar bills. With Maisie leading the way and Ethan and Tessa on either side of me, we walked through the quiet square toward Oak Avenue when I heard Bean's bell ring. A black figure jumped on to one of the tables on the café's patio.

The hat had been unusually quiet then I remembered I had silenced her. Mostly glad I had, I wondered if she'd heard something I hadn't. I watched Bean clean his paws, the little bell making small *tink tink* noises. Had he sensed something? Was that why he led me behind the stage? So far, the little furball had been right about quite a few things.

Maisie crossed the desolate street before us, leaving the wagon outside the fence and scooped Bean up to nuzzle her face in his fur. I walked past them to unlock the door to the café.

"I'll be quick." I stacked the cupcake boxes in my arms. Ethan held the door open for me, I walked back into the kitchen.

I placed the boxes on the island, opening the refrigerator, then reversed the silencing spell.

It's about time! The woman huffed.

"Did you see anything?" I whispered as I slid a box onto the bottom shelf.

I'm a hat. I don't have eyes, she responded.

I clenched my jaw. "That has never stopped you from being nosey."

True ... but I didn't see anything. Though, there is something unnatural going on in this town right now.

Placing the last box, I had to force the refrigerator closed with my back. "You're one to talk about unnatural."

The chime on the front door rang.

"Riley, you almost done?" Maisie's voice carried through the quiet café.

"Coming!" I yelled to Maisie, then in a whisper said, "We'll talk later."

Chapter 28

We walked in silence the whole way home. Maisie held Bean as if he was her security blanket. Ethan held my hand. There wasn't much to say. I think we were all feeling a bit dazed by what had happened. At least I was, and to be honest, I just wanted to get home and hide behind the bolted doors. Wildewood no longer felt safe.

Climbing up the porch steps, I unlocked the front door and Bean jumped out of Maisie's arms to get inside. His bell rang as he rushed past us. I kind of liked being able to hear him. It would make it harder for him to sneak around now. Maisie walked inside, leaving the door cracked as I turned to face Ethan.

Ethan ran his hands down my arms. He squeezed my hands then lifted my chin. Our eyes met. "Do you want me to stay?"

Yes. No. I shook my head in a slow up and down movement. I didn't like feeling scared. I didn't want to admit it but I was. I knew too much and I was afraid of what Aaron would do next. I was a loose end.

Ethan placed his lips against my forehead. "I'm gonna run home and grab some things." He pressed his lips against mine. "I'll be quick."

He took off down the stone walkway. Once inside, I shut and locked the door. Maisie was leaning against the island. She had her arms crossed, her back bowed, and was staring at her shoes. The tip of one of her boots drew imaginary lines on the ground.

"He's going to stay the night," I said, tossing the hat off my head onto the couch and walked past her to open the refrigerator on autopilot. I wasn't really hungry but I didn't know what else to do. Biting the inside of my cheek, I stared at the empty shelves. There was a row of random condiments and a gallon of milk. I wasn't much of a cook and I was rarely home long enough to prepare a meal, so I lived off of cereal and take-out.

"Good," Maisie commented. I guess him staying over would make her feel safer, too.

Closing the door, I opened the pantry and took a few boxes of cereal out, and placed them on the island next to her. "This is pretty much all I have."

She grabbed a box of chocolate rice cereal. "These are my favorite."

Pulling two bowls out of another cabinet and grabbing the milk, I smiled. "Mine too."

After pouring a smaller portion of the cereal than my usual filled-to-the-brim amount, I leaned against the sink and my stomach rumbled loud enough for Maisie to hear. She raised an eyebrow and I shrugged. I guess I was hungrier than I initially thought. I shoveled a large spoonful into my mouth. Come to think about it, I hadn't had a chance to eat anything during the entire festival besides a few pieces of funnel cake.

"I can't believe there is a murderer in Wildewood," Maisie broke the silence. She stared into her bowl leaning over the island counter. Pulling her cat ear headband off, she set it next to her on the counter. I glanced at the hat I had casually tossed onto the couch having forgotten momentarily there was a woman ... er ... spirit possessing it. Bean sat on the coffee table, staring at the hat as if he was expecting it to do something. I'm going to take a wild guess and say those two have a history.

Turning back to Maisie, I asked, "Do you know anything about Trey?" A little part of me wondered if there was a history between them. I believed her when she said she hadn't broken into the café. I was convinced it was Aaron trying to stop the wedding and mostly convinced he murdered Trey.

Maisie stood up straighter and scrunched her brow. "I have never even spoken to him except for the few times he came into The Witches Brew."

"I heard he was having an affair with someone," I commented. Even if Maisie hadn't set the Bakery on fire, or broken into the café, she still could have been the reason he stopped coming into the café. Or was it just a coincidence?

Maisie raised an eyebrow and laid her spoon on the side of her bowl. "But he was getting married ..."

Maybe she really didn't know anything and it was nothing more than a coincidence. I gave a slight shrug. Turning to the sink, I rinsed my bowl out and set it quietly into the basin. I needed to shove away the idea of Maisie being involved. I needed to trust her.

I pulled a can of tuna out of the cabinet. As I opened it, Bean raced across the floor toward me. I poured it into a small bowl and laid it on the floor. I needed to go get some cat food tomorrow. That was the last can of tuna.

"He's a strange cat." Maisie smirked, running her nails from his shoulder blades to his tail.

You don't even know the half of it, the hat said.

I closed my eyes to suppress an eye roll.

The clock on the oven said it was well after midnight. "Are you coming into work tomorrow?" I asked, hoping she'd want another shot.

"Really?" Her eyes widened.

I took that as a good sign.

"I'd like to have a do-over," I replied. "Would you?"

She caught me off guard as she jumped off her stool and wrapped her arms around me. "I'd really like that." She took a step back, her arms falling to her side. "I'm sorry for how terrible I was. I—" She sucked in a shaky breath and looked down, wringing her hands together. "I was jealous of your life."

"How many years were you in the system?" It was my turn to catch her off guard.

Her mouth opened and her brows creased. "Eighteen."

I could tell by the sagging of her shoulders it hadn't been easier for her.

"Me too," I admitted.

She glanced up and stared at me as if she was trying to comprehend what I had said.

"My life didn't turn around until I came here," I reassured her, then curiosity struck. "How did you find out about me?"

She held up her index finger and walked to the guest room off the kitchen. Her voice was loud as she spoke, "I received a letter a few months ago." I moved to see what she was up to. She picked up her duffel bag and poured its contents on the bed.

Rummaging through the pile of clothes, she found a leather-bound notebook and walked back into the kitchen. She untied the strap around it. I followed her back to the kitchen island as she pulled a folded note out of the pocket in the front. She unfolded it and handed it to me.

It was written in cursive and the ink was slightly smudged.

I read the letter out loud: "In Wildewood, you will find your sister, Riley Jones."

There was no signature. No way to know who had sent it. But someone clearly wanted Maisie to find me. Someone was trying to bring us back together. I looked at Maisie and refolded the note. She placed it back into her notebook and tied it closed.

The doorbell rang and I shrieked, my hand quickly clapping over my mouth. Maisie walked with me to the door. I pressed my eye against the peephole. It was Ethan. Of course, it was. He said he wouldn't be gone long. I opened the door and, before I could usher him inside, Maisie flung her arms around his shoulders.

"I'm so glad you're staying here," she mumbled, letting him go.

Chuckling, Ethan smiled and gave her a sideways hug in return. "Happy to be here."

"Sorry." Maisie tucked her hair behind her ears, her cheeks a little redder. "I'm just really freaked out."

"Me too," I agreed, taking Ethan's hand in mine.

Maisie grabbed her notebook and hugged it against her body. I glanced at the hat still lying on the couch as Ethan put his bag beside it. I wondered, the woman had said sisters should be together, so could she have mailed it to Maisie? Was it possible for spirits to do something like that? And if it wasn't the woman in the hat, then who? Someone purposely separated us and now another was trying to bring us back together.

"I'll leave you two alone." Maisie grabbed a cup of water. "That bed is calling my name." She backed into the room with a smile and shut her door.

Ethan looked at me from his spot on the couch. "Do you

have a blanket I could use?" He picked up the hat, dropped it, and shook his fingers.

Did she just shock him? How petty. I glared at the hat as if she could see me. He tried again and moved it to the coffee table.

"Are you staying on the couch?" I asked, a little disappointed.

He cocked his head and shrugged. "I just figured—"

Licking my lips, I stuttered, "I'd like it if—" I took in a breath. "You could—" I pointed toward the stairs.

"You sure?" He stood slowly. "I didn't want to assume."

Assume away. I nodded.

I walked up the steps with Ethan behind me and turned on the little lamp beside the bed. Ethan sat down at the end of the bed, digging through his bag and produced a pair of basketball shorts. I opened a drawer of my dresser and stared at the ratty pajamas I owned. I picked out a thin black camisole that had a hole near the neckline hem. Real sexy, Riley. I glanced up at the mirror in front of me and saw Ethan pulling his sweater over his head. His chest was broad, his muscles defined. It looked like he did more than just jog every day.

Pulling out the matching pair of pajama pants, I regretfully excused myself to the bathroom before he could remove his pants. Changing quickly, I splashed water on my face. The mascara I was wearing was waterproof and I was too tired to mess with it. I used the light switch to turn off the lights in the living room and kitchen then walked back up the stairs feeling nervous. This was the first time I would have a man sleepover who wasn't a result of a drunken decision. I was completely sober and my anxiety was on the rise.

Ethan was lying under the comforter as I stepped into the loft. His chest was bare, except for a small tuft of hair between his pecs. He was on his side, propped up on an elbow. His eyes lit up as he saw me in my thread-bare outfit, causing my nipples to pebble as if he had physically touched me. I tried to slow my breathing, but it was a wasted effort. I looked down at the ragged clothes I had put on. If this was going to happen more frequently, I was going to need to invest in new pajamas.

I climbed in next to him and his arm slid under my neck, his other arm around my waist. He pulled me close. I shifted to lay on my side, my back pressed against him. His hand crept under my shirt and his fingers traced my ribs, right below my breasts. I felt a heat rise inside me, waiting for his hand to move further up. Instead, he pressed his lips below my ear and whispered goodnight.

He was keeping his promise about waiting until after he took me out on a date. I would be lying if I said I wasn't a little disappointed but the heaviness in my eyes told me it was for the best. I allowed myself to relax into the warmth of his body. Nuzzled in the curve of my neck, his breath was hot on my skin. I could feel the slow rise and fall of his chest, his breathing deepening as he fell asleep. Safe in his arms, I realized I'd never had someone who felt the need to protect me. I closed my eyes, feeling safer than any magical protection could make me feel.

Chapter 29

Ethan wasn't beside me when I woke, instead, a note telling me he had to get to the clinic was on the pillow he'd used. It was probably for the best. I hadn't brushed my teeth the night before and my mascara had clumped.

There was a gloom hovering in the air around Wildewood. Through the large window in the front of the café, I could make out the police tape wrapped around the crime scene. The entire town was stunned. I had never seen so many long faces at once during the morning rush. Usually, after a few sips of Hocus Focus, the crowd would be buzzing but it seemed that not even my awakening spell was doing the trick this morning.

Leah seemed to be taking it extra hard. I had prepared a little speech about Maisie coming back to work knowing how Leah might react, but she never gave me a chance to use it. She hadn't even questioned Maisie's presence. In fact, she had walked around on autopilot, barely uttering a word.

Standing behind the bar, I looked up from the to-go carrier I was filling with foamy coffee drinks and looked toward the hallway when I heard a sniffle. Leah came into view wiping her eyes with a tissue. They were red and her mascara had been rubbed off. That was the third time this morning. She scrunched the tissue in her hand and touched the exposed skin above her low-cut shirt. I saw the realization on her face, her necklace was not there. The clasp must have come undone again. Her brows furrowed and she ran the back of her hand under the nose.

"Leah," I whispered as she came behind the counter to stand near me.

She turned the water on in the small sink hidden by the counter and scrubbed her hands harder than necessary. "I'm okay." She took a sharp inhale.

I wasn't convinced.

Before I could say another word, the chime on the door rang. I looked up to see Connie Fields. Her silver hair was pushed back by her big glasses positioned on top of her head. The lines in her face were deeper than the last time I had seen her but she was right on time as I snapped the lid on the last cup.

"Hey, Riley," she spoke softly as she rested her arms on the counter.

I gave her a small smile. "Do you want any muffins today?" Connie had two employees I'm pretty sure were her college-age granddaughters. They looked like they could be related, but she refused to let anyone know her real age, though I'm sure Eliza knew. My guess was a young sixty.

She shook her head, her glasses slipping. She placed them on the tip of her nose. "No. The girls just want coffee. No one seems to have an appetite today." She glanced at the display case. It was still half full, a rare sight to see in the morning.

I pushed the carrier toward her and she looked around the room before returning to me. Leaning closer, she peeked over the rim of her glasses and whispered, "Have you heard anything about the M-U-R-D-E-R?"

Shaking my head in response, I wrote her order total on the ticket. "No one is talking much this morning." It was so quiet even our whispers felt loud.

She scooted onto the stool and leaned further over the counter. She whispered so softly I barely made out what she said, "Eliza told me a woman wearing white was seen next to Trey right before the blackout." She scrunched her nose and pushed her glasses up.

I leaned closer. We were almost ear to ear. "Did she say who it could be?"

Sitting back on her stool, she shrugged. She wrapped her fingers around the carrier's handle. "No one knows."

Standing, she patted the counter as a goodbye and took the ticket to the register where Maisie was.

Maisie smiled accordingly and thanked her for her business. I think it was going to take some time to adjust to this new Maisie. She was turning over a new leaf at the café and might just give Leah a run for her money.

Leah scurried through the café toward the hallway. Her hands were covering her face. I let out a sigh and followed. Knocking lightly on the door, I could hear her crying over the running water.

"Just a minute," she choked out the words. The water turned off.

"Leah." I rattled the handle. I kept my voice down, "I think you should take the rest of the morning off."

The door cracked open. She looked at me with puffy eyes. Her lips were turned down in a deep frown. "I don't know why I can't get it together. It's just so upsetting that someone was murdered right across the street." She dabbed her eyes with a tissue.

Pushing the door open further, I rubbed my hands on her

arms. "It's okay." I stepped out of the doorway. "Take the rest of the morning off. If you want to try to come back this evening, just let me know."

Leah bobbed her head, sniffling.

I followed her out of the hallway. She made a B-line for her purse and shoved the apron under the counter. Maisie was still standing near the register and raised a brow. "Is she going to be okay?"

"Yeah." I chewed on my lip. I hoped so. "They went to school together. She just needs some time."

The door chimed again and this time Tessa stepped inside. She scanned the room, her head slowly moving from the left to the right until she spotted me in the back corner. Waving, I watched her grab someone's coffee cup. What the hell was she doing? She tapped a spoon on the side of it. It made a loud noise and the whispers stopped as everyone looked at her.

She placed the cup back down on the table. She mouthed a sorry to the gentlemen whose cup she took. Clearing her throat, she spoke loudly, "Mayor Miller is calling a town meeting. All residents are asked to come. It's at eleven-thirty in the meeting hall."

She apologized to the man again, waved to me, and quickly ducked out of the café. The whispers picked back up, louder than before. They had something new to talk about—something else to gossip about.

I glanced at Maisie. "I bet it's about the M-U-R-D-E-R."

The meeting was only an hour away. I found myself curious about what it was about. Then I wondered if Aaron was going to be there. He was, after all, the mayor's assistant and a possible murderer. Wait … Connie said the rumor floating around was that a woman in white had been seen fleeing the scene. Could

Aaron be innocent of this crime? It was just a rumor though. I closed my eyes and rubbed my temple trying to remember who had been wearing white.

My eyes popped open at the sound of the register being shut. Samantha. She had been dressed as an angel. It was hard to imagine her as a killer but the last time I had seen them together, she had been really angry. No, she couldn't have done it. Could she? I suppose one never really knew what someone was capable of. Anger made people do stupid things all the time. Did the police know about their premarital problems? Who am I kidding, the whole town knew.

I followed the last customer to the door and flipped the sign over to closed. We'd find out soon enough who the killer really was.

Chapter 30

The meeting hall was filled beyond capacity. Even with the rows of gray, plastic chairs cramped together, there was still a crowd of people standing in the back of the room. It looked like the entire town had shown up for the announcement. Someone opened the big, double doors and cold air filtered through. Thank God. It was beginning to get unbearably hot with so many bodies squished together. Maisie and I sat next to Tessa near the back. We had made it just in time to snag seats, though we were collectively sharing two seats. I had drawn the short straw and was scrunched between the two of them, sitting precariously on the edge of both chairs. Hopefully, no one moved, otherwise, I might find myself on the floor.

Looking around the room, I spotted Ethan on the opposite side. He was standing against the wall next to his sister, Jennifer. His arm was around her shoulder. Jennifer wiped at her eyes with a tissue and he squeezed her shoulder tighter as he bent his head to say something to her. He looked up and our eyes locked. Even from across a crowded room, I could feel lustful hunger radiating off of him. My breath caught in my throat as a smile crept over his face before his attention returned to his sister.

Even with the door cracked open, I was sweating. Every few minutes I would catch Ethan looking at me and I would quickly stare at my hands, otherwise, I was liable to jump over the crowd and into his arms to do God knows what in front of a group of strangers.

Finally, I saw Esther move through the room wearing a black, long-sleeved dress. Behind her followed a man I had never seen before and Sheriff Vargas. Samantha, who was usually right on her heels, was MIA. I scanned the crowd and couldn't find her or Aaron. Oh, darn.

Taking her place behind a large podium, Esther tapped her finger on the microphone. She adjusted the small, black hat positioned off-center on the top of her head. Its black netting draped over her eyes. The two men stood on either side of her as she began to speak, "Thank you for coming." She pulled her white handkerchief from her clutch and dabbed under her eyes as tears formed. Clearing her throat, she continued, "As most of you already know, Trey Brewer was murdered last night." She sniffled. "He and Samantha had not yet been able to walk down the aisle together, but he was already a son to me. I am taking this loss as a very personal, and urgent matter. His father, William Brewer, has a few words he would like to share."

Esther stepped aside and William moved forward. This was sounding more like a funeral than a town meeting. William gripped the edges of the podium until his knuckles turned white. "This is a travesty." He sucked in a deep breath. "Trey was my only son and the heir to the Northern Georgia Bank and Trust founded here in Wildewood." His voice bellowed from the microphone through the room.

Hmm, that's interesting. I leaned close to Tessa and whispered, "That explains why Esther was pushing for this marriage."

She glanced at me with a frown. "What do you mean?"

Keeping my eyes on William as he went on to talk about how great of a son Trey was, I explained as quickly as I could about the conversation I'd overheard between Esther and Samantha. She had wanted out, but Esther wouldn't hear it. If Esther could marry her daughter into one of the richest families in Wildewood, it would help secure her position as mayor.

Tessa shook her head. "I don't know. I think in their own way, they really did love each other." She chewed on her lip. I don't think Tessa had ever considered there was an ulterior motive for their engagement.

Placing my hands in my lap with my elbows tucked tight against my body, I leaned back against the seats and glanced at Maisie. She was propped up with her chin resting on her fist, elbows on her knees, paying close attention to William's speech.

His voice boomed around the room as he leaned a little too close to the microphone, "If anyone saw anything, please call the police hotline. If any tip leads us to find his killer, a twenty-thousand-dollar reward is yours."

My mouth fell open. Maisie sat up straight. That was a lot of money. The crowd seemed to agree as a collective gasp filled the room. Chatter quickly followed, growing louder. I suppose, for a grieving father who owned one of the largest banks in North Georgia, twenty-thousand was nothing as long as it helped find his son's killer. A knot began to form in my stomach. How was he going to feel if the killer ended up being his son's fiancé?

William returned the podium to Esther, taking his place to the side of her. She wiped at her eyes again. "Due to the recent rise in crime, the town council has decided to set up a neighborhood watch. If you are a resident of the town, please stop by the sign-up sheet in the back of the room. We need as many volunteers as possible, starting tonight. We must be vigilant in catching these criminals."

So, Esther assumed it was more than one person? I suppose it was possible she hadn't connected the burglary of The Witches Brew to the other two crimes. She thanked us for attending and she and William Brewer walked through a door held open by Sheriff Vargas.

"Have you heard from Samantha?" I asked Tessa as we stood. I found it a little strange she wasn't here. Even if she was Trey's murderer, I'd think she would at least try to keep up with appearances to throw the police off her trail. If she had been standing with her mother, or his father, and looked like a widowed woman, it would be pretty convincing she wasn't involved.

"No." Tessa pulled her thick, crimson-colored jacket on. "I've been calling her but she isn't answering. She's probably too distraught to talk. I know I would be."

Unless you were the one who killed him, I thought.

"I'm going to go over there later with some food from Mike's." She pulled her hair out from under the jacket and we followed her to the sign-up sheet.

Tessa took one of the first slots for tonight. Maisie and I signed up for tomorrow. I had never been a part of a neighborhood watch. I had always thought the neighborhood watch signs were just a ruse to deter criminals and not a real thing. The shifts were only two hours long and hopefully, we hadn't chosen an exciting one. I'd had enough excitement to last quite a while.

As we walked from the meeting hall, Tessa checked the time on her phone. "We still have enough time to take down our booths before your café reopens."

Maisie buttoned her jacket. "You guys go ahead. I'm going to grab Bean some food."

At least one of us remembered.

Waving goodbye to Maisie, Tessa and I walked across the street toward the center of Town Square. On a normal day, the square would be filled with children playing, couples walking hand-in-hand, even some walking their dogs. Today, there were only a few people scurrying around, dismantling the remains of the festival. The silence of Wildewood felt eerie. The police tape caught my attention as it fluttered noisily in the wind. I closed my eyes for a split second and could see Trey's lifeless body lying on the ground.

Tessa stopped walking. The wind pushing her wavy hair in front of her face as she stared at the spot. Her arms were wrapped tightly around her body.

"I can't believe this happened in the middle of a crowd and no one saw anything." She pushed her hair out of her face and behind her ear.

"The lights had gone out," I reminded her.

"Still," she rubbed her hand underneath her nose, "someone had to have seen something." Her eyes widened and she snapped her finger. "I bet Jack got a picture of the moment right before—"

Jack! I hadn't even thought about Jack. He had been taking pictures of the band, so it was possible he had accidentally caught who Trey was last seen with. I gave Tessa a tight hug. She looked at me with furrowed brows. "You're a genius," I whispered. "Come on. Let's get those booths down."

I started to pull her away from the spot when something shiny caught my attention.

"Hold on," I said and jogged over to the police tape. I picked up a silver chain and held it up. It was Leah's cameo necklace. It must've fallen off when she and Jack had been taking pictures of the band. No matter what she said, I bet her and Jack had been dancing and it loosened the clasp.

"Riley." I turned around to look at Tessa. She was pointing to Town Hall. Officer John Russell was walking out of the front entrance with Samantha. She had her face buried in her hands. We watched as he escorted her down the steps, his hand on her elbow, and walked her next door to the station.

"Come on." Tessa pulled on the sleeve of my jacket. Her mouth was turned down, clearly upset by the sight of her friend going into the police station. "I want to get this over with."

Chapter 31

The evening shift at the café was over before I knew it. Maisie and I hadn't had one moment to stop while we tried to keep up without Leah's help. She came in just long enough for me to give her the necklace then burst into tears. She tried. I appreciated it, but she needed more time. I hadn't known Trey the way she and the other people in this town had. I hadn't grown up with him. Hell, I hadn't even realized what family he was from and I used the bank they owned. Hopefully, tomorrow would be a better day for Leah and she'd be able to make it through a shift. I hoped so. Maisie was doing well, better than expected, but she wasn't Leah.

When the last customer left, I felt I could breathe. My feet and my back were killing me. Man, I hadn't had to work this hard since the café first opened and it was just me. I walked to the door and flipped the sign to closed. As I was about to lock the door, a hand slapped the window and I screamed, my body jolting as if I'd been shocked with electric volts.

Tessa stood on the other side. Her eyes were wide, she shouted, "Samantha is in the hospital!"

I flung the door open. "What happened?"

199

"I'll tell you on the way. Come on." She motioned with her hand for me to come with her.

Maisie ran from the back, worry written on her face. "What's wrong? What happened?"

"I'm going to the hospital with Tessa." I pulled the keyring from my pocket and tossed it to her. "Please lock up. I'll see you at home."

I pulled the door closed behind me. Tessa's cream-colored sedan was parked right outside the café in a tow zone. I slid into the passenger seat and as Tessa climbed into hers, I asked, "Is Sam okay? What happened?"

Tessa turned on the ignition and made a sharp U-turn. Her wheels ran up on the opposite curb and caused me to bounce around in my seat. I grabbed at the seat belt, wishing I had put it on before she took off.

"She was attacked." Tessa threw on her blinker.

I took a glance at her. Tears were hovering in the corner of her eye and I felt the car pick up speed. "What do you mean attacked?"

"Someone tried to kill her. She was stabbed." Tessa sniffled. "Just like Trey. Someone is trying to kill her."

I stared out the window as we drove in silence toward the hospital on the edge of town, right before the bridge connecting Wildewood to the rest of the world, and went over my suspect list. Maisie had been crossed off, leaving Aaron and Samantha. I was certain Aaron had caused the fire at Just Treats. I was pretty certain he had stolen the mixers at The Witches Brew, even without any proof. I suspected Aaron or Samantha to have murdered Trey and based on the woman in white rumor, I had been leaning toward Samantha. But now she had been attacked.

What if Samantha faked the attack? It would throw the

police off her trail if she too was a victim. Or … could Aaron have attacked her? The way he was holding her after Trey's body was found made me wonder if there was something between the two of them. I scrunched my brows, tapping my finger against my lip. Things weren't adding up, but I had something up my sleeve. Taking another glance at Tessa, I wasn't sure I'd get the chance to test it out.

Without slowing, Tessa turned into the hospital parking lot. I grabbed the bar on the ceiling as her tires squealed. My seatbelt locked as she slammed on her brakes and threw the car into park. She flung her seat belt off and bolted out of the car. I had to run to catch up with her.

The fluorescent lights of the hospital were bright as I came up behind her at the receptionist's desk. "I'm looking for Samantha Miller." She slapped her hand on the counter a few times.

The nurse in pink scrubs looked up from her computer screen, obviously not appreciative of Tessa's impatience, and took her time to look for the room number. Tessa tapped her fingers, looking up and down the hallway.

"Room Ten." She pointed to the left set of doors. "Through the double doors and take the first right."

Tessa spun on her heels and ran to the doors. She slammed her hand against the large metal button for the power-assisted doors. This was so unlike Tessa. She was rarely short with people.

I gave the nurse a small smile. "Thank you."

As we turned into the next hallway, Officer John Russel nearly collided with us.

"Hey, John." I stopped quickly and, surprisingly, Tessa did the same.

"Riley." He nodded. He wasn't a chatterbox like Pete. I noticed he was holding a large, clear bag with a red strip of tape at the opening that said "*evidence.*" It had burgundy colored fabric in it. The velour sweatsuit I had seen Samantha wearing the morning of the fire.

"Is that Samantha's?" I asked, pointing at the bag.

"Yes." He was obviously not interested in a conversation. He held the bag up and switched it to his other hand. I spotted the same black goo that had been on the knife that had killed Trey. What the hell was that? It definitely hadn't been icing. The way it looked, the texture and the way it shimmered, it wasn't anything I had seen before.

I was about to ask John if he had any idea what the goo was when Tessa tugged on my arm. "Come on, Riley." She began to walk again.

I waved to John, he nodded, and I caught up with her.

Halfway down the hallway was room ten. Coming to the door, Tessa slowed her pace and took in a deep breath through her nose. She knocked gently, the first gentle thing she had done since retrieving me from The Witches Brew.

"Sam?" she whispered as she pushed the door open slowly.

Sitting beside the bed was Esther. She was holding Samantha's hand, her thumb brushing back and forth along Samantha's skin. Her other patting gently. Esther turned as we walked closer. She stood, letting Samantha's hand go and whispered, "She's sleeping."

"Is she okay?" Tessa asked quietly, taking a few steps toward the bed.

Esther smoothed the wrinkles out of her light-brown blazer. "She will be."

She walked to Tessa and placed a hand on her arm. "I'll let you guys have a moment."

I watched Esther walk to the door. She gave me a weak smile

as she left the room. She wasn't herself. Her presence wasn't as large as it usually was. It was giving me the heebie-jeebies. I turned back toward Samantha. Her black hair was pulled back in a ponytail. She had a bruise forming on her cheek and her right arm was in a sling. There was a large bandage on her other forearm. It looked like she had tried to stop whoever had attacked her.

Samantha stirred and her eyes blinked open.

Tessa sat in the chair Esther had been in. "Hey, Sam," her voice was quiet. She reached out to touch Samantha's arm but hesitated and pulled her arm back to her side. Shuffling my weight from one foot to the other, I was feeling out of place as the two of them shared a moment. Samantha blinked away tears as Tessa spoke softly to her, "Do you want anything to eat or drink?"

"Some ice water would be nice," Samantha replied then cleared her throat.

Tessa looked at me as she stood. "Will you stay with her?"

Repressing my urge to say no, I nodded instead. I didn't want to be in the room, alone with a possible murderer but it looked like I was about to get my chance to find out what really happened after all.

"I'll get you some coffee, too." Tessa touched my arm, her eyes pleading with me to stay, then she walked from the room.

I stood in silence for a moment as Samantha's eyes fluttered closed. The noise of the IV dripping pounded in my ears—or maybe that was the sound of the adrenaline flooding my body. The machine behind it beeped reading her pulse. It wouldn't be more than a few minutes before Tessa was back. I closed my eyes and took a deep breath. It was showtime.

"I'm sorry about this," I whispered. My heart skipped a beat.

"*Verum Dicere.*" I moved my hand in the air as if I were wiping steam from a mirror then brought the same hand to my mouth and blew hot air over my palm at Samantha.

I cleared my throat and Samantha opened her eyes. "Who attacked you?" I got straight to the point.

Samantha shook her head. "I don't know. The lights had gone out."

"Did you kill Trey?" I asked. I didn't have much time. The hospital wasn't that big.

Scrunching her brows, Samantha sat up in her bed, wincing from the pain of her arm. She looked at me, her eyes small slits, nostrils flared. "Why are you asking me that?"

I cocked my head, confused, and searched her face. Had my spell not worked? Maybe I hadn't waited long enough. "*Verum Dicere,*" I repeated then asked again, "Did you kill Trey?"

"Nurse!" she yelled and reached for the phone next to her bed.

Shit! Shit! What did I do wrong? Maybe I needed to say it three times, so I said it again.

Samantha pressed a button and glared at me. "Get out of here, psycho!"

Me? Psycho? My mouth fell open. At least I wasn't a murderer. What was going on? My spell wasn't working. I took a few steps back and looked at my hands. Why hadn't it worked?

"Your magic doesn't work here."

I spun around and saw Esther. My eyes widened. I felt sick to my stomach. What did she say? Did she see me cast the spell? I felt paralyzed. What do I do? I searched Esther's face, not knowing what my next move was. She closed the door and the click rang in my ears. Shit. This was bad. Her lips were thin as she walked further into the room. I looked back down at my hands and then at the mayor. Wait a minute … how did she know my magic wouldn't work?

"Put the phone down, Samantha," she demanded.

Samantha placed the phone back in its cradle.

Esther pushed past me and I watched her repeat the spell I had tried. Her hands moved just as mine had. She looked at me over her shoulder, her eyes narrow, then back at Samantha. Her voice gave me goosebumps as she asked, "Did you kill Trey?"

Instantly, Samantha's eyes glazed over. Her head rose to look at her mother. With a listless voice, as if she were in a trance, she answered, "No."

"Does she know who was trying to stop their wedding?" I exclaimed then quickly pressed my hands over my mouth. My heart was racing. I had been exposed. There was no turning back now. But just as terrifying as someone finding out about me, I had found out something bigger: the mayor was a witch. The mayor was a fucking witch.

"That's enough. She doesn't know anything," Esther growled.

"It was Aaron," Samantha calmly explained. "He loves me."

We both looked at her. I knew it! I took a step closer and threw all caution to the wind as Samantha continued to blink lifelessly at the wall behind us.

"So, Aaron *did* set the fire." I pushed my luck by taking another step. "Did he kill Trey also?"

I heard Esther exhale. She repeated my question, "Samantha, do you know who killed Trey?"

Her head turned slightly; her eyes focused on her mother. "No."

Esther snapped her fingers and whispered a word I couldn't make out. Samantha shook her head. She groaned and placed a hand on the side of her head as if she had a headache

Esther looked over her shoulder at me. "You need to leave. Tell Tessa Samantha fell back asleep."

"But—" I watched Esther cup Samantha's face in her small hands. She whispered in her ear and Samantha leaned back against the pillow. She closed her eyes and her head rolled to the side.

"Go," the mayor quietly hissed at me as she pulled the thin blanket around Samantha's shoulders.

I opened the door, stopping in my tracks as the mayor called after me, "Riley, you will not speak a word of this to anyone."

I swallowed. That felt like a threat. I closed the door behind me and leaned against it. My heart was beating loudly in my ears and I could barely catch my breath. Mayor Miller was a witch and she knew I was one too. "Your magic doesn't work here." She had already known. She knew more about me than I did.

"Riley?"

I almost screamed as Tessa appeared out of nowhere. She stood in front of me with a water bottle in one hand and a Styrofoam cup in the other.

"You scared me!" I sucked in a deep breath and ran a hand over my mouth.

"Everything okay?" she asked, handing me the steaming cup.

"Yes," I blurted out. Clearing my throat, I added, "Everything is fine. Samantha fell asleep. The mayor wants us to come back later." I took the coffee from Tessa and sipped the water-downed drink trying to look like it was delicious as it burned my throat going down. "Thanks."

"You're welcome." Tessa's voice was distant as she peeked into the window on the door. "I guess I'll stop by in the morning."

As disappointed as her voice sounded, I was ready to get as far away from the hospital and the mayor as possible.

This time it was me rushing to Tessa's car. My head was pounding, stomach acid was rising in my throat and I was pretty sure it wasn't from the hospital coffee. What had I been thinking? Casting a spell in public like that. A nurse could've walked in. Tessa could have walked in. But no, the mayor had. I slammed the door to Tessa's car and strapped myself in. I had learned something. Samantha had not killed Trey. Only the truth could be spoken during that spell. She knew Aaron had been trying to stop the wedding, but would he have told her if he was the one who murdered Trey? And what about the woman in white?

I stared into the Styrofoam cup, wishing I had tossed it.

How had the mayor known I was a witch? How was that possible? Holy shit. I cannot believe the mayor was a witch.

Chapter 32

Running up the steps to the house, I slammed the door behind me and leaned against it to catch my breath. The drive had been anything but comfortable. Tessa was trying to figure out who could have hurt Samantha. She had been asking so many questions. Questions I was pretty sure I knew the answer to but didn't want to divulge. I closed my eyes, wondering if I should've just told her everything I knew. If I had, at least I would've been able to get it all off my chest. I needed to take a chance and tell her about *me*. What was the worst that could happen?

"Is Samantha okay?"

My heart jumped into my throat and I let out a little squeal. My eyes focused on Maisie. She was staring at me from the couch, her legs tucked underneath her, and Bean was curled up beside her. She blinked. "Are you okay?"

I nodded, pushing away from the door and walked to the living room. "She'll be fine." I wasn't sure if I was going to be fine though.

"Good." Maisie ran her hand between Bean's ears and one of them flicked as if it tickled.

I sat on the opposite end of the couch and pulled a throw

pillow into my lap. I stole a glance at Maisie. Was it too soon to unload everything about myself to her? We were just getting to know each other. Would she think I was crazy and leave? Why was this secret all of a sudden beginning to feel like a huge burden?

I buried my face into the pillow and let out a deep breath. I needed to talk to the woman in the hat. Okay, I was losing it if she was my only option.

"Are you sure you're okay?" Maisie questioned.

I looked up from the pillow. Bean jumped from her lap and padded into the kitchen to swat at his empty tuna can.

Maisie followed him into the kitchen and grabbed two boxes of cereal out of the pantry. Could I trust her? In my heart, the answer was yes but the anxiety welling up inside me said no. It's as if I couldn't form the words to just tell her, *I'm a witch.*

"All you have left are these fruity marshmallow ones." She held them out in front of her. I pointed to one. With the box under one arm, a bowl, and a spoon, and the remaining half-gallon of milk hooked on two fingers, she brought them to the coffee table in front of me.

I opened the cereal box and stared at its colorful contents. "Have you ever had a secret you felt like you could never tell anyone?" I pried, tipping the box over the bowl. I picked up the milk, and it sloshed onto the side of the bowl as it hit the colored loops.

"Doesn't everyone?" She leaned against the arm of the couch. Stiffening, Maisie raised an eyebrow. "You aren't about to tell me you're a murderer, are you?"

Almost choking on my food, I shook my head. With my mouth full, I responded, "No. It's not that bad." At least, I didn't think it was that bad.

Maisie shrugged. "Everyone has a secret, Riley." Bean jumped back into her lap. The fishy aroma clinging to him wafted into my nose.

Swallowing, I looked down at my cereal and pushed the bowl away.

"I'm sure even he has a secret." Maisie rubbed a knuckle under the cat's chin.

Oh, I'm positive he has a secret and as if he could hear my thoughts, Bean turned his head slightly and looked at me before closing his eyes to relax against her touch.

"Do you think you could cover for me for an hour or so tomorrow morning?" I asked as I carried the uneaten, mushy contents of my bowl to the kitchen sink. My appetite was gone. I don't know if it was the smell of the tuna or everything else on my mind, but the thought of eating was turning my stomach.

"Sure." Maisie stood, holding Bean in her arms. "Are you sure everything's okay?"

"Yeah." No, not really. My stomach knotted as I rinsed the milk from the bowl, the water turning cloudy. "I just need to run an errand."

I wasn't feeling very chatty. I was tired and confused, so I told Maisie goodnight then walked up to the loft. Okay, I chickened out. I might as well start flapping my wings and peeking at the ground. I was chicken. I was scared. I wanted so badly to share my secret with her but I couldn't work up the nerve. What if she rejected me? I'm not sure I could handle that.

I sat on the bed and kicked off my shoes. I could hear her tinkering around in her room below. Bean's bell softly jingled. The sound got louder and I looked up to see him sitting on the top step. I rubbed my fingers together and he came to me. I picked him up and nuzzled his soft body. "At least I don't have to worry about you leaving. You already know I'm a witch," I whispered. So had Esther, apparently. I knew there was something magical about Wildewood, the moment I stepped foot in the town. I just never realized it was the residents who held it.

Setting Bean on the bed, I grabbed a pair of pajamas and started toward the steps when I heard the shower turn on. I was going to have to get used to having another person in the house. Everything was changing, for better or worse.

Chapter 33

The chatter in the café was surrounded around the mysterious woman in white. It seemed like Eliza and Connie had done their due diligence the day before and spread the rumor far and wide. I had listened closely, like a fly on the wall, at the gossip to hear anything new. But so far, no one had any idea who the woman could've been. It was as if no one had actually seen this person. She was only a ghost, made up to fill a missing piece of the story. Whether or not there was any truth to the gossip, I would find out soon enough. I was headed to the Wildewood Tribune in search of Jack Hanson with a box of bribe muffins.

I crossed my fingers and hoped he had captured something in a picture as I stepped into the four-story office building. I made my way to the directory sign in the middle of the lobby. Searching for the *W*s, I located The Tribune and made my way to the stairs. They shared the building with other small businesses, most of which didn't need a large storefront. I huffed up the last set of stairs until I reached a long corridor. I looked up and down it and spotted The Tribune by the big gold sign next to the door.

Was I supposed to knock? Could I walk right in? The door opened and I came nose-to-nose with a petite brunette. She had a tag hanging from her pocket on her blue shirt that read, "*Portia Daniels, editor*."

"Can I help you?" She looked me over, unimpressed.

I shuffled out of her way. "I'm looking for Jack."

She tilted her head back. "Down the hallway. Make sure you knock." She moved past me and walked to the bank of elevators. Are you kidding me? I groaned. I could've taken an elevator instead of four flights of stairs.

With the box in hand, I walked down the hallway and found his name engraved on a gold nameplate eye-level on a door. I hadn't enhanced these muffins but I was hoping dropping by unannounced would do the trick. It was wrong, I know, but I knew how Jack felt about me and I was taking advantage of it. I could hear mouse clicks coming from the room and the sound of gunfire. Could he be working on some top-secret footage? I knocked softly.

"Come in," he yelled through the door.

Pushing the door open slowly, I peered into the dark room. The only light came from the computer screen where Jack was sitting. His back was bowed as he stared intently at the screen with his nose only inches away, his finger repeatedly clicking the mouse. Oh, I mouthed in disappointment. He was playing a game.

"Hey, Jack." I shut the door behind me.

He swiveled in his chair; the jerkiness of his movements caused the mouse to fall from the desk where it hung by its cord. He looked up, blinking his eyes rapidly. He was obviously not expecting me. Good. "Riley. What are you doing here?" The noise from the game he had been playing continued.

I set the box on his desk. "I thought you could use some muffins while you went through the pictures from the festival."

I opened the lid to show him the *hopefully* irresistible blueberry muffins.

He looked at the box, and I swore he stopped himself from licking his lips before looking back at me with a raised eyebrow. "Thanks?"

Maybe the muffins weren't as irresistible as I thought. The look on his face was confusion. I guess my dropping by unannounced was not working the way I had hoped. I had never, not once, stopped in to bring him muffins. Before my cover was blown, and he started asking questions, I blurted out, "I'd love to see the pictures from the festival. It was pretty good. Well," I scrunched my nose, "Until, ya know ..." I trailed off with a shrug.

Jack reached into the box and took a muffin, turning back to his game. "I'd love to show you."

Thinking he was going to close his game and pull up the pictures, I moved closer to peer over his shoulder. "I'd like to see the pictures of the band." And to not sound so suspicious I added, "And any my booth were in."

Jack pressed the spacebar on his keyboard and the game paused. He peered over his shoulder to look at me, our faces very close together. I saw his eyes drop to my lips and I straightened. "I said I'd love to show you but I don't have them."

Crossing my arms, I looked over his cluttered desk, confused.

Jack unpaused his game and continued to battle the alien-looking monsters on the screen. His character died and Jack leaned back in his chair with an exaggerated groan. I cleared my throat and he turned. "The mayor took the memory card from me this morning." He explained.

Oh? "Why would she do that?"

He raised his shoulders in a quick shrug as he took

214

another bite from the muffin. With his mouth full he mumbled, "Probably for the same reason you're looking for the pictures."

My jaw dropped. Cover blown. Abort mission. Abort mission!

He cracked a grin. "I'm kidding. She probably thinks I caught something incriminating."

Well, since he brought it up. "Did you?" I asked.

Jack spun his chair back toward the computer and restarted the level he was on. "Honestly, I hadn't even had a chance to look."

I flicked my eyes to the ceiling. Now how would I figure out who this woman in white was? Or if it was just the gossip mill? "I hope you enjoy the muffins." I turned to leave.

The noise from the computer paused. "Hey, Riley …"

I knew what he was about to ask. I glanced over my shoulder as my hand turned the doorknob. Before he could say another word, I interrupted, "You should ask Leah out." I opened the door and stepped through. "I know she's a little cold right now but you guys looked great together." I shut the door before he had a chance to respond and rushed out of the office.

The elevator doors opened and I stepped out into the lobby. Why would Esther confiscate the photos? Was she hiding something? Oh, shit—what if Samantha had something to do with Trey's murder and she was covering it up? I rubbed my temple as a headache began to form. What in the world was the mayor really up to?

Chapter 34

I walked past the Square toward the grocery store. The festival was almost completely dismantled. All that was left of the hay maze were bits of hay covering the grassy area where they had been placed. The stage had been taken down and the remaining canopy tents removed. Someone was dragging a wagon with pumpkins toward a truck to toss them in the bed. All signs of Trey's murder were gone as if it never happened. But it had. I wondered if the police had any suspects I had overlooked. I had been hoping Jack's pictures would shed some light but apparently, I wasn't the only one with that idea.

Come to think of it, Esther had been wearing white at the festival.

Oh. My. God.

I stopped walking and looked behind me. Could she be the woman in white? No. I shook my head. As much as I wanted to run with that idea, that would mean she would've attacked her own daughter and I just couldn't see her doing that. They were attached at the hip, even if they disagreed about the wedding. Looks like Samantha won that argument ... but just how far had she gone to win?

I stepped inside the cold store and Eliza looked up from the register and waved. The flowers had been changed. The bouquets had more cream flowers than the ones just a few days prior. Connie had probably come by this morning. Her flowers always seemed more vibrant than any other cuts I'd ever seen. Grabbing a cart, I eyed the arrangement suspiciously. I wonder if she was a witch, too?

Walking to the cereal aisle, I scolded myself. I needed to stop suspecting people. With the mayor knowing who I was and now knowing what she was, it was hard not to. Filling the cart with more cereal than two people needed, I glanced over at the fresh produce section. I didn't know what other types of food Maisie liked, so I took a guess and threw some bananas and a box of strawberries into the cart. If nothing else, they would taste good in the cereal.

"Did you sign up for the neighborhood watch?" Eliza asked as she scanned the groceries. She looked at me with a raised eyebrow as she punched the number for the bananas into the register.

"Yeah." Oh, that reminded me. I walked to the endcap and grabbed two mini flashlights hanging next to small packs of batteries and placed them on top of a fallen box of cereal. "Maisie and I have a shift tonight."

"I hope they find the mur—" she fell quiet as the front doors slid open. Waiting until the man had moved past the registers, she whispered, "The murderer."

"Me too," I responded and paid for the groceries.

"You girls be careful out there tonight," she said as she helped put the bags in my arms.

Over the top of one of the large brown bags, I told her we would then walked through the sliding doors. Well, we'd try.

Esther was making it harder for the police to find the murderer. It had to be someone close to her, if not herself. Was it, Aaron? Samantha said no, but that only meant he hadn't told her. She said she didn't kill Trey … so … dammit. No one could lie under that spell. Okay, Samantha was officially crossed off the list. That only left Aaron. What had he been wearing? Damn. I had been so startled catching him looking at me that I couldn't remember. Maybe Maisie would remember.

Wait—I turned around and walked back inside.

"Forget something?" Eliza asked.

I shook my head, though I wasn't sure she could see it over the bags. "No. I was just curious if you knew where the town kept old records?" Not only was Eliza the gossip queen but she had lived here her whole life. She would have some idea.

"The library, most likely," she answered.

I yelled thanks over my shoulder and hurried to the café. Locking the groceries in my office, I found Maisie in the kitchen washing dishes from the morning shift. Leaning against the wall with my arms crossed, I watched her. I had never tried to figure out anything surrounding my—our—birth. Maisie looked over her shoulder at me and hummed.

"Have you ever tried to find your original birth certificate?" I pushed away from the wall and began to dry the dishes she was rinsing.

Maisie shook her head and handed me a clean plate. "I just assumed I didn't have one."

I had a birth certificate. It was mostly filled in with guesses. No one knew what day I was actually born or where I was born. The only thing I had never questioned was my name. I chewed on the inside of my mouth. "Would you mind coming with me to the library? I want to look through the old newspapers."

I finished drying the last plate. "Didn't people use to do birth announcements?"

"Sure. But—" Maisie turned the water off and dried her hands. "Why would there be an announcement for abandoned babies?"

She had a point but I didn't have any other ideas. "Humor me?" I begged with a forced smile.

Maisie untied her apron from around her waist and grabbed her jacket. "Okay. But I don't think we're going to find anything."

The library was quiet when we stepped inside. A middle-aged woman with her nose in a book sat behind the circulation desk in the center of the room. She glanced up, blinking her eyes into focus, and pushed her glasses up her nose. She turned the book over with its spine open and laid it down on the desk. It was mid-day and we were the only visitors she had.

Walking up to her, I placed my hands on the edge of the counter. "Where can we find older records of the town?"

"Old records of what?" She wiggled her nose as her glasses slipped back down.

"Birth records," Maisie piped in, her voice echoed around the bookshelves.

"And news articles before everything went digital," I added in a whisper, glancing sideways at Maisie.

The woman opened a thin drawer underneath her and took out a key. She stood, pushing her chair back. "You'd have to go to the hospital to find birth records, probably. Now, the gene-alogy of Wildewood, you can find that here." She moved from around her desk. "Follow me. The archives are back here." Her long, paisley skirt flowed back and forth as she shuffled across the building in a pair of black crocks to a large wooden door behind the young adult section.

She put the key in the lock and it made a loud click as she turned it. Pushing the handle down, she looked at me. "The door automatically locks when it closes so if you leave, you won't be able to get back in."

We thanked her as she moved away. She stopped and added, "Nothing leaves that room."

Nodding, Maisie and I walked inside. The door slid closed with a loud thud that echoed throughout the brightly lit room. It had a large window that peered into the library. I walked toward it and pulled the blinds shut. In the center was a large rectangular table. Bookcases protruded from around the perimeter of the room. Across from us was a microfilm reader sitting on top of another table with dozens of drawers underneath that had small labels of years printed on them.

"Where should we start?" Maisie looked around, walking to a bookcase. She ran her hand along the old books.

I took in a deep breath of the musty smell. "Twenty-eight years ago?"

"Do you really think we'll find anything?" Maisie looked up from a book she'd pulled out.

"I don't know. We'll probably just have to go to the hospital—" I stopped. "Assuming we were even born in a hospital."

Maisie slid the book back into the bookcase. "You think there are no records of our birth?" The trip to the library had clearly sparked some hope in her.

"Like you already said, we were abandoned, so your guess is as good as mine." I walked to the microfilm reader.

Maisie pulled another book out then pushed it back in. This may have been a wasted trip to the library, but it was a start. Inspecting the drawers under the table, I pulled one open dated twenty-eight years ago. Finding the first box from January of that year, I placed it on the table and turned the machine on. It lit up underneath where the film was to be placed. Uh, now what? I looked around and spotted step by step instructions taped to the wall above it. After a moment of confusion, I finally had a large, black and white image of the first page of the newspaper dated January first, nineteen-ninety-one.

Slowly moving the knobs on the apparatus, a picture of a woman wearing a long, white dress came into view. She was lying on the ground, the bottom half of her body submerged in water. Leaves were embedded into her dark hair. Her eyes were open but void of life. I turned another knob to make the image larger. It was hard to tell, but it looked like a waterfall in the background. I wondered if that was one of the falls separating Wildewood from Twin Falls.

"Who's that?" Maisie asked from behind me.

"I have no idea." I glanced over my shoulder at her.

Maisie returned to the bookcase where she'd been and replaced the book that had been in her hands. If I knew exactly when we were born, this would be a lot easier. I removed the film and replaced it in the drawer. Grabbing a new box labeled May, I fed it into the machine. I had been found on the twenty-fourth, but before I could turn the knob, the film jumped to May thirteenth. What the hell? I glanced at Maisie to see if she had noticed but her nose was in a book.

That was weird, but what wasn't these days. Okay, Mister Microfilm Reader, what are you trying to show me? I slowly turned the knob, pretending this was normal, and as the first page came into view, I read the bold print caption: *Woman Found Dead*. All right, another dead person. This seemed to be the theme for the week. Scrolling down, I saw a picture that caused me to suck in a breath. I recognized the woman.

No. It couldn't be.

Police stood around the bottom of a grand staircase. A woman's body was on the ground with her face halfway covered by hair. I zoomed in. Holy shit. The woman was wearing a daisy print shirt and jeans.

In small font under the picture was the sentence, *"Agatha Wildewood-Law found after having committed suicide."*

The woman in the hat.

"Find something?" Maisie asked. I turned to look at her peering from around a different bookcase. She started toward the machine.

I shook my head and pushed the image away with a quick turn of the knob. "No, just another dead body."

Except that hadn't been *just another* dead body. Agatha Wildewood-Law. Was that my Agatha? I flicked my eyes to the ceiling. Great, I was referring to her as 'mine.'

Wait … Maisie's last name was Law. Was that our mother's last name? Hold up. Were we Wildewoods? What the actual f—

"That sounds pretty dismal." Maisie plopped a book on the table and sat down in a chair. She propped her feet up on another chair and flipped open the book to what seemed like a random page.

"Yeah." I blinked, feeling a bit disoriented. I had come to find some record of our birth, not to find out that we might be related to *the* Wildewoods, the founders of the town. I rotated the knob until I reached the birth announcements and, at this point, nothing could top what I had just found.

I take that back, I thought, as another picture came into view.

"Mais—" my voice trailed off.

The chair Maisie was sitting in scuffed the floor as she

pushed it to stand. She lowered her head near mine and looked at the bright screen at a large picture of a young Esther Miller. She was holding two swaddled babies. Babies who almost looked identical.

"The mayor?" Maisie murmured as she recognized the woman in the picture.

I read the caption out loud, "Mayor Miller aides in the relocation of twin girls abandoned at Wildewood Memorial."

"How did we end up outside of Wildewood with two different last names?" Maisie stood up straight and crossed her arms.

I shut the machine down. "I have no idea." But I don't think we were supposed to find our way back.

Chapter 35

Locking the door to my office, I left the café in the capable hands of Leah and Maisie. Hopefully, Leah would make it through the evening shift because I needed a moment, or two, maybe even three, to clear my head. I propped my feet on my desk, the chair squeaking as it leaned back, and rubbed my temple in a circular motion. What the actual fuck had I just found out?

Not only had the mayor already known I was a witch, but she had found me and Maisie as infants. She had helped relocate us. We had been abandoned by our mother and then again by the mayor. How the hell had I ended up at a fire station? Or was that a lie? Some type of cover-up? What the hell really happened twenty-eight years ago and what had she gained from removing us from Wildewood?

I bet Agatha knew. *Boy*, the first chance I could find to talk to her was she going to get an ear full. She was, what, our aunt? She looked young. Actually, she looked our same age. But she was hiding something. I couldn't think of any other reason why she couldn't have come right out and told me who she was or who I was. A freaking Wildewood.

I wanted to talk to the mayor and ask her, but until the murder was solved that could wait, though for how long? With the mayor confiscating potential evidence, how much longer would it take the police to solve the murder? Even though I knew who set the fire at Just Treats, I couldn't just go to the police with it. What exactly would I tell them? The mayor cast a truth spell ... yeah, that would go over well. But I wasn't worried about them figuring it out because they had found blood on the glass. I was certain the same person stole my mixers. Aaron was behind both of those.

However, the black residue left on the murder weapon and on Samantha's shirt didn't exactly point to Aaron. It was nothing I had ever seen before. It didn't look like oil or grease, and honestly, I bet he didn't even know how to pop the hood of a car. It was a weird paste-like substance. It shimmered but looked dense. It didn't drip or move. If I hadn't seen it with my own eyes, I would think it wasn't real.

A knock came and I lost my concentration. The office was small enough that I only had to lean over and unlock the door. Ethan poked his head through the opening. Oh! I tried to turn the chair toward the door with a foot, but instead pushed a little too hard and me, the chair, and any dignity I had left went toppling backward.

I stared up at the ceiling from the floor, the back of the chair cushioning my fall. But it did nothing for my pride. As if I had any at this point. Ethan chuckled as he towered over me. He grabbed the sides of the chair and pulled it back up onto its wheels, with me still in it.

"I didn't mean to startle you." He leaned against the desk; his lips pressed together but I could see he was trying his damndest not to laugh out loud.

I cleared my throat. Pretending I hadn't just made a fool of myself *again* and looked at him. "What can I do for you?" Really, Riley?

"Well." He licked his bottom lip, his eyes flicked down for a split second before meeting my gaze. "I'd like a date with the most beautiful girl in the room."

I took a look around the tiny office. Was there someone else with us? Glancing at Ethan, his smile had spread to his eyes. I crossed my arms, leaning backward. "Very smooth, Mr. Mitchell."

He held his hand out to me and I gave him mine. Pulling me up out of the seat, he wrapped his arms around my waist. My hands went to his chest. His lips trailed along my neck, causing a shiver to run down my spine.

"I was thinking tomorrow evening," he whispered against my skin.

I nodded, my brain turning to mush as his hands slowly moved down. Clearing my throat, his hands stilled, resting on top of my back pockets. "It'll have to be a little late." My heart rate sped up. Stay cool, Riley. I was ready to get this date over with so we could get some other things over with. Well, we could take our time for that.

"How about eight o'clock?" he asked.

"Sounds great." I gave him a small smile.

Walking out of the office, Ethan held my hand. I couldn't remember the last time I'd held hands with a boyfriend. Hell, I couldn't remember the last time I called someone a boyfriend. Wait, was he my boyfriend? Did I just jump to a conclusion? We stopped in the doorway and he leaned down to kiss me, I stood on my toes to meet him. His musky, vanilla scent filled all my senses as he pulled away. "Pick you up here?" he asked.

"I'll be here," I responded. I think I would like to call him a boyfriend. It had a nice ring to it.

"See you tomorrow, Miss Jones."

As he moved through the café, I heard a little snicker. Maisie was standing next to the register with a big grin plastered on her face. Oh. She had seen that. Looking around the café, I saw a few other people glance at me and my cheeks heated. I hadn't even noticed anyone else around. This boy was going to get me in trouble.

"I like him," Maisie said quietly.

"Me too." I covered my smile with fingers pressed against my lips. I felt like I was floating on cloud nine as I watched him leave the café. Was this what people felt when they were falling for someone? But I found my smile fading when I remembered tomorrow was the day Samantha and Trey were supposed to be getting married.

Chapter 36

Shortly after the café closed, Maisie and I began our shift on the neighborhood watch. The instructions were simple—watch for anything out of the ordinary. So far, as we stepped on to the deserted street to take a walk around the square, I saw a cat following us, except I didn't think that's what the mayor meant.

The mayor had enforced a ten o'clock curfew until Trey's murderer was brought to justice. I handed Maisie one of the miniature flashlights. I clicked mine on. It was a little eerie how empty the town was. By nine, most of the shops were closed, the restaurants were usually still open, just not tonight. It was dark, the only lights coming from the dim lamp posts. It was quiet except for the sound of our shoes hitting the ground and the occasional shake of leaves from the wind.

"I've been wondering ..." Maisie clicked her flashlight on, sweeping the ground with the thin light. "If we were found together, why were we separated? I was left at a hospital in Twin Falls and you?"

"Fire Station," I responded. Taking a peek at her, I saw frown lines set deep in her forehead. "I don't know why they separated us." I wished I had a better answer.

I had known many siblings in the system who had been kept together, and some who weren't. But they knew of each other. They had been allowed contact, even if it was just over the phone. We should've known about each other, but in my gut I knew, someone hadn't wanted that. The only person I could think of who would purposely make sure we never knew of one another was Madam Mayor herself. I just didn't understand why.

Maisie kicked a small pebble off the sidewalk. It bounced from the curb and fell into a nearby gutter. The echo of it hitting the bottom rang loudly around us. "Did our father ever mention me?" she asked.

There was no easy way to answer that question. "No," I simply stated.

"Hmm. That explains why you had no idea about having a sister."

Bean ran a few steps ahead of us and Maisie followed him with her flashlight.

"Andrew, our dad, told me our mom didn't even tell him she was pregnant," I started to explain, but I could tell by her sniffle her feelings were hurt.

She peered at me; an eyebrow raised. "What?"

I had been just as shocked when I found that out too. "He said the last time he saw her he'd noticed her belly looked swollen. He guessed she was a few months pregnant." I nudged her with an elbow. "He asked if she was, but she wouldn't answer as if she didn't want him to know." Bean stopped in front of me and I swerved around him. He crouched in the middle of the sidewalk, moving his paw to cover a bug.

"That's pretty messed up," Maisie muttered.

I couldn't agree more. If she didn't want us, I believed Andrew would've taken care of us. He said he always wanted to be a father but it just never happened. "He told me she vanished after he started asking questions. He filed a missing persons report and he and Pete Kelley searched for her, but she was never found. She just vanished without a trace."

Bean hissed and we stopped walking. I turned around to look for him. His back was arched and he drew his legs up under his body.

"Bean?" Maisie took a step closer to him.

Oh, shit. I recognized that posture. I rushed to him but he raced across the grass of the square. I shoved the flashlight into my jacket pocket and chased after him, Maisie by my side. The last time he had done something like this, he had led me to … I just hoped this time it wasn't another dead body. I don't think I could handle another one anytime soon, or ever again.

We followed him through the street, our feet beating against the ground as we tried to keep up. Wheezing, my calves were on fire and I wasn't sure I could run much longer when Maisie abruptly stopped in front of me. Almost knocking her over, I stumbled and doubled over to suck in a deep breath. I hated running.

"Where did he go?" Maisie shined the flashlight on the ground.

We were in front of Town Hall. I looked over the porch and heard his bell coming from the left of the building. Maisie pointed; she had heard it too. We slinked around toward the back. There were no lights on inside, it seemed just as desolate as the rest of the town, but for some reason, the hairs on the back of my neck were standing.

The light from my flashlight reflected in Bean's eyes and I pulled Maisie toward him. As we neared, Bean jumped on to a large trash can situated behind the building. His tail twitched back and forth watching us. What was this cat up to? He jumped from the can onto a larger dumpster and began to pace.

Exchanging a look with Maisie, I walked to the dumpster. Shooing Bean out of the way, I pushed one of the lids open. Okay, now what? What did he want me to see? I looked around at the multitude of white trash bags. Picking Bean up, Maisie set him on the ground and pushed the other lid open.

"Riley," she whispered.

Following the light from her flashlight, I saw something reflecting from underneath a bag. Wrinkling my nose in disgust, I didn't want to dig through a dumpster but pushed the bag aside. My mouth fell open as her flashlight hit the stainless-steel surface of one of my mixers.

"What are those doing here?" She pulled the large mixing bowl out of the trash. Moving another bag aside, she found a second one.

Before I could answer, the little bell attached to Bean's collar jingled. I turned to see him pad up the back steps of Town Hall. Now what? I pulled on Maisie's jacket and dragged her toward him. He perched beside the bricks below a partially-open window. Oh, hell no. I rubbed my thumb and index together and clicked my tongue hoping to attract his attention.

It was bad enough he made me go dumpster diving, but there was no way in hell I was going to break into Town Hall. No. Way. I couldn't use magic to stop him, because last time I had used a spell on him it had rebounded. Plus, Maisie was with me. I tried to coax him again but Bean shrugged his way through the opening and made his way to the other side.

"No!" I ran to the window, trying to force it open but it wouldn't budge.

Maisie stuck her hand through the opening, trying to grab at him but he jumped on to a large oval table in the middle of the room.

"What are we supposed to do? We can't just leave him in there." Maisie cupped her hands against the glass to look inside.

Sure, we can, that's exactly what we're going to do. "I have no idea."

I watched Maisie push away from the window and walk to the door. Hearing her mumble, she jerked her head in my direction with a grin on her face. "It's unlocked." She turned the knob and walked inside as if she had been invited.

Great. We were breaking and entering. I flicked my eyes to the dark sky. This was not a good idea, but I quickened my steps to follow her through the door. Shining my flashlight around the empty hallway, I could hear his little bell jingling. Maisie went toward the noise but curiosity struck. I moved the light to shine on the door to the mayor's office.

Should I? My steps faltered. If I was going to jail for rescuing that damn cat, I might as well make it worth my while. I crept toward the door. Pushing it open, I took a look behind me. Maisie was in the doorway of the conference room. Just a quick look, just long enough to see if Jack's memory card was inside.

My heart was beating loud in my ears as I swiped the light back and forth across the mayor's desk. I had never been much of a rule-breaker and yet here I was. Riley Jones, The Criminal Witch of Wildewood. That wasn't a title I wanted to own. I walked further inside, not having seen anything on the desk, and shined the light on the computer tower.

There it was. I bent to retrieve it when I heard a floorboard creak.

"Maisie?" I whispered, looking up only to see Aaron standing in the doorway.

I froze, the flashlight falling from my hand. My heart rate accelerated. Aaron had his arms crossed over his chest. "What are you doing in here?" He turned the office light on.

Recoiling from the blinding light, I blinked my eyes to focus. "I was—well, my cat—"

He looked around the room. "I don't see a cat." His chest rose as he took in a deep breath.

I wrung my hands together, trying to stop them from shaking. I had never thought of Aaron as anything more than a scrawny, maybe even geeky errand boy for the mayor. But now—I found myself scared to be in the room with him.

I spotted Maisie behind him with Bean tight in her arms. She had her hand pressed against his bell so it wouldn't ring. I raised my hand and pointed. "I'm sorry. I'll go." I emphasized *go* hoping she would take the hint.

"Oh, no." Aaron fumbled around in his pocket then pulled his cell phone out. Maisie moved out of sight and I prayed that meant she'd caught on. "I'm calling the cops."

Shit. How was I supposed to get out of this one? Pressing my lips together, I wracked my brain for something, anything to distract him. "And tell them what?" I clamped my mouth shut. I hadn't thought this through. I should've just told Maisie no, and left Bean. I'm sure he could get himself out of trouble.

Aaron looked up from his phone, his eyes small slits. "Excuse me?"

I sucked in a breath. Here goes nothing. "Are you going to tell them you murdered Trey?"

Aaron's mouth opened. He slid the phone back into his pocket. "Why would I tell them that?"

I took a step around the desk, throwing caution into the wind and possibly becoming his next victim. "I know you're

233

behind the fire and the burglary. You were trying to stop their wedding."

Aaron's eyes searched me, then he turned and walked out of the office. I followed him like a damn idiot just begging to be the next murder victim in Wildewood.

"I was trying to stop the wedding. But—" he took a glance at me from over his shoulder. "I didn't kill Trey."

"Why would I believe that?" I poked. Shut-the-fuck-up, Riley!

Aaron grabbed a folder from his desk and handed it to me. "You don't have to believe me."

Staring at the manila folder in his outstretched hand, I asked, "What is this?" He gave it a slight shake and I took it from him. Opening it slowly, I saw pictures from the Halloween Festival. These must be from Jack's camera, the illegally confiscated photos.

"Look at them." Aaron leaned against his desk with his arms crossed.

Scanning through the pictures, I stopped. I brought one closer to my face. On the left side of the stage, where the pumpkin carving booth was, I could see Trey in his devil's costume. Oh God, these were the last images of his life. A small pit formed in my stomach. I glanced at Aaron and he motioned for me to keep looking. I flipped through the pictures. Trey was still on the same side of the stage, but this time he was talking to someone in a wedding dress. I shook my head. This couldn't be right. Trey and ... Leah? The scrunched, frustrated looks on their faces combined with the way their arms were held out to their sides didn't convey a very friendly conversation.

Was that Leah? Her image was grainy as if the camera had lost focus but only on her. I looked at the next image in the folder but it was dark. The lights must have gone out when Jack took this one. All of the people in the image were nothing more than streaks from the flash. I took in a breath as I looked at the very last picture in the folder. Trey was on the ground, the knife in his chest.

Closing the folder, I blinked slowly, trying to wrap my head around what I had seen. Was Leah the woman in white?

The sound of a crash came from down the hall. I jumped, shrieking. Aaron rushed past me, cursing under his breath as he ran to the back door. He flung it open and I took that as my cue to leave and ran in the opposite direction to the front door. My boots stomped down the steps. As I hit the grass in front of the building, I saw Maisie and Bean running.

Chapter 37

"What the hell was that about?" Maisie shrieked as we burst through the front door.

We had run all the way to Cattail Road. The fear of Aaron coming after us made me not want to stop until I reached the safety of my own house. Sure, he could easily figure out where I lived. He might even already know, but at least there was some distance between us now.

I sucked in a much-needed breath and tossed the manila folder on the floor. In all honesty, I had forgotten it was in my hands. Unbuttoning my jacket, I wiggled it off and pulled my sweat-drenched shirt away from my body to let in the cool air.

"Which part?" I finally responded, my lungs had been overworked and my heart didn't want to slow down. I was so out of shape.

"The Aaron part." Maisie tossed her jacket onto the kitchen table and rushed to the sink. Turning the faucet on, she leaned her head under and gulped water. She wiped her chin with the back of her hand. "Did he kill Trey?"

I kicked my boots off and they hit the wall next to my jacket. My feet instantly cooled on the hardwood floor. I shook my head and took another deep breath. "No."

This time taking a cup from the cabinet, Maisie filled it under the faucet then offered it to me. "But I heard you say—"

I grabbed the folder off the floor and walked to her to take the cup. Drinking too fast, water ran down my chin, dripping onto my shirt. Setting the cup on the counter, I wiped the liquid off with the back of my hand. "I was just trying to catch him off guard." It wasn't totally a lie. I had suspected him, but I just wanted to give Maisie a chance to get out.

Maisie's face scrunched and she held her hands out by her side. "But he admitted to—"

Oh, crap. She'd heard more than I realized. I briefly closed my eyes and pushed my hair behind my ears. I should just tell her everything. And I mean everything.

"Riley?" I opened my eyes to see her searching me, her head tilted to the side and her arms crossed. "What aren't you telling me?"

I motioned for her to follow me to the table. "I don't even know where to start." I sat down, tapping my fingers on the folder.

"Try the beginning?" she suggested as she leaned back in her chair across from me.

The beginning, right. I squirmed a little. "The fire at Just Treats ..."

I explained everything to Maisie starting with the clues from Just Treats. I also admitted to her I thought she had been the one having an affair with Trey.

"Gross," she curled her upper lip.

How I connected those dots, she seemed to understand even with the occasional gags coming from her side of the table.

"Then the café got broken into." And well, I had also thought that had been Maisie. Good grief, she probably felt I thought she was the worst person in all of Wildewood. But the timing had been just right.

"Well, now we know it was Aaron," she commented.

I nodded in response. We did now because he admitted to it. I had just assumed everything was connected, and my assumption had been right. I decided to omit the weird black residue because I still hadn't figured that out. Why? Because I was chicken.

"I thought Aaron had killed Trey, but—" besides the information I'd heard at the hospital, I pushed the folder toward her.

Maisie eyed it suspiciously, just as I had when Aaron handed it to me. I opened it and motioned for her to look through the pictures. Scanning the pile of images, I waited quietly until she reached the bottom of the pile. Maisie laid her hands on the table and raised her head; her mouth was open and her eyes wide.

"Leah?" She pushed the pictures back to me and shook her head slightly.

Gathering the images, I placed them neatly back in the folder.

"We have to tell the police," Maisie finally spoke after a moment of silence.

I bared my teeth and shook my head. "I just don't know if she really did it. It could just be a coincidence." I didn't want it to be true. I just couldn't imagine Leah ... I wasn't ready to call the police, not yet.

Maisie stared at me, the creases in her forehead deepened. She opened her mouth, but then snapped it shut. I could see she didn't understand my need to wait. Leaning over the table, I looked Maisie in her eyes—eyes that were the same as mine. "I want to find out the truth. Just give me until tomorrow evening," I pleaded, feeling my face slacken, "and then we'll call the police."

She thought about it for a moment but eventually agreed. Standing, she added, "It's going to be weird working beside her tomorrow."

Ain't that the truth.

Going up to the loft, I threw the manila folder onto my dresser and grabbed a pair of pajamas. While I was changing, I heard someone clear their throat. Spinning around with my shirt pressed to my bare chest, I didn't see anyone. I turned in a slow circle, my eyes landing on the hat sitting on a pillow at the head of the bed. I'm pretty sure I hadn't left it there. Pulling the shirt over my head, I picked it up.

About to place it on my head, I paused. I had no idea when I was talking to Agatha if it was in my mind or out loud. Looking down the steps, the house was dark and I could hear water running in the bathroom.

She can't hear you, Agatha's voice spooked me and I jumped.

"She won't be in the shower forever," I kept my voice low.

Fine. Say 'auribus tantum' and draw a large circle in the air, she sounded annoyed.

I closed my eyes and while moving one arm in a large circle, I whispered, "*Auribus Tantum.*" My fingertips began to tingle and I drew the circle again. When I opened my eyes, I wasn't sure if it had worked. I didn't see anything, though I wasn't sure what the spell even did.

It worked. She can't hear us, now put me on, she demanded.

You could at least say please, I thought as I sat down on the bed and placed the hat on my head. Agatha appeared in front of me, wearing the same clothes as the last time I'd seen her. Hands shoved into the high-waisted pants, she paced. Noticing me, she clapped her hands in front of her, a large grin spreading across her face. "Have you told Maisie yet?"

"Told her what?" I folded my arms across my chest.

Her shoulders sagged, her arms falling to her side. "That you're a witch."

I rubbed the back of my neck and shrugged. "No, there's been a lot of stuff going on and I haven't found the right time."

Her posture went rigid. "You have to tell her."

"Why do I have to?" I didn't understand the urgency. Sure, I'd love to tell her and I would at some point. But why did it matter so much to Agatha?

She waved her hand in the air, shifting her weight back and forth. "Because—" she paused. "Sisters shouldn't keep secrets from each other."

She was one to talk about keeping secrets. So far, she hadn't shared a single piece of information about herself with me. "Since you're so worried about keeping secrets, why don't you tell me how you died, Agatha?" I blurted out. The newspaper had said suicide but I wanted her to tell me.

She jerked her head back, her mouth falling open. "How did you—" her voice was shaky.

"Don't you think it's time you shared something with me?" I questioned.

Her chest rose and fell slowly. "I will, but first you have to tell her."

Clearly, we were just going to go back and forth, so I pulled the hat off my head and she faded from view. I knew she was hiding things from me. It was pretty obvious she didn't want me to know anything about her. I laid down on my bed and stared at the ceiling. What was so crucial about Maisie knowing? I flicked my wrist and pointed at the dresser. The hat rose from the bed and floated across the room. The hat dropped onto the dresser and knocked my deodorant onto the floor.

Entertaining the idea of telling Maisie made me feel nauseous. I rolled over on to my side and held the extra pillow against my stomach. I had no idea how to even strike up that conversation. We might be sisters, but we barely knew each other. If I told her would I lose her? I couldn't take that chance.

Chapter 38

The café was supposed to be closed, but after the wedding had been canceled, I reopened. My stomach had been in knots throughout the entire evening shift. It was hard not to stare at Leah. Actually, I take that back. It had been hard not to stare, but I had done a pretty good job avoiding her. Whatever room she was in, I would excuse myself and go to another. My kitchen was spotless and my office was clean for a change.

Walking out of my office with a wad of cash, I found Maisie scrubbing down a table in the middle of the room. She looked up at me, her eyes darting toward the kitchen where Leah was. "What's up?" she asked.

"I forgot to get cat food yesterday. Do you think you could run to Eliza's for me?" I held out the money to her. Please take the hint. Please, take it.

Maisie took a second glance at the kitchen. The water was on and I could hear plates hitting the sink. She shook her head, understanding and removed her apron. Taking the cash from my hand, she shoved it in her pocket. "Are you sure you don't want me to stay?"

"I'll be okay. See you at home?" I lied. I was not okay, and

I wasn't going to be okay. It felt like fireworks were going off in every nerve of my body.

Maisie walked to the door and looked back. "Are you sure?"

I nodded, feeling stomach acid rising in my throat as she left the café. Drawing in a deep breath, I scurried behind the bar and grabbed a clean, white mug. I had come up with a half-assed plan while cleaning my office. I was going to use the same truth spell I had tried on Samantha, but I was going to tweak it a little.

Pouring coffee into the mug, I stared into the dark liquid. I took in a deep breath, brushing my palm above the lip of the cup then brought the same palm to my mouth and blew across it. "*Verum dicere*," I repeated once more. The liquid rippled. I took that as a good sign.

"Leah," I called to the swinging doors, "could you come here for a moment?"

The water turned off and a moment later she was pushing through the doors. My heart skipped, the nervousness turning to fear on top of guilt.

"What's up?" She gave me a smile and a wave of guilt washed over me.

Please let the pictures be wrong, I prayed. I handed the coffee cup to her. "I'm working on a new drink. Would you tell me what you think?"

Leah gave a slight shrug then picked up the mug. I licked my lips, my mouth becoming unbearably dry. I watched as she brought the cup to her mouth. My pulse raced. Act normal, Riley. This wasn't the first time I'd asked her to try something new. She trusted me. The pit in my stomach grew. This had to be a mistake. There was no way Leah was the murderer.

She pulled the cup away from her mouth and a droplet fell from the rim and landed on her necklace. Placing the cup down,

Leah scrunched her brows. "Uh, Riley ... this just tastes like black coffee."

"That's odd." I mimicked her facial expression and tapped my finger on the counter. I picked up the cup and pretended to inspect it.

Leah reached for a napkin, pausing as the lights flickered. She looked up at the ceiling until the flickering ceased then brought the napkin to her necklace. I barely noticed the lights as I watched movement past her raised hand inside the cameo. What the fuck was that? My eyes widening, I clamped my jaw shut tight, forcing myself not to scream, as I watched the head of the carved woman in the necklace shake furiously, making her features blur. It was so quick I could barely focus on it. The shaking stopped abruptly and her eyes turned black, staring straight at me, causing me to catch my breath. A menacing smile spread across the small face. Flinching, the cup fell from my hand. It hit the ground and broke into pieces.

"Are you okay?" Leah turned to grab the small dustpan from under the counter.

I rubbed my eyes. What the hell just happened? Had I really seen that?

Leah stood, the dustpan falling to the ground by her feet. She was still. Her shoulders rose and fell as her breathing deepened.

"Leah?" I tiptoed around her to see her face void of expression.

The spell had taken effect. I swallowed and glanced down at the cameo. The woman was just as still. Blinking slowly, I licked my lips and cleared my throat. Had I imagined it?

"Leah," I took in a deep breath, trying to force my nerves to calm, "did you kill Trey?"

The corners of her mouth turned down. "I couldn't stop

her," she whispered so softly I almost didn't hear her. A single tear rolled down her cheek then dripped from her chin.

Time felt like it slowed as I watched the tear fall onto the white image of the cameo. The movement began again, faster this time, her head shaking back and forth. I took a step back in horror as the woman's arms reached out from the pendant. Her image grew as she pulled herself from her confines. My back hit the counter, unable to move any further.

A chill wrapped around me and I could see my breath as if the temperature had dropped. I froze, paralyzed as the woman hovered in front of Leah. Her long, wedding dress gray from age and in tatters around her bare, muddy feet. The dress clung to her body as if it were wet. Black tears stained her cheeks. Her body jerked, her image flickering in and out of view. She shrieked, the sound piercing my ears. The pendant lights above the bar exploded. Screaming, I covered my head and turned to shield myself from the glass as it rained down around me. It hadn't been a power surge this whole time. It had been ... her.

Peering under my arm, I saw Leah throw her head back and a throaty cry came from deep inside her. The spirit, whatever the hell it was, turned into a thick, black cyclone of smoke. I fell onto the floor, pulling my legs against my body and watched in horror as the cyclone forced itself into Leah's mouth. Her screams filled my ears.

Leah convulsed. Her arms wrapped around her stomach and she bent over, falling to one knee. Her hands reached out to stop herself from hitting the ground. She choked, a gagging sound as if she was trying to throw up. I could hear the sound of glass crunching and saw bloody handprints from the shards piercing her palms.

"Leah?" I whispered. What do I do? What was I supposed to

do? My breathing quickened and I crawled back away from the counter.

Leah jerked her head up. A cry tore out of me as I watched her eyes flash black. The veins under her pale skin pulsed as the black spread throughout her body. She opened her mouth and a deafening growl rang out.

Leah stood, her black eyes blinking. She moved past me, heading to the door.

"No!" I yelled, scurrying to a standing position and slipping on the glass.

The fairy lights above her popped. The café was dark, the only light came from the kitchen and a single strand of fairy lights. "I loved him so much," the woman cried.

It didn't sound right, as if two voices were being used at once. "He was supposed to marry me." She turned to face me. "Me!" I covered my ears, the pitch of her voice so high I thought my eardrums would burst.

I had to do something. I had to stop her but I didn't know what to do. I had never used any defensive magic before. I didn't even know one single spell. I was a fucking terrible witch. I really couldn't defend myself and now this thing was going to be let loose on the town and there was nothing I could do. I looked around, searching for anything nearby that would hurt or distract it when I heard the chime on the door.

Maisie. Oh, shit! No!

I opened my mouth to yell at her, to tell her to run, but before I could get the words out Maisie dropped the grocery bag. Its contents spilled out on the floor. She held her hands up, palms to Leah. "*Restringunt!*" she shouted.

The air in the café changed, the temperature rose. Holy fuck. Maisie was a witch. She was a fucking witch! Tears stung my eyes as I watched Maisie step toward Leah. She repeated the spell. Leah staggered, unable to move her feet.

The image of the woman flashed over Leah. Her upper body struggled as she tried to move forward. The muscles in her neck strained. I finally recognized her. She was from the newspaper at the library, the one who'd died at The Falls. Leah threw her head back and screamed. I covered my ears but a sharp pain radiated in my left ear. I felt something wet and warm. Bringing my hand into view, blood covered my fingers.

Leah's feet began to move. She had broken through the spell. Mimicking what Maisie had done, I used the same spell. The amount of magic pulsing out of my hands almost sent me backward. I watched as the ripple of air bounced off of Leah and came back toward me at such speed, there was no way to stop it.

Like a ton of bricks, the spell blasted me. My legs locked and I began to fall backward. Knocking a table over as I landed on the ground, my head hit the seat of a chair. Loud ringing in my ear disoriented me. I looked around and saw Maisie moving in my direction.

I shook the stars out of my eyes, screaming, "Stop her!"

Maisie stopped in her tracks and turned her attention back to Leah. She balled her hand into a fist, bringing it toward herself. "*Iniuriam!*" She threw her fist in Leah's direction. I had no idea what she had said or what she had intended, but the glass on the front door shattered into a thousand tiny pieces without harming Leah.

Leah turned her head. Black tears ran down her cheeks. Her eyes were still black and I wasn't sure if the real Leah was in there anymore or not.

"I can't live with this pain anymore." She stepped through the broken door.

The lamps outside of the café popped, the bulbs exploding in bright orange. Maisie ran to me and grabbed me by the elbow to pull me onto my feet. Together we ran out of the café to the edge of the patio. Leah had already made it to the end of the street. She was fast, she wasn't human anymore. We had to stop her before anyone else got hurt. Including Leah.

Chapter 39

There was no way we would be able to catch up to Leah on foot. The laws of physics seemed to have no effect on her. She was nothing more than a stream of white light as she floated, or ran, or whatever she was doing. She was just too fast while the ghost was possessing her. This was one of those times I wished I had a car. Except … I did have a form of transportation. I glanced at Maisie. My hand slid into my pocket and I felt the little broom keychain.

It was possible we could get in front of her.

"Maisie." I pulled the keys out of my pocket and held them by the broom. "I need you to trust me."

She pulled her attention from the trail of busted street lamps and looked at my hand. "Okay?"

Dragging her into the alley between the bookstore and café, I unclipped the broom from the keychain. Maisie scrunched her brows. Her mouth opened but I held a hand up to stop her. She'd figure it out soon enough. I placed the miniature broom on the ground between us and without the worry of anyone hearing, recited the spell making it grow into its original size. As soon as it was over, I picked it up.

"What the—" Maisie blinked.

"Trust me. This is the only way," I urged and straddled the broom. This would be an interesting ride since I'd never had a passenger weighing more than a cat.

"Are you serious?" Maisie took a step back.

I took in a deep breath and motioned for her to hurry. "Just come on. We have to stop her."

Scooting onto the handle, Maisie grabbed my waist. "This is the most ridiculous thing I think I've ever done," she mumbled.

"Just think of it as a bike ride," I tried to reassure her. Here goes nothing. "*Subvolare!*" I ordered.

"I don't know how to ride a bike!" she bellowed as the broom began to rise into the air, slower than usual.

Gritting my teeth, I pleaded with it, begging it to carry our combined weight as it inched higher and higher. Debating whether or not this was going to work, it felt like the engine kicked on as we reached the roof and we were almost thrown off.

Maisie's grip was making it hard to breathe. I could hear her cussing as we flew toward the last spot I had seen Leah—the other side of the square. I held the handle so tight my knuckles were white. Pulling us higher into the sky to conceal us, I noted the streets were empty. Everyone was scared, and from what I just witnessed, they should be.

Glancing around, I strained my eyes but couldn't see Leah. We sailed through the air in the direction she'd gone but the trees were getting thick. I could barely see the ground.

"Where did she go?" I yelled. The wind was loud in my ears.

Maisie hesitantly took one arm from my waist and the other squeezed twice as tight. She pointed. Past the edge of the town, the street lamps were out. I pulled the handle of the broom in that direction. Another set of lights burst. She was running toward the town bridge. Shit. She was leaving Wildewood.

"We can't let her get out of the town," Maisie yelled in my ear before wrapping her arm back around my waist.

Whispering sweet nothings to the broom, I begged it to pick up its pace. It was going faster than I usually asked of it but I needed more speed.

My thoughts went back to the newspaper article I found in the archives. The woman possessing Leah had been found in water. The Falls. We had to get to The Falls before she did. We had to stop history from repeating itself. I had to get that necklace off of Leah. The clasp was broken, so hopefully, it wouldn't be difficult. I just had to get to her first.

Swerving, Maisie's grip caused me to gasp. We were going to take a more direct route. Leah was on the streets, but we were in the air. We didn't have to follow the same path. She was still human, to some extent, and couldn't pass through solid objects. Or, at least I didn't think she could.

We shot past the hospital to get in front of Leah. The Falls were not too far away. I felt the broom drop a few feet and Maisie's scream made my ears ring. What the hell? I repeated my spell, trying to put magic back into the broom. Nothing happened. We were losing velocity. Oh, shit! The hospital … Esther told me my magic didn't work there. I thought she just meant inside the hospital.

"What the fuck is happening?" Maisie yelled over the wind; her grip pushed the air out of my lungs.

Grabbing the handle tight, I tried to pull it back up into the air with all of my might but it just wasn't working. "We have a problem!" I yelled back, noticing the ground getting closer and closer with each moment we were airborne.

I spotted the shimmer of the lake between the two waterfalls. Hopefully, we had enough magic left in the broom to get us at least to the water.

"Come on, baby," I pleaded.

I looked over my shoulder. Maisie's eyes were closed tight enough to form wrinkles around the corners and she was gritting her teeth. She was going to hate what I was about to instruct.

"We have to jump!" I even hated my suggestion.

Her eyes popped open. "What? Hell no!" Her arms constricted me like a python.

"We have to!"

The broom was quickly descending, headed directly for the bank of the lake. If we didn't jump, we would die. The broom started to tilt forward and it took all of my strength to keep us from sliding off.

"Now!" I screamed.

When Maisie refused, I pushed her off and jumped right after. Screaming as I fell, I heard the broom hit the rocks. An explosion of wood.

As my body hit the water, my arm collided with something hard and I yelped. My mouth filled with water as I sank into the lake. I jerked trying to stop the descent. I needed oxygen. I tried to swim but my arm wasn't working. It hurt. God, it hurt. Kicking my legs, wagging only my right arm, I reached the surface.

Sucking in a deep breath, I coughed the water out of my lungs. I looked around for Maisie. I needed help. I could feel myself sinking, it was difficult to keep my head above the water with only one arm.

"Maisie!" I tried to yell as I choked, water filling my mouth.

The rushing water from the waterfall was pushing me further away. Straining to keep my head above the surface, I screamed Maisie's name again. I kicked my legs, desperate for air. My left arm was useless, my right arm burned with fatigue. Sinking, water filled my mouth, but as I coughed, more replaced it. I sank below the surface, straining to see in the dark lake. My lungs felt as if they would explode.

My body sagged. I looked up, reaching toward the surface but I couldn't get to it. This was it. This was how I'd die. I blinked, the remaining air escaping in bubbles from my nose. My thoughts drifted and I closed my eyes.

An arm wrapped around my waist; my legs kicked. Reaching the surface, my lungs burned and I coughed up the water that had forced its way down into my lungs. I saw Maisie, her face strained as she pulled me to the shore. Her image faded out of view. I reopened my eyes and touched solid ground. I rolled onto my side, pain shooting through my arm. Without any warning, my body heaved and I threw up into the rocks.

Forcing myself into a sitting position, Maisie rushed past me. Straining to focus my eyes, I saw another figure in front of her. "Leah!" I tried to scream as she headed toward the rocky edge of the second fall.

I slipped on wet rocks trying to stand. Maisie stopped abruptly. I heard her shout with her hands outstretched. Her magic failed. She turned to me, looking dumbfounded, her eyebrows scrunched together and her mouth wide open.

"We're powerless," I tried to explain, my voice hoarse.

Maisie repeated her spell, but again nothing happened. Confusion flashed across her face. "Why?"

I shrugged, my arm stinging from the movement. "I don't know." And I really didn't know. It made no sense to me. I stepped past Maisie. The image of the ghost inside Leah flashed into view. The clouds above moved and the light from the slender moon shone brightly on the rushing water of the fall as it cascaded down into the lake below. A haunting cry came from

Leah, causing the air on my arms to stand. Her body swayed as she took a step closer to the edge.

"Please," I begged, wishing I knew the name of the ghost. Leah was no longer in charge. The ghost had taken over and I wasn't sure if Leah was aware of her actions. She hadn't murdered Trey. The woman holding her captive had. If history was repeating itself—if this was going to play out the same way I had read about, then—

Leah looked at me from over her shoulder. Her blonde hair swept across her tear-stained face, her eyes still absent of color. "It's the only way." She turned back around. Her feet teetered on the edge. The sound of the water hitting the rocks below thundered.

"No!" I ran, reaching my arm out to grab her. I needed Leah to take control. I needed to take the necklace from her. If I could get her to hear me, maybe this would end differently.

"It's too late." She took a step.

Without a sound, she fell. I slid to the edge, landing on my knees and screamed as I watched as her body hit the water with a small, quiet splash. The lake quickly consumed her. She was gone.

Chapter 40

Maisie pulled me away from the edge as my screams turned to sobs. We rushed down the steps that led to the lake. My shoes slipped on the last step, and I fell to my knees. Trying to stop my fall, I had reached out to grab the railing with my hurt arm and howled in pain. If it wasn't broken, it sure as hell felt like it was.

Maisie helped me stand, wrapping her arm around my waist. The ground was muddy and sandy and my shoes weren't meant for the terrain. I stumbled toward the shore, seeing Leah's lifeless body floating. Trudging through the water to reach her, my vision blurred with tears. The pendant floated beside her; the chain still wrapped around her neck. It shimmered in the moonlight. The woman's picture had returned, Leah's body was no longer useful to her.

I grabbed Leah's arm and pulled her to shore. Maisie helped me get her out of the water. Sitting on my knees beside her, I pushed her hair from her face. Leaves were tangled in the blonde strands, just like the woman from the newspaper. The story had played out again. I couldn't stop it.

I pulled her head into my lap and slumped over her, pressing my forehead to hers. My whole body rocked violently as my sobbing turned into howling wails. This wasn't right. It wasn't supposed to end like this. I should've been able to stop it, but something had prevented me. My cries turned silent. Why hadn't my magic worked? I could've saved her.

I felt a hand touch my back. "Riley," Maisie's voice was hushed.

I looked up, wiping tears from my eyes. Maisie was pointing at Leah's chest. My eyes drifted down until I spotted the black residue oozing out of the necklace. It looked like small, black tendrils creeping, searching for a new host.

Maisie reached for the necklace and a voice shouted, "Don't touch that!"

I jerked my head up to see Esther climbing down the stairs with Bean at her heels. She waved her hand in the air and the necklace flew away from Leah's body and landed at her feet. She picked it up with a white handkerchief and wrapped the necklace in the fabric securely.

I stood. "You knew?" my voice was loud and scratchy. She knew the whole damn time and she just allowed this to play out!

Esther shoved the necklace into her pocket. "No. I didn't know."

"Bullshit!" I yelled and took a step forward.

"Wait." Maisie grabbed my wet sleeve. "She's a—" she paused, letting me go. "Why does your magic work here but ours doesn't?"

"We don't have time for that conversation right now." She looked down at Bean for a moment and I barely made out her whisper but I swore I heard her say, they don't need to know yet before her gaze landed back to us. What did we not need to know? "The police have been called; you two need to leave."

"No," I refused and dropped back to my knees beside Leah. I tried to hold her hand between mine, but a weak cry escaped me as pain shot through my arm. Her body was cold. Maisie stood protectively beside me. Her hands clenched into fists.

The mayor let out an exasperated breath then spoke, "That looks pretty bad." She nodded at my arm.

"It's fine." My arm could wait. I wasn't going to leave. She would have to drag me against my will.

The mayor waved her arms in a large circle while chanting words I couldn't comprehend. Everything around me went black. It felt like I was being sucked into a vortex. I heard Maisie yell my name but it was distant, muffled by the whirlwind all around me. Before I could figure out what was happening, my feet hit concrete. I dropped to my knees from the impact and teetered forward. Maisie grabbed my shoulder from beside me.

"What the—" I looked up and saw the door of the animal clinic. "What are we doing here?" Better yet, how the hell had we gotten here? I groaned and stood. Every bone in my body felt bruised.

Ethan's image came into view as he pushed the door open. He was dressed for our date. A pair of faded blue jeans and a crisp, white button-down shirt. He bent in front of me, his hand going to my face, then to my shoulder. "What happened?" We were covered in mud and soaking wet. I hissed as he touched my left arm. "Is your arm broken?" He helped me to stand and ushered us into the clinic.

"She fell," Maisie lied, though it wasn't far from the truth. I had fallen. From riding a broom.

The clinic was cold, forming goosebumps on every inch of my body. My jaw started to chatter and I tried my best to keep it quiet. Maisie came to my side, her hand finding mine. I peeked at her and saw her eyes were red. I hadn't even noticed her reaction with Leah. I squeezed her hand, and another set of tears ran down my cheek.

"We need to get you to the hospital." Ethan grabbed his keys from behind the front desk.

I tensed. "No hospital. Can't you do something?" A hospital would ask too many questions. There would be a record of us being there. I think I was starting to understand why Esther had sent us to him.

"Of course, he can," Esther spoke from behind us.

I yelped, turning to face her. "Stop doing that."

Ignoring me, Esther walked past us. She stepped in front of Ethan. "Mr. Mitchell, please fix her up without asking too many questions."

Ethan's eyebrows scrunched. He opened his mouth but instead of responding, his upper lip curled slightly and he audibly snapped his jaw shut. His shoulders tensed and he looked past Esther. "Follow me."

Maisie tugged me forward, our hands still locked together. We followed him into a back room. Glancing at Esther, her expression was cold. What had that been about? Ethan handed a pair of light blue scrubs to Maisie. He motioned to a separate door. "Bathroom's around the corner."

Maisie's grip on my hand tightened.

"I'll be fine," I tried to reassure her.

She took the clothes and I walked into an exam room with Ethan. Closing the door, his Adam's apple bobbed slowly as his eyes roamed over me. "What happened?" his voice was low, probably so Esther couldn't hear.

I could feel tears stinging my eyes, but I shook my head. I didn't know how to tell him what happened. I had no idea how to explain how I ended up at his clinic soaking wet and covered in mud. I sucked in a breath, but it caught in my throat and I could feel the little composure I had beginning to slip.

Ethan reached out and wiped a tear from my cheek. He looked so sincere, so worried. I wanted to tell him everything. I wanted him to hold me and tell me everything was okay but I just couldn't. Not yet. "Let me help you get cleaned up." He pressed his lips to my forehead and the dam nearly broke.

"It hurts to lift my arm," my voice cracked.

"I'll help." His fingers traced the hem of my shirt, moving it up to expose my midriff.

I could only pull one sleeve off. Ethan grabbed a pair of scissors and cut the other sleeve away. He tossed the ruined shirt into the trash. When he turned around to look at me, I swore I saw his eyes flash gold before he glanced away.

Shimmying out of my wet jeans was not an easy task. They wanted to cling, and having only one hand was problematic. I couldn't unclasp my bra. It was wet and uncomfortable. Ethan wrapped his arms around me, his fingers trailing along the thin fabric and unhooked it. Licking my lips, I could hear his heart beating. This was not exactly the way I wanted our first date to go.

He pulled the damp cloth away from me, and as a gentleman kept his eyes locked with mine as he helped me pull a dry scrub top on. I pulled the stretchy pants on easily and threw the rest of my clothes away.

Grabbing my waist, Ethan picked me up and helped me onto the exam table. He turned to open the cabinets and drawers, gathering supplies for the cast. They had an X-ray machine in the room and he took a picture of my arm to find the break. Surprisingly, it was only fractured. But it still hurt like a bitch.

"Hurry up, Ethan," The mayor called from the front of the clinic.

Ethan grunted in response. He cleaned my arm then proceeded to form a black cast around my thumb and forearm. "Riley," he took a glimpse at me as he finished, "what happened?"

I shook my head. "I'll explain everything later." I wasn't sure if I was lying to him or not. I suppose at some point, if our relationship was going to continue, I would have to tell him.

He rinsed his hands and I slid from the table. My arm was still throbbing, but hopefully, with some pain medicine, it would be tolerable.

Gently pushing my hair behind my ears, his hand dropped to lift my chin. His lips were warm against mine. If we could stay in this moment for a while, maybe the pain of the last hour would disappear. But Esther called again and Ethan tensed. What exactly did she have on him? Agatha and Bean had both mentioned they didn't like him, but why?

Ethan opened the door for me and I stepped out to see Maisie standing with the mayor, her arms crossed over her chest. I turned to tell Ethan goodbye, but he was gone. My heart sank. What was he hiding?

"Let's go." The mayor pushed the front door open.

Linking her hand in mine, Maisie and I followed Esther. My ears picked up a quiet jingle. Bean must be nearby.

"Are you going to tell us what's going on?" I could feel anger bubbling back up into my throat.

Esther walked ahead of us in silence. We took the alley past The Witches Brew and as we neared the large oak tree in the center of Town Square, Bean jogged to Maisie. Flashing blue lights caught my attention.

Across from us, an officer emerged from the car and walked

up the front steps of Town Hall. His knock was loud and it echoed in the quiet night. Aaron opened the door and was immediately apprehended.

"I was wondering when they'd figure it out," the mayor mumbled under her breath, watching the scene unfold.

With his hands behind his back, the officer led Aaron next door to the police station. The same police car sped away in the opposite direction.

"They are going to find Leah's body and will claim the murderer has been found," she explained.

"You know that's not right." I clenched my jaw. Leah wasn't the murderer!

"What would you have me tell them?" She glanced at me. "A ghost was the killer?"

I wiped at my eyes, my frown deepening. I knew she had a point. I didn't like it and I didn't want to agree with it but unfortunately, someone had to take the blame. At least Leah wasn't alive to deal with it. I swallowed and my eyes filled with tears. She shouldn't have died. We could've stopped it—if only my magic had worked.

The mayor began to walk again, her heels clicking on the pathway. We followed her because, at this point, I didn't know what else to do besides climb into my bed and cry. She hurried us into Town Hall and down the basement steps.

"What are we doing?" Maisie asked.

"It's time to show you two something." She unlocked a large, vault at the bottom of the steps using only a wave of her hand to spin the wheel. As it shrieked open, large fluorescent lights lining the ceiling flashed on.

The room was filled with wooden crates and glass cabinets. Esther took the necklace out of her pocket, unfolded the handkerchief and carefully placed it inside a small glass box on a table in the center of the space without touching it to her bare skin. She closed the lid and pressed her finger on the seal. The opening glowed bright red as it welded closed for good.

Whispering, she patted the top of the box, "You won't be hurting another person again."

Moving further into the vault, I tried to take in all the items sitting on the shelves in various sized glass boxes. Other pieces of jewelry, chalices, folded articles of clothing, and even large stones. Some of the items were tucked into glass boxes, some were not. The room looked like a museum of old artifacts.

"What is all this?" I turned to Esther from the back wall lined with shelves of books.

"These are all the magical items that have found their way into Wildewood for generations. It's my job to contain the chaos they create." Esther picked up the box with the cameo necklace and set it on a shelf. "Unfortunately, a few have snuck in without my knowledge."

A soft thud caused me to look past her. Maisie was stepping backward toward me as Agatha's hat jumped around on its brim in the doorway. Bean hissed and jumped from her arms. The hat began to spin. Faster and faster it spun like an upside-down, wooden top. It rose off the floor while a dark cloud formed underneath it.

The mayor cursed under her breath, shocking me at the words she chose. She had to understand what was going on, unlike me. I watched as the black cloud faded then disappeared. Agatha stood in front of us with the hat resting atop her head.

"Finally." She stretched her arms up then behind her back. Her reddish-brown curls bounced. "It's so nice to see the Wildewood Twins together, in person." She bobbed her head from side to side and clapped her hands in front of her.

Even though I had seen her before, my mouth opened seeing her in front of us. There was no black void. She was here. In the flesh. Well, mostly. I could slightly see through her.

Maisie looked at me, obviously shocked. She threw her hands up. "What the hell is going on? Wildewood Twins?"

Esther cleared her throat. "This is Agatha Wildewood-Law," she began, "your mother's twin sister."

I jerked my head to look at Esther. My mother's twin sister?

But she wasn't finished, "You two are the last remaining twins of the line of Wildewood witches," Esther spoke through clenched teeth and narrowed her eyes at Agatha.

I was getting the suspicion they knew each other. Had Esther been the one to trap her in the hat?

Agatha scowled in the mayor's direction. She walked toward us and put an arm over each of our shoulders. I felt Maisie jump. "It's about time you two found your way back, many thanks to Madame Mayor here." Agatha gave an unfriendly look at the mayor. She squeezed us together. "I have been waiting a long time to see both of you, but now, we have a lot of work to do."

Maisie wiggled out from under her arm. Backing up, she held her hands up. "What work?"

"Some family business that needs to be addressed." Agatha started to pull me toward the door.

"Not just yet." The mayor was quick on her feet, moving around us to block our exit.

Agatha dropped her arms to her side. "What now?"

Those two definitely did not get along.

"Riley," Esther ignored Agatha, "do you know where Leah got the necklace?"

Chewing on the inside of my cheek, I thought back to when

I first saw it. "She found it at Odds 'n' Ends. It was inside an old trunk." I gave a quick nod toward Agatha. "She was in it, too."

Esther's chest slowly rose then sank. Her eyes closed momentarily. "I need you to call Tessa. We need to see if there are any other magical items in it."

"Do you know what else was in the trunk?" I asked Agatha.

She dramatically looked up at the ceiling and pointed with both hands at her eyes. "I was a hat—no eyes."

Esther let me use her office phone. It only took me a few minutes to explain to Tessa that the mayor needed to get into her store right now because she might have an heirloom that found its way inside Odds 'n' Ends. I hated lying, but I couldn't tell her we were looking for magical items.

Surprisingly though, Tessa didn't ask too many questions. By the time we reached her shop, she was waiting for us inside her little sedan parked at the curb. Agatha had gone back inside the hat, unwillingly I might add. Her human form was slightly translucent and I didn't want to freak Tessa out. Maisie was eyeing the hat suspiciously. I didn't blame her; I had felt the same way.

Tessa climbed out of her car and met us at the door. "I hope I have what you're looking for." She unlocked the door and let the mayor inside first. Tessa glanced at Maisie and me. "What the hell happened to you two?"

Groaning, I whispered, "I'll tell you later."

"Riley said you have an old trunk in the store." Esther scanned the floor.

Tessa glanced at me again and scrunched her brows. I wish I could explain everything to her, but for now, I just shrugged. "The only trunk I have is in my office. I was going to go through it tomorrow."

Tessa unlocked the office door and stepped inside. A moment later, she walked out empty-handed. "It's gone."

The hat wiggled out from under my arm and bounced away as I tried to grab it. Horrified, I watched black smoke swirl underneath it again. My eyes flicked to Tessa. Her mouth opened, eyes wide as Agatha came into view. I pushed my hair back over the top of my head and turned to Tessa. How in the world was I supposed to explain that?

"Riley?" Tessa never took her eyes off Agatha.

"Can we go now?" Agatha motioned her hand to Maisie and me, completely clueless of Tessa's reaction.

Tessa looked at me. "What the—" she looked at the mayor. "Who is—"

I shook my head, I needed to confess everything. I didn't feel there was any other way to explain what she just saw. "Tessa—" I started.

The mayor interrupted before I had a chance to continue, "These are the Wildewood Twins and that," she pointed at Agatha, "is their aunt, Agatha Wildewood."

Tessa turned to me; her eyes wider than before. "The Wildewood Twins?"

I scrunched my brow. Did that mean something to her? I watched as confusion then recognition swept over her face. Finally, it went slack with worry.

"Will someone please tell me what the hell is going on?" I demanded.

Tessa shuffled on her feet then straightened her posture. Her attention bounced between me and Maisie. "My grandma used to tell me a story about the curse of Wildewood."

"Curse?" Maisie's voice was hushed as she came to stand beside me, our shoulders touching.

Tessa nodded.

"We don't have time for this right now," the mayor barked.

Tessa stopped her, "They need to know the truth."

"I agree with her." Agatha crossed her arms. She rose a few feet in the air to sit on top of the counter near the register. Nobody batted an eye as if the presence of a ghost was a normal thing.

"Fine." The mayor raised a hand in the air, telling Tessa to continue.

"A long time ago, a line of witches, the Wildewoods," Tessa nodded at me, "found the source of infinite power. The witches born into this family always came in pairs, twin girls to be exact. As they grew, so did their powers. The twins had the potential for greatness, but all power corrupts. As long as both twins lived, their power knew no bounds, but there was a price to pay. The heart of one twin would slowly blacken." She licked her lips and glanced at the mayor. "The Keepers, another line of witches, cursed the Wildewoods' magic to the town. As long as they remained within the boundary, they would have their power. If they ever left the town their powers would stay in Wildewood, awaiting their return. The Keepers begged the Wildewoods to give up their magic, to keep the world safe, but the only way to break the curse and save the heart was to make the ultimate sacrifice."

"And no one ever would," Agatha commented. "Except for me, but the curse wasn't broken."

I looked over at Agatha and hesitantly asked, "What exactly was the ultimate sacrifice?"

"My life." She leaned back on her arms and crossed her legs at the ankle.

Her suicide.

The mayor cleared her throat. "Girls. We have to find the items in that trunk. Tessa, do you know what was inside?"

Tessa shook her head. "I hadn't looked through it yet."

Agatha jumped from the counter to stand beside Maisie. "Oh, well. We have more important things to deal with. Let's go." Her hand reached for Maisie's wrist.

"Nothing is more important than the safety of the town." Esther took a step toward Agatha, her eyes narrowed. Her angry outburst caused me to shrink-away, moving closer to Maisie. Esther flicked her wrist in the air and lashed out a chain of foreign words.

Agatha opened her mouth, but before she could make a peep, she turned back into black, swirling smoke. Esther snapped her fingers and the smoke dissipated in the air in a shock wave around us.

"What did you do to her?" Maisie mouthed, her eyes searching the dark store.

Esther's wrinkles deepened as she walked past us. "She'll be back." Before she stepped through the doorway, she spoke in a low voice, "Something dark has been set free in Wildewood."

To be continued…

Acknowledgements

Thank you to my father-in-law for answering all my police procedure questions without asking me why even though that is a little concerning.

To my husband, who helped me brainstorm and gave me ideas when I found holes. Without you I wouldn't have found my ending. You are my rock.

To Shannon, who always told me not to doubt myself when I would start to sink pretty low.

To Katie, who forced me to give myself breaks when I was obsessing and constantly let me bounce ideas off her.

To my kids, who created chaos and made me lose my train of thought right in the middle of a stream of consciousness. I love you all, I swear.

Thank you to every person I met along the way and who helped guide me through this process. Writing this could have been so much harder without each and every one of you.

And a huge thank you to my family and friends for always believing in me.
I love you all so very much!

About the Author

R.M. Connor lives in Georgia with her handsome hubby and their four children. She has been a writer since her early teens and has always dreamed of becoming a published author. She spends her days chasing small children and daydreaming about her books. She loves metal, rock music, carnivorous plants and is a huge Trekkie.

Follow her to stay up to date for the next book of
The Deadly Series

Instagram: @R.M.Connor_writes

Facebook: R.M. Connor

Website: www.rmconnor.com

Lightning Source UK Ltd.
Milton Keynes UK
UKHW040636080321
379977UK00001B/38